Praise for Serial D

"…Berkom is a   e
nuances of plot,   ɔ
create complex, sympathetic characters….it's unapologetic
camp of the best kind, sure to keep you glued to the page
as you try to guess what comes next, who did what to
whom, and whether or not the guy will get the girl…"
~ *BloodWrites*

"…This book is without a doubt one of the most
engaging, complex and enthralling mysteries that had me
totally in its grip. I was swept into this story so much so
that I finished it in one sitting…Serial Date has
everything a mystery/thriller needs to be successful, fast-
paced and action packed, strong and memorable
characters and a story that will grab you from beginning
to end…" ~ *Confessions of a Reader*

"Basso and Santiago sizzle. This romantic suspense- is
full of snapping, realistic dialogue that never, ever spells it
all out for you: brilliant… [There's] enough suspense to
arrest the real world until you arrive at the finish line, nail
bitten and wrung out…"
~ **Ruth M. Ross**, *Editor & Reviewer*

"Now this, this is what thrillers are made of: grit, spunk,
no-nonsense and 100% unputdownability….Quite simply:
Brilliant." *~Cath 'n' Kindle Book Reviews*

"*Serial Date* was a surprisingly entertaining read with witty
writing and dark humor. The prose is sharp and
gritty…In short, I highly recommend *Serial Date* to those
who enjoy murder mysteries with a touch of satire."
~Seattle Post Intelligencer

Serial Date

A Leine Basso Thriller

D.V. Berkom

SERIAL DATE
Copyright © 2012, 2015 D.V. Berkom

Cover by Deranged Doctor Design
Second Edition

This book is a work of fiction and any resemblance to any
person, living or dead, or any place, event or occurrence is
completely coincidental. The characters and story lines are
created from the author's imagination and are used fictitiously.

All rights reserved. Printed in the United States of America
ISBN: 0692493263
ISBN-13: 978-0692493267

For Mark

CHAPTER 1

PETER BRONKOWSKI PEELED himself away from the prop closet. He needed air. The onlookers parted to give him space.

Oh my God, oh my God, they're going to shut us down. When this gets out the motherfuckers are going to crucify me. All the hard work, the hustling, the endless lunches listening to that blowhard Senator Runyon, all of it would be for nothing. Peter shook his head to clear it. His breath came out in fast gasps, threatening to hyperventilate.

At first, Peter thought it was a grotesque looking mannequin with fake blood stains down the front and side of its torso. The moment reality clicked, a jolt of shock split him, pooled behind his eyes and slid to his gut. With dawning comprehension, Peter realized the blood was real. And it was no mannequin.

It was Mandy.

Peter turned back to the prop closet. Everyone stared at him, as if he had the slightest idea what to do now. Fuck. He couldn't see a way out of this. Too many people had seen the body. He thought of his brother, Edward, but brushed the idea away.

Mandy was dead. Murdered. Sweet, small-town-sexy Mandy. *Who would want to kill her?* Now Tina, yeah, he could sort of see that, she could be quite the bitch. But Mandy? And which one of the cons did it? No getting around it, he'd have to call LAPD. They'd be swarming all over the place. Better find another home for Edward. He wasn't going to like that one bit. Edward didn't do well with change.

Gene Dorfenberger walked toward him, pushing people out of his way.

"Give him some room! The man can't think with you crowding him like that." Reluctantly, the small crowd began to disperse, a few stealing one last look at the gruesome sight.

Gene glanced at Mandy's body and shook his head. "Now why would somebody go and cut off her arm?" He edged closer, squatting to take a better look. "And an ear? What kind of sick fuck would do that?"

Peter froze. "Her ear's missing?"

"Yeah."

Peter shook his head to clear it. *It can't be.* He took a deep breath to try to stop the dizziness. Everything was spiraling out of control.

Originally slated as low-cost filler for summer, Serial Date had turned into the most watched reality show on television. Less than a year and a half ago he couldn't get the mailroom clerks to return his calls much less the now regular invitations to private parties and dinners with the network brass. They all wanted a piece and Peter had happily parlayed the lust for the extraordinary profits generated by the show into extra bargaining power.

This is it. It's over. We'll never recover.

2

"It's going to be rough. You're going to have to do some major damage control." Gene's sharp gaze traveled from the massive amount of blood soaked into the costumes scattered around Mandy back to Peter.

Peter nodded, his expression grim. "We've got to get somebody legit in here so the cops'll think we're taking steps to keep the contestants safe."

If Gene took offense at the comment, he didn't show it. "I think I know just the person. It'll take some doing, but I hear she's strapped for cash."

Peter looked at Gene with disbelief. "She? Gene, we need somebody who'll keep the fucking cops at bay, not another broad on the set."

Gene shook his head. "Oh, this one ain't just another broad, believe me."

CHAPTER 2

LEINE BASSO DROPPED her purse on the floor, kicked off her shoes and stalked across her apartment to the kitchen. She opened the refrigerator door and grabbed a beer. The old appliance clanked in protest.

Holding the cool bottle to her forehead, she walked over to the couch and dropped onto it, sighing with relief. Three down, two to go. God, she hated looking for a job. Especially when it seemed like everyone and their brother was out there doing the same thing.

Leine set the bottle on the thrift-store maple coffee table, leaned back and hiked up her skirt, struggling to peel off her pantyhose. It wasn't easy. The oppressive heat and the high humidity was fairly unusual for Seattle, even if it was the middle of August. Didn't matter if she took a shower or not; once she stepped outside, she was as damp as if she had.

Why didn't I just stay at the last job? Leine paused for a moment in her battle for freedom from the polyester and nylon blend. *Oh yeah. Because you didn't like the creep masquerading as your boss and he ended up on the floor with a broken collar bone when he tried to grope you.* A real player. Not only that, but he was a few heads shorter than Leine's five-foot-ten inches and she knew from experience that the guy would continue to be on her ass, one way or another, in order to prove himself the alpha dog. A lot of short guys had a chip on their shoulder. Except her husband, Frank.

Correction: her ex-husband.

The marriage hadn't exactly worked out. She made it four years.

Giving up on her stockings for the moment, she crab-walked back into the kitchen, opened the freezer and stuck her head in. Too bad her whole body didn't fit. Between the sound of her breathing and the death rattle of the fridge, she barely heard her cell phone go off.

She backed out and shut the freezer door, stuck her hand in her purse and grabbed her phone.

"Leine Basso."

"Leine? It's Gene Dorfenberger."

That was a blast from the past. *Why would Gene be calling her?*

"Hey, Gene. It's been a while."

"Yeah. Hey I got a line on a sweet job that you'd be perfect for. The only thing is, it starts right away and it's in L.A. You available?"

L.A. Not her first choice. Too many memories and they weren't happy.

"Depends on the job, Gene. I'm not freelancing anymore."

"No, no, nothing like that. See, I work for this guy named Peter Bronkowski. He's got a small problem and I was thinking you could fix it for him. He needs some special protection for his TV show. Ever heard of Serial Date?"

"I never watch television." Leine walked back to the freezer and stuck her head inside again.

Crappy airless one bedroom apartment.

"Oh. Well, it's this gigantic hit reality show that uses ex-cons as dates for really hot looking women, only the guys are billed as serial killers."

"This is a hit show?" Last time she had a TV, she emptied her gun into it after watching a sitcom. Apparently, she hadn't missed much.

"Yeah, the biggest. Anyway, one of the contestants was killed and ..."

Leine brought her head up, barely missing the edge of the old Hotpoint. "How do you know she was killed?"

"Pretty obvious. I don't know of anybody who'd cut off their own arm and ear before killing themselves. Van Gogh she ain't."

"Any ideas who might've done it? I mean, you've got how many ex-cons on the set? Did you check their records to see which ones did time for violent crimes?" Had the world gone crazy while she wasn't looking? Employing ex-cons wasn't usually a big deal, but putting them in close proximity to a bunch of beautiful women and having them act like serial killers made no sense at all.

"Not yet. Peter's delaying the call to the police until I talk to you. What do you think? Interesting?"

Interesting wasn't the word.

"Why me? Why not some off-duty cop or something?"

"Because I trust you. I don't trust anybody else when it comes to family."

"What do you mean?"

"You remember my sister, Ella?"

Leine remembered that Gene was holy-shit-scared of Ella, with good cause. A fierce lady, she didn't take kindly to Gene's bullshit. He had the scars to prove it.

"Ella's kid's working on set as a gopher and I can't keep an eye on her all the time. I figured with the two of us we'd be able to make sure she stayed safe."

"So you think the killer's still hanging out on the set?"

"I don't know. Nobody has a clue, but obviously there are a lot of suspects. I'd feel better if you were here to back me up."

"How much and how long?"

"Peter said to offer you two large a week if you could start right away. It runs until they find who did it, maybe longer."

Two-thousand a week was a hell of a lot better than what she made now, which was nothing. And it's not like it would be a tough gig. She could probably get used to L.A. again. Mainly, she didn't like the people and she knew how to avoid people.

"I'll take it."

CHAPTER 3

DETECTIVE SANTIAGO JENSEN was having a bad day. Not only did he and his partner, Don Putnam, draw the Serial Date murder case along with the prospect of the media climbing up into their shit, but his ex-wife was making noises that he was going to have to fork over more money to keep her in the lifestyle she deluded herself she deserved. Jensen could have kicked himself for caving in to the breast implants. She was an actress. He thought the boob job would help her secure regular employment, get her off his back. Now she thought he was the never ending spigot of wealth.

He should've bought her acting lessons.

The forensic team headed for the men's dressing room. Jensen sighed. He didn't have the energy for this. These guys were hardened criminals; they weren't going to give their permission to search the lockers easily. Luckily, Putnam was always ready for a fight. Jensen was happy to give the part-time pugilist free rein in all matters testosterone. He preferred dealing with the opposite sex.

"I see you all have padlocks on your lockers. I applaud how security conscious you actors are, but here's how this works." Putnam watched the small group of ex-cons gathered in the room with a belligerent expression. Jensen knew he was itching for a reason to cuff somebody. "You can give us the keys or tell us the combos and then give us consent to search, or we all stay here until individual warrants come through."

One of the cons, a big one named Reginald, propped his foot up on the bench that ran between Putnam and the rest of them. "Fuck that. Get your warrant. I got rights." There were several murmurs of agreement among the men. Jensen leaned against a wall of lockers, enjoying the show. Putnam's expression morphed from belligerent into what Jensen referred to as his 'happy face' which was anything but.

"Then you're gonna be here a long time. Is that what you all want?" Putnam shrugged. "Make it easy, make it hard. It's no skin off my ass."

One of the men, a blonde-haired guy built like a brick shithouse with matinee idol looks stepped forward and said, "I got nothing to hide. Go ahead and search."

"Shut up, Graber," a guy next to him hissed. Graber turned to him with a look that said, *don't mess with me*. The other guy backed down.

"Now, see? That's all we ask; a little cooperation from you fine, upstanding gentlemen." Putnam eyed Graber, sizing him up, then turned his attention to the rest of the group. "Before you say no, let me just say we're not interested in anything that you smoke, snort or stick in your arm. Make us spin our wheels while we get the remaining five warrants and we will take a serious interest in your little contraband stashes. I will make it my sole mission in life to ruin each and every one of your days."

All but Graber grumbled and got pissy, but in the end, Putnam had his way. By the time they made it to Graber's locker, they'd found the usual stash of cocaine, methamphetamines and ecstasy, along with several pornographic magazines, a crack pipe and anal prong. Putnam opened Graber's locker and stopped.

"Santa, come here."

Jensen walked over next to Putnam to see what he'd found. He pointed to a single diamond stud earring, tucked into a piece of foam rubber glued to the locker door.

It matched the one on the victim's remaining ear.

Putnam and Jensen exchanged looks. Jensen stepped back from the locker while Putnam held up the earring for Graber to see. His expression hardened.

"This your idea of a sick joke? Huh? Some kind of messed up kill-trophy?" Putnam shook his head, disgust obvious on his face.

"No—" Graber's eyes widened. Sweat beaded on his forehead. Panicked, he looked from Putnam to Jensen to the offending piece of jewelry. "It's not like that. S-she gave it to me—"

"Gave it to you?" Putnam sneered. "You mean after you raped and killed her? Right."

"No—I swear I didn't do it. I-I loved her," he finished, quietly. There were a couple of snickers from the other men in the room.

"Twisted way to say I love you, don't you think?" Putnam glanced at Jensen as he handed the earring to one of the guys on the forensic team. "Looks like we'll get to interview you all one more time." A chorus of groans erupted from the group. "Especially you." He glared at Graber.

"Do what you gotta do. I didn't kill her, man. I would never do that."

"Sure, whatever you say." Putnam leaned in close, getting in Graber's face. "You'd best make yourself available anytime, day or night. Cause we're gonna be so far up your ass, you'll think a prostate exam is pleasant."

Graber lifted his chin as Putnam brushed past him and walked out. Jensen watched him for a moment, noticed the weariness in his stance as he stared at his locker. Then he left to catch up to Putnam.

"What do you think?"

"Fucking dirt bag, that's what I think." Putnam turned to look at Jensen. "What? You think he didn't do it?"

Jensen shrugged. "I don't know. The guy gave us consent to search. If it's a trophy, why let us find it so easy?"

"Because he knew we'd find it eventually whether he gave us consent to search or we got a warrant."

"True. Still, an earring's not much. I watched him when you opened his locker. He was pretty code four when you went for it. He didn't react until you called it a 'kill trophy'."

Putnam snorted. "Jesus, Santa, he's an actor. I got a reaction because I called it for what it was. He had to appear shocked."

At that moment, Felix Ditterand, a rookie officer everyone gave the crappy jobs to, walked toward them wearing gloves, booties over his shoes and a paper suit. He looked like he'd been standing next to an exploding blender. Carrot and potato peelings dropped off of him with each step, littering the floor, and there were several unidentifiable stains that climbed up his pant leg. He carried a plastic evidence bag with what looked like a blood soaked rag inside.

"What you got there, Dits?" Putnam eyed the bag, wrinkling his nose at the rotten food smell emanating from Ditterand's attire.

Ditterand handed it to him and said, "Bloody towel. Kind you use at the gym. Found it in the dumpster two doors down behind the Thai place."

"Good work. Anything else?"

Ditterand shook his head. "Not in that one, or the other two I searched."

Putnam nodded, waving his hand in front of his face. "You're stinking the place up. Go get changed and when you book the towel, tell the lab we want a rush on processing. We got a good suspect."

Ditterand grimaced and headed down the hallway toward the back door, muttering something about the glamor of law enforcement. Putnam turned to Jensen.

"At least now we're getting somewhere. I'll lay five to one it's the vic's blood. And," Putnam's smile lacked levity, "we could get lucky and find us some killer DNA."

CHAPTER 4

THE EXTERIOR OF Serial Date's building teemed with law enforcement. Badges and yellow crime scene tape crisscrossed the attractively landscaped grounds.

Lukewarm sweat ran in rivulets down Leine's back, made worse from the short walk from her rental car, staining her cream colored blouse. She hated hot weather. It was the reason she moved to Seattle. No sweltering. And, no one from her past life could bother her. Well, except for Gene the bullshit machine. Being in L.A. also put her within spitting distance of Frank, but he rarely bothered her anymore. Apparently, he took to being a free agent a lot easier than Leine did.

It was annoying as hell.

And now, here she was back in La La Land. What was she thinking? She'd locked down her apartment in Belltown, gave the key to her neighbor, Del, and grabbed the first flight out of SeaTac to LAX. Oddly, it felt good, reminiscent of the old days when she'd get the call with the target's identity and the clock started ticking. Made her feel alive. But reality had set in as soon as she'd touched down and looked out the window of the 737 at

13

all the brown crap Los Angeleños affectionately called "air."

She left Seattle for this?

"Leine." Gene hustled up to her on the sidewalk, dragging a tall, not-bad-looking-if-you-went-for-that-type-of-guy behind him.

"So, you've done this kind of work before?" the tall man asked. "You don't look like you could fend off a chihuahua, much less keep things from hitting critical fucknuts around here."

Leine felt a muscle in her eye spasm. Gene took a step forward, putting distance between them. "Leine, meet Peter Bronkowski. He's the brains behind Serial Date."

More like the ass, she thought, but extended her hand.

Peter ignored her and raked his fingers through his streaked, California-blond hair.

"It's insane. Cops everywhere, the girls—I mean, contestants—are scared to death. Until they catch this guy, we're gonna be sucking air. Gene told you all the bachelors are ex-cons, right?" He paused for a breath. His lava red face looked like a stroke might be imminent. "I don't have a holy motherfucking idea what's going to happen when we air this week. Our ratings are gonna tank."

"I think I can handle it," Leine replied. This boy needed to calm down. He'd stress out the Dalai Lama. She turned to Gene. "Can we get him a Valium or something? He seems a tad overwrought." Best to keep things on a professional level for as long as possible. There'd be plenty of time to piss off this idiot down the road.

Gene looked at Peter. "Yeah. You're right. C'mon, Peter, we need to get you away from here and into a drink."

"No—it's all falling apart. I can't relax now." Peter sank onto a bench next to them and stared at the sidewalk. The skin around his eyes sagged. Leine wondered what kinds of pharmaceuticals he indulged in. In her experience, most producers had some kind of an addiction, and it was usually the white, powdery kind. She did a quick inventory: no facial scarring, no broken veins, and his teeth were in good shape although, that wouldn't be too hard to fix. Not with his money. His hands twitched, but that could be due to the high stress situation.

Something about this guy didn't sit right, but she couldn't figure the reason. Hell, she didn't like much of anybody anymore. She should probably give him the benefit of the doubt.

At least for now.

"Mr. Bronkowski." Leine's voice came out soft but carried weight. As though against his will, Peter's complete attention shifted to her, like a rat eyeing the mast of a sinking ship. Pretty good response for someone who was close to meltdown.

"You need to relax. You're freaking out everyone around you. Let the professionals handle this. I'm sure the ratings won't be as bad as you envision. You need to rest. Wait this thing out. Once the dust settles, the police will more than likely have caught the killer and everything will go back to normal." As far as normal could be on this freak-fest of a show.

He nodded, rubbed his eyes. A uniformed officer was heading toward them. Gene turned his back to him and motioned for Peter to get up.

"C'mon, boss, time to go." Gene pulled him to his feet and led him toward the parking lot. The cop watched them go and then turned his attention to Leine.

"You need to move along, ma'am."

"I'm here to see the detective in charge." Leine dug in her purse and handed him her driver's license. The officer checked it and relayed the information into his shoulder mic.

A disembodied voice advised them to wait. He returned her license and Leine had a seat on the bench. Minutes later the same voice came back on the radio, granting them clearance.

"Follow me, please."

Leine followed him toward the front door of the building. What was she going to tell the detective? That she was an ex-insurance investigator who'd been hired to keep an eye on things along with Gene? And how was it that Gene wasn't a suspect? His priors read like a bad novel. No murder, but plenty of check kiting and forgeries. Leine thought she remembered something about grand theft back in the eighties, too.

She shifted her handbag to her other shoulder as they neared the perimeter tape. Every so often, one of the show's employees scurried past, identifiable by a Kelly green vest with the word Serial Date stitched in vibrant yellow across the upper left front. The excitement on their faces was unmistakable. It's not every day someone is dismembered at work.

They came to a stop just inside the tape. A man in a dark blue suit broke from a small group of uniformed officers and headed their way. Must be the detective, Leine thought.

The man was tall, over six feet, with dark hair and large hands. He flicked his gaze over her as he walked toward them.

Wow. Those are some gorgeous green eyes. She felt a little trill of sexual interest run through her, but squashed it like a bug on a windshield. It had been a long time since her last fling. She could wait until someone more appropriate came around, say, a corporate raider or a mobster. Fucking a cop would be like going to confession, only without the added bonus of absolution.

She never forgave Frank for being legit. Everyone she knew had assumed he was Mafioso, including her. She didn't want or deserve an upstanding member of society. Not after what she'd done.

The detective stopped a few inches away, closer than she liked. She took a step back and hiked her handbag higher on her shoulder.

He eyed the cop standing next to Leine. "Go ahead and sweep the area for folks that don't need to be here."

The officer nodded. "Sure thing."

"And who have we here?" The detective's intense gaze bored into her. Leine squared off, tilted her head back and looked directly at him.

"Leine Basso. I've been hired on as additional security. Are you the detective in charge?"

His mouth twitched in apparent amusement. Leine found herself staring at his lips.

"Leine? That's an unusual name. Detective Santiago Jensen." He held out his hand.

She shook it and replied, "It's short for Madeleine, which I despise. Yours is interesting. The height and eye color says Jensen, but the dark hair and olive skin tone screams Santiago."

He laughed. "Yeah, the product of a Norwegian father and Mexican mother. I'm partial to Lute Fiske and tortillas."

"Together? That's a pretty gruesome fish taco."

He laughed again. His teeth were white and straight. She liked that in a man.

"So what do you need from me? Name, rank and serial number?"

"Nah. Bronkowski gave us your information earlier. You're about as clean as they come."

Nice to know that Eric, the bastard, had kept his word. He'd promised to scrub her past, leave her clearances intact, hoping to make good. The rest she wasn't willing to forgive. Not now. Not ever.

Leine shrugged. "What can I say? I live right."

A slight frown flitted across Detective Jensen's features, quickly replaced by his hundred-watt smile. Leine wondered briefly if he'd run across anything that might make him want to delve further into her past. Doubtful. Probably his cop-radar kicking in. What could she say? Years in the profession left its mark. Not everybody noticed. Just the ones who bought the ticket and took the ride.

"So, detective, how can I help the investigation?"

He smiled, his eyes half-closed in a way that had Leine rethinking her decision to skip happy-sack with the detective. She felt like a small planet being drawn into his orbit. Maybe she could be persuaded.

"Well, ma'am I can think of several—" His attention shifted, over Leine's shoulder. "I'll have to get back to you on that." He slipped past her like a wave and was gone. Leine checked herself from drifting along behind him. She turned to see what made his demeanor change.

The shouting hit her eardrums as though breaking through the surface from underwater. At the end of the walkway on the other side of the perimeter tape, a red-faced, barrel-chested man stood toe-to-toe with one of the cops, his face raw with emotion. Rage, as far as Leine could tell, mixed with despair so deep, it made her catch her breath. Jensen intercepted the man before his imminent detonation and moved him off to one side, talking to him in soothing yet authoritative tones.

Further down the walkway, a tan, slight woman with white blond hair and glowing white teeth gripped one of the show's young employees by their green vest, tears streaming down her face. The woman, probably family, most likely the mother, choked, sobbed her grief onto the kid's vest, staining it like sweat. The kid gripped her shoulders and pushed her to arm's length. The poor guy looked panicked as he scanned the area, searching for someone to help him. One of the cops standing nearby started for the two.

Calming the woman down was going to take something other than a police officer and a kid. Leine walked toward them and caught the cop's eye. He lifted his chin in acknowledgement and stepped back. The kid's eyes met hers and she gave him a slight nod. Relief flooded his face. He bowed his head and said something to the sobbing woman. Her unfocused gaze skated first to him, then to Leine, the moist confusion in her eyes a match to her mascara-streaked face.

"She was only nineteen. Nineteen! This was her first real break-" The woman looked ready to collapse.

"Is there somewhere I can take her?" Leine asked the kid. He nodded and motioned toward a secluded courtyard a few steps down to their right.

She placed her arm around the woman's shoulders and guided her toward the courtyard. The woman cried softly, her face buried in Leine's armpit, using her thin shirt as a de-facto tissue. She led her to a bench near a fragrant honeysuckle bush and gently peeled her arms from around her neck, lowering her to the seat with great care.

The woman's cries replaced now by occasional ripples of emotion, Leine dug inside her purse for a small pack of tissues and placed them beside her on the bench. The woman shook her head as fresh sobs bubbled over.

"Why? Why Mandy? She was so vibrant, so full of life. S-she was going to be an actress, you know." The woman grabbed a tissue and blew, her head bowed as though she couldn't bear to see the world. She glanced at Leine briefly, before her eyes lost focus again.

"They told me she died sometime last night. Stan and I were home in bed when she was..." She rocked back and forth. "I can't help her. I have no way to help her. She won't know where she is. She'll wonder where her momma is..." The tears fell, attempting to wash away a mother's guilt for not being there to protect her child.

Leine looked away. The sting of tears pricked at her eyelids. What could she say? This grief had no match in Leine's world. Her daughter was still alive. Where, she had no idea, but reports from friends assured her. The last sighting was a few months back, in Amsterdam. Leine's grief grew from another vine, entirely.

Knowing your child didn't want you in her life.

Ever.

CHAPTER 5

ETER WALKED PAST the couple sitting at the front table, a plate of linguine and clam sauce between them, and headed for the back room. Several people stood at the crowded bar, singing along to Warren Zevon's *Werewolves of London*. The pretty, model-thin bartender kept pace with the drink orders shouted at her, a smile never leaving her face.

The further back in Bonanno's Peter got, the smaller the crowd, until he came to an open doorway flanked by two large men in pony tails wearing identical black tee shirts, cargo pants and combat boots. They checked his I.D. and parted to let him pass.

Buzz Runyon sat in the far corner, his back against the wall. The senator showed vestiges of his former athleticism, but time and power had done their best to obscure most, if not all of his youthful vigor. His double chin and expanding waistline mocked his tanned features and expensive haircut, giving him the appearance of someone who came late to the party of the L.A. fitness-obsessed. On the other hand, he kept pace quite well with many of the über powerful in regard to their unusual proclivities.

Peter knew from past experience that when the senator needed to get his freak on, nothing was sacred. This included forays to a little-known organic farm outside of L.A. that raised free-range livestock. The senator referred to his little expeditions to the farm as a 'trip to bountiful'. The memory of the senator's favorite pastime would forever be seared onto Peter's retinas. He figured the recurring nightmares were the price he had to pay for access.

"Sit down." The senator nodded at the chair next to him. Peter took the seat across from him and ordered a shot of Grey Goose from the waitress who appeared at his side.

The senator waited until the waitress left, then leaned forward, anxiety spiraling off him in waves.

"What the hell happened, Pete? I'm in a closed meeting all damn day and I come out and my aide tells me a contestant's been murdered on the set? I thought you said you had security handled."

"I did. I do. It happened last night, after everybody left. No one was supposed to be near the set. They found the body this morning in the prop closet after they finished filming a promo. Apparently, the rent-a-cop out front fell asleep on the job. It was his first late shift. He doesn't remember hearing or seeing anything unusual." Peter had wondered how the guy could miss the sound of a power saw being used to dismember a body, not to mention Mandy's screams, but realized he wouldn't have heard a thing from a soundproof set.

Senator Runyon stuffed some pasta in his mouth and washed it down with a swallow of red wine. Peter glanced at the huge plate of fettuccine swimming in butter and his stomach churned. Ordinarily he wouldn't give the artery-clogging meal a second thought. Not tonight.

"I can't let this bury me, Pete."

Peter took a deep breath, steeling himself to manage the impending meltdown. "Senator, I realize this means-"

The senator cut him off. "What this means, Bronkowski, is we might have had a problem before, but this compounds the original reason I called this meeting."

"And that would be-"

"I'm a shoo-in for the L.A. County Make a Difference Award, but that slime ball Lopez is getting press for the shit he did for all those inner city kids last year, so I'm running a distant second for the Los ANGELenos Award. Being connected to the show's gonna sink me, unless you can find some way to spin it."

Peter leaned back. As usual, it was all about the senator. The Los ANGELenos Award was on par with the Congressional Medal of Honor as far as a southern California politician was concerned. The last three Governors and several senators and representatives had won the award, and it was rumored to be the magic bullet when it came to winning over the hearts and minds of multiple constituencies.

Runyon jabbed at the pasta in front of him. "Losing is not an option. Word is, that cocksucker Lopez is gunning for my seat and if he gets the award, it raises his profile to an unacceptable level." He wiped the grease off his lips and took another sip of wine. "I was gonna have you ramp up a media blitz on the ex-con rehab project. Obviously, that's no longer an option."

The waitress returned with Peter's drink. He drained the glass before she could leave and ordered another.

"So, who was it? Tina?" The senator dabbed at the corners of his mouth with his napkin, looking at him expectantly.

"No, it wasn't Tina." Peter couldn't decide whether to inform the senator and risk meltdown status and possibly another trip to the farm, or wait and let the media do it. A trickle of sweat slid down the back of his neck. If he waited and didn't get into the particulars, he risked alienating his most powerful ally. On the other hand, the police seemed confident they'd crack the identity of the killer in no time and Peter didn't want to alarm the senator unnecessarily. He opted for a combination of the two.

Peter pivoted toward Runyon, keeping his voice down. The senator leaned forward, his garlic-and-cigar breath enough to make Peter gag.

"There's more to it than what the media reported."

The senator's expression shifted to one of anxiety. Peter rushed to put him at ease.

"The LAPD's confident they'll be able to make an arrest, so there's no reason to be alarmed." Not exactly what they said, but if it avoided a breakdown, it was worth the small white lie.

"What happened?" It was the senator's turn to sweat.

"Nothing to be worried about. If it gets to the point where things don't develop as planned, then you'll be the first to know, I promise. Right now, the less you know the better."

The senator's face flushed deep red. Uh-oh, Peter thought. *He's going to lose it.*

"I'll be the judge of that, Pete. What the fuck is going on?"

Peter sighed. *I should've kept my mouth shut.*

"The killer dismembered the victim."

"Dismembered? As in, cut off body parts?"

"Yes."

"Who?"

"Amanda Milton."

Senator Runyon collapsed back in his chair with a stunned expression. He wiped the perspiration from his forehead with a linen napkin. The color in his face had faded to a pasty shade of gray. Alarmed, Peter wondered if he should call 9-1-1.

"This isn't good, Pete. This is very bad, in fact. You said Amanda Milton?"

"Do you know her?"

"Know her? Christ, I've been banging her every Tuesday, for God's sake." He leaned forward, elbows on the table and put his head in his hands. "Fuck me. Fuck fuck fuck. I'm dead."

Peter couldn't believe it. *Amanda and the senator?* Thinking about the two of them together made him want to vomit. Mandy with her young, nubile body and perky tits, and the flaccid old senator, who had a hard time getting it up without a farm animal nearby. This definitely complicated things.

"How long?" Peter asked, his morbid fascination growing.

"A couple of months, tops." The senator's gaze locked on his as though he alone could hold back the tide. "You have to make this someone else's problem, Pete. If this gets out, I'm finished. There's not a media consultant alive who can spin me out of this one."

Yeah, Peter thought. *That, and the Hereford incident and I could totally bring you down, motherfucker.* He kept his expression impassive.

The senator's eyes widened. "Aw, Jesus. What if I'm a suspect? My finger prints are all over her apartment." He blinked, once. "Janet will finally get proof of what she's been bitching about all these years. There'll be no reason for her to stay, not if I'm finished." He closed his eyes. "Knopf has been on her for years to write a book. Offered her seven figures."

Good God, Peter thought. The man could obsess. What about him? Didn't the senator owe his illustrious career to Serial Date? He'd still be the Mayor of Podunk, California if Peter and the show hadn't given him a platform by agreeing to tie everything in with the California penal system. It had been a pain in the ass, working with the State and Runyon, but in the long run it was a win-win for everyone. Peter accepted the occasional request for a tour of the set from the wardens, and looked the other way when a favored ex-con was promised a slot for the next season.

"As I said, the LAPD assured me that they'll keep information about the investigation to a minimum for as long as they can. No one has to know about your involvement with Mandy."

"What about your people? You have a lot of employees running around on that set. What if she talked? Can you absolutely guarantee that this won't hit the tabloids?"

Peter had been stressing about that himself, but it wouldn't do any good to convey that to Runyon. Peter answered with a voice that sounded much calmer than he felt. "Everyone's on board, senator. Don't worry. I have a tight rein on my people."

"You damn well better." The senator pulled out his phone. "I'm calling Shank. He'll know what to do with this pile of shit."

Jack Shank was a high-powered attorney to the stars whose specialty was helping his clients avoid unnecessary publicity and/or jail time. Ever since he'd worked his magic for the internationally known televangelist with a penchant for smoking crack and banging male prostitutes, he'd been the go-to guy for anyone with a serious problem. He had his hands full with Runyon.

"Jack? Buzz here. Yeah, fine, fine. Jack, I got a problem I'm gonna need you to run interference on. What? Yeah, it's about the murder." Runyon glanced at Peter. "He's right here. You want to now? Hold on." He held out the phone. "He wants to talk to you."

Peter took the phone. "This is Peter."

Jack Shank's soft voice slithered through the earpiece.

"So the shit finally hit the fan." There was a faint click in the background followed by a deep inhalation. "I warned the senator it was only a matter of time until something went wrong, but he wouldn't listen. Should never have gotten involved with the show." Shank started to cough like he was about to hack up a lung.

The coughing subsided and Shank's voice came back on the line.

"Talk to me."

Peter told him about the murder and what the LAPD said about the investigation. Jack Shank listened in silence, the occasional damp cough punctuating Peter's sentences. When he came to the part about the senator's involvement with the victim, Shank cleared his throat, but didn't say anything for a moment. Peter fidgeted in his chair.

"Well? What do you want to do?" Peter asked.

There was a long pause, then, "I'll tell you what you should do. After I do that, I want to speak to the senator."

Shank ran down a list of comments Peter could use when the media got hold of the full story, and explained a few other options. "And Peter? When they run with this,

and I guarantee they will, then you roll with it. Spin it like there's no tomorrow. I'll take care of the senator."

Peter handed the phone back to Runyon, pushed his chair back and stood. The waitress returned with his second shot of vodka. Peter indicated she leave it with the senator. He waited for a moment, but Runyon was so absorbed in the conversation with Shank that he didn't look up or acknowledge Peter.

He left without saying goodbye.

Detective Santiago Jensen slapped the folder on the desk in front of him and sighed.

Nineteen years old. *What a waste.* He flipped open the file and glanced at the crime scene photos of Amanda Milton. Peter Bronkowski had some kind of pull if he'd been able to operate the set of Serial Date with only Gene Dorfenberger as security. Jensen rubbed his eyes. It was a damned miracle something hadn't happened before now.

He'd had Garcia pull files on every ex-con even remotely associated with the show. Both he and Putnam were amazed at some of the lowlifes Bronkowski employed. Their rap sheets ran the gamut of burglary, assault, domestic violence. How did the show ever get enough female contestants? Yeah, they got paid, but it wasn't a huge amount. At first blush they thought these guys were serial killers. He shook his head. Apparently, the all-American guy wasn't cutting it for the modern American woman.

Bronkowski made them all sign a waiver that explained who they'd be working with and that the show couldn't be held responsible for anything that happened outside the confines of the studio. He'd been floored when Bronkowski told him maybe one out of fifty contestants opted not to sign.

Putnam was certain Graber did the deed, but Jensen wasn't so sure. To add to everything, there was mounting pressure from above. Murders were up twelve percent in the city of Los Angeles alone. The Mayor and the City Council had been climbing all over the Chief's ass to bring the numbers down. Departments were stretched tight.

Election years sucked.

Jensen thought about Leine Basso, the woman Bronkowski hired to beef up security. Her most recent gig had been working as an insurance investigator. He'd read something in her file about doing security for a couple of government hacks, but Jensen got the feeling if he dug a little deeper, he'd find out a lot more about Ms. Basso.

She'd been married briefly to a successful businessman named Frank Basso, but ended up dumping him. Jensen wondered why she'd leave such a dick gig. Huge house in Bel Air. Influential friends. Bi-annual trips to Vegas, Europe, New York. Most women he knew would climb over the bodies of their dead grandmothers to snag a rich husband like Frank, and it intrigued him.

She carried herself the way his buddies in Special Forces did; relaxed and calm on the exterior, like nothing could phase her. Jensen sensed another kind of tension in her, more emotional, one that pulled at the calm exterior. She exuded mystery.

And he really wanted to fuck her.

"Hey Santa." Putnam tapped him on the shoulder, breaking into his thoughts. "They got some kind of letter down at the freak show. Bronkowski sounded pretty messed up."

Sighing, Jensen slid Amanda Milton's file in the desk drawer and grabbed his badge.

Showtime.

"There. It's right there." Peter Bronkowski jabbed his finger at the offending piece of paper on his desk. "Fuck. He's going to do it again, isn't he?"

Jensen slid on a pair of latex gloves before he picked up the letter and read the wandering manifesto. When he finished, he handed it to Putnam and gave Bronkowski his serious, calm look. Putnam finished reading and stepped back, remaining quiet.

"We're doing everything we can, Mr. Bronkowski. He won't be able to get to any of the other contestants, not now." Security was tight. The contestants couldn't visit the toilet without a shadow. Luckily, the women lived together in a house a few blocks away from the set while taping the show, so it would be easy to keep an eye on them all. Especially since the house was already wired with cameras everywhere except the bathrooms.

Jensen re-scanned parts of the letter, looking for something that might give him answers to the writer's identity. The letter went on at length about how watching reality shows and eating factory farmed meat killed off people's brain cells and made everyone stupid and fat. The loss of intelligence would be devastating to the country's brain-trust as a whole. According to the author, this couldn't be tolerated.

The obvious remedy was to foster public awareness by eating younger, free-range meat that hadn't experienced the long term, adverse effects of heavy metals and toxins absorbed from the environment. Although, not too young. The author preferred some seasoning to his protein, and referenced Ms. Milton as a prime example.

Enter Serial Date, the perfect outlet for his protest. His reason being if he culled the contestants from the most offensive show, it would bring attention to the plight of the television-watching public. As an added bonus, the contestants, being healthy and fit specimens, allowed him to make his point succinctly, while exercising his right to enjoy a healthy, delicious meal. He apologized for not taking more choice cuts from the body and leaving so much waste, but had been unable to remove it from the prop closet without being seen.

Wonderful, Jensen thought. *A cannibal with a social agenda.*

Leine Basso walked into the office. "You called?" she said to Bronkowski. Jensen tensed.

Bronkowski pointed at the manifesto. "The killer sent a letter. He's a fucking cannibal..."

"Mr. Bronkowski," Jensen warned, his voice terse. He looked pointedly at Leine and Peter. "This isn't general knowledge and is key evidence, unique to this crime. You can't discuss this with anyone outside the investigation."

Putnam added, "If this is leaked to anyone, we'll hold you both responsible and file charges. Do you understand?"

"You won't hear it from me, detectives." Leine's gaze swept over Jensen.

A surge of electricity headed straight down his belly and into his dick. She wore her dark brown hair loose and it fell just below her shoulders. Sexy.

Definitely have to follow up on this one, Jensen thought.

"No, no. Of course not. I don't need this getting out any more than you guys do." Bronkowski waved at the air, dismissing their concerns.

"Is there anything I can do?" Leine asked, looking first at Jensen and Putnam, then Bronkowski.

"If you find out anything about an ex-con or contestant, no matter how inconsequential it may seem, my partner and I would appreciate it if you'd let us know." Jensen picked up the letter and placed it into an evidence bag. "We pulled the personnel files from both seasons, but nothing beats a visual—it'd be great if you could keep an eye on everyone else on set and report any suspicious activity. The more bodies we have looking out, the better."

"Of course, detective. Anything else?"

Everything about her said "business only." What would it take to get those panties off? Jensen smiled his most disarming smile. Piece of cake, he thought. Turn on the ol' Santiago charm. Make her think she's part of the investigation, get close to her. A little wine, a little dinner... then, look out, Mamacita. Give her some red-hot salsa.

"That's all for now, Ms. Basso. We've got your number."

CHAPTER 6

THAT'S THE LAST one, Edward." Peter set the moving box on the dining room table and wiped his forehead with a tissue.

Edward raced to the box, opened it and checked the contents. With a deep sigh, he visibly relaxed once he'd made sure nothing had broken. Peter felt a twinge of sadness. The new meds didn't seem to have much of an effect.

"Edward, I need to ask you something important, okay? It has to do with the blackness."

Edward stiffened. He began to rock back and forth and shake his head. The humming began almost immediately. Peter put a hand on his arm. Edward quieted.

"Don't worry, it's a simple question. You only have to answer yes or no, all right?"

Edward nodded, though he still acted wary. Peter knew anything that had to do with what Edward referred to as the blackness could set him back months, and he didn't bring it up lightly.

"Edward, I need to know if you've experienced it recently and whether you've told anyone."

Edward shook his head. "No, no, Peter, not recently. Not recently. The blackness isn't here anymore." Peter took in Edward's agitated hand movements and the telltale facial tick, and his heart sank.

"Edward, are you still taking those pills Doctor Shapiro prescribed?"

Edward rocked his head up and down. "Yes. I take them every day, just like you said." He opened a box next to him and proceeded to search the items inside.

Peter sighed. He knew the move to a new place would screw everything up, probably send Edward off his meds, but he couldn't chance the police finding out about him. Peter had worked diligently to keep his younger brother under wraps ever since he'd found Edward at the age of sixteen, standing over their stepfather's dead body, holding a bloody baseball bat. A brutal alcoholic, their stepfather enjoyed ambushing Peter when he came home from his afternoon job at the local newspaper. On one occasion, he nearly broke Peter's neck. This did not sit well with Edward who had a near reverence for Peter. Peter had been the only one who understood why Edward punished the mean dogs in the neighborhood. In Edward's mind, killing his stepfather counted as payback for Peter's friendship.

"Edward, you know you have to take the pills or the blackness comes back, right?"

Edward avoided Peter's eyes and continued to dig inside the box.

Peter went into the bathroom and came back out with a full bottle of pills in his hand. Edward backed away, shaking his head.

"No. You can't make me take them. They make me someone else inside, Peter. Please don't make me take them."

Edward described the blackness once as being trapped in a dark basement with only a small glimmer of light visible overhead. His thoughts during this time scared him and as a result kept to himself. People passed him off as extremely shy. He told Peter that when he was around, sometimes the door to the basement opened and the light poured in and he felt normal. As Peter became more successful and had less time to spend with Edward, the blackness became more prevalent, until it could only be controlled with medication.

Peter placed the bottle of pills on the table.

"You have to take these. Something happened at work and there are cops all over the place. If they find out about you and what you've done, they're going to come down hard, believe that you're the bad person they're looking for."

Peter took a step forward. Edward edged back until the wall stopped him.

"You haven't been on set again, have you Edward? Like at night when everyone's gone home?"

He shook his head. "No, Peter, I only did it that one time, I swear. I never do it anymore because you told me not to."

Peter nodded. Edward was covering something up, that much was obvious. He knew if he looked in the freezer, he'd probably find plastic bags filled with small animal parts, but he didn't feel like looking today.

"Fine. I believe you. But you have to promise me you'll take your medication every day."

Edward broke into a relieved grin. "Yes, I will take the medication, Peter, I promise."

CHAPTER 7

L EINE WATCHED AS Billy maneuvered in for Tina's close up, using a handheld camera to achieve the show's signature documentary feel. Personally, Leine got a queasy stomach whenever she watched the playback. She didn't do so well in the back seat of a moving car, either.

"It's an incredible adrenaline rush to think that I could be next," Tina said with a breathy sigh. She turned to look at Javier and playfully wiggled her petite foot at him. On cue, Javier looked into the camera and grinned. He lay stretched across a layer of cream-colored satin pillows as he painted Tina's toenails shell pink, bobbing his head and shoulders to the incessant beat of techno dance music.

A sultry Asian beauty with dark, kohl-lined eyes, Tina's shock of white-blonde hair and sparkly, hot pink mini dress contrasted sharply to Javier's dark good looks, black tux and flawless tan. The magic of body makeup.

They were filming Tina's 'confession' for that week's show. She appeared unperturbed as she recited her lines on camera, although Leine noticed she alternated between gripping the arms of her chair and smoothing her hair back.

The process of shooting a reality show may be interesting to some people, but the well-scripted performances put Leine in escape mode. She'd had enough lying and subterfuge in her old life and deception now set her teeth on edge. It didn't matter that the audience was more or less complicit.

Then there were the contestants. X-ray thin, the way they stared at a hoagie made Leine eat her lunch off-site. What would make a young, attractive woman take a chance on making a love connection with a known felon? Sure, they knew the men weren't actual serial killers once they signed the waiver, but still. Leine couldn't imagine her daughter being quite so naïve.

The bachelors didn't do much for her, either, but she watched them closely. Her gut told her the killer remained nearby, curious to see the effect of his actions. She'd never been tempted to stick around. Once she'd completed a job, she disappeared.

But that was business. This type of kill was personal. Leine never let things get personal.

Tina finished her piece and Billy handed the camera to a grip. Javier said something to her and laughed as he walked away toward the concession table.

Billy sat down in the director's chair and slid what looked like a script from his back pocket. One of the electricians walked up to him and started chatting. Leine waited until they were finished, then made her way over and sat next to him.

"Nice work."

Billy nodded, smiled. "Thanks." He eyed her for a moment, then, "You're Gene's friend, right?"

"Yeah."

"He said you worked as a bodyguard for some government agency."

"Something like that. Have you always been a cameraman?"

Billy shifted in his chair. A strand of dark, wavy hair fell across his face and he tucked it behind his ear. "No, but it's my favorite, so far. Right up there with director."

"From what I hear, you're pretty good."

Billy smiled and looked down, obviously pleased with the compliment.

"What did you do before this?" Leine figured it took years to become proficient in handling a video camera and he didn't look all that old. She guessed late thirties.

He shrugged, looked into the distance. "I tried teaching. Couldn't deal with the bureaucracy. Then I experimented with a couple of other gigs that didn't work out and here I am." He returned his attention to Leine. "It's a shame about Mandy. What are you planning to do about it?"

The abrupt change of subject surprised her.

"That's for the police to decide. I'm just here to help make sure everybody's safe."

Billy folded his arms across his chest. "They know who killed her?"

"Not yet. The police are working a couple of leads. Hopefully they'll know more in the next twenty-four hours." Leine didn't mention Gene told her they'd narrowed the suspects down to two main persons of interest and interviewed them both that morning.

Leine had been watching each of the bachelors on set and eliminated most of them in her own mind. Gene gave her copies of their personnel files, but none of them struck her as the violent, mutilating kind. One of the two men the cops singled out, Devon Winston, said he'd been having dinner with his mother at the time of the murder. Leine thought the alibi convenient, but figured his mother would break down under questioning if the story wasn't true.

That left Charles Graber, the main bachelor for the season and usually on set. According to the files he was the least violent of the two, but had a shitty alibi. Gene thought the cops found some evidence linking him to the murder. Still, Leine didn't feel one way or another about him.

Billy folded the script and returned it to his back pocket. "Tell me about being a bodyguard. You ever smoke anyone?"

"It wasn't like that. I mainly did low level bureaucrat types."

Billy studied her for a moment. "Why don't I believe you?"

Leine smiled. He's bluffing, trying to punch up his idea of what kind of person I am. I'm not that transparent.

"You can believe what you want, Billy, but I haven't had to kill anyone." Technically true. She could have turned down any of the targets, but that would have cost her the reputation she'd worked so hard to build.

Billy's lips curled up at the corners and his eyes danced.

"Whatever you say, Leine." He got to his feet and held out his hand. "I need to run. Let's talk, soon."

She shook his hand and he headed for the exit, a bounce in his step.

That's one odd duck, Leine thought. She'd forgotten what L.A. creative types were like. You never knew where you stood, primarily because most of them didn't know, either.

Tina had been hanging out, watching them from the other side of the set, and chose that moment to approach. Her face appeared frozen in time, like a statue. Leine wondered if the young woman used Botox. They certainly started early, she thought.

"You're the new security guard, right?"

Leine nodded. "And you're Tina?"

Tina smiled. Her cheeks barely moved. "That's right." She slid onto the director's chair. Leine's eyes watered from the onslaught of her perfume.

"Do you think they'll catch the guy soon?"

"They seem to think they're close."

"It's really hard on the other girls."

"I can imagine. There's plenty of security on you guys, though. It'll be over soon."

"It's not that. It's hard for us to not say anything to the press. They're everywhere, and offering a lot of money. A bunch of us have boyfriends and they're wondering why we aren't allowed to see them. Naomi's boyfriend already threatened to break it off with her. He thinks she's lying to him, seeing one of the bachelors on the side."

"Well, it's pretty important to the case that they know where the contestants are at all times. I'm sure the boyfriend will come around once the killer is caught and she can explain it to him."

Tina looked away and chewed on her lower lip. She turned back to Leine.

"One of us might have let something slip," she said, her eyes cutting to the side.

"Oh? Like what?"

"Like telling someone about the-the missing body parts. I think they even paid for the information."

Nice, Leine thought. Won't be long now before the press picks that up. "I'll have to let the detectives know. It's going to impact the case."

Tina's kohl-lined eyes widened and she reached over and touched Leine's arm. "You didn't hear this from me. The rest of the girls would rip me apart if they found out."

Heather and Tina were the top two contenders on the show. Leine figured the information was Tina's way of eliminating the competition. Leine didn't plan on naming anyone, except maybe Tina.

"How many people outside the show know?"

Tina hesitated a moment. "Not more than three, I think."

"I'll be sure to let the police know." Leine got up to leave.

Tina looked disappointed. "Aren't you going to ask me who they are?"

"If the police want more information, I'll tell them who told me." Leine had a pretty good idea which contestants Tina would single out as leaks.

"Do you think the killer will try again?"

"They're doing all they can to prevent that."

Almost to herself Tina said, "I wonder why he chose Mandy and not me?" She held up a well-toned arm for Leine to see. "I work out, too. She definitely wasn't the most cut, by far."

Leine took a deep breath. *Wow*. "I'm sure he had his reasons."

Tina nodded. Leine couldn't be sure, but it looked like a frown struggled to make its appearance.

"Great piece today, by the way."

"Hmm?"

"The confession Billy just shot. That was some good acting."

Tina smiled, evidently flattered. "You think so? I've been taking classes."

"It shows."

CHAPTER 8

THE ARREST OF Charles Graber didn't go exactly as planned. Once word reached the Chief that the bloody towel had Graber's DNA on it, Putnam, Jensen and two uniformed backup units were given the go ahead and descended on his West Hollywood home. The Los Angeles Sheriff Department was all too happy to allow the LAPD to step in and make the arrest, even though it was their jurisdiction.

Putnam assigned Felix Ditterand and his partner to cover the rear of the small Craftsman-style home, in case anyone escaped. The suspect burst through the back door at full throttle and Ditterand pursued on foot. Graber cut down an alley, heading for Santa Monica Boulevard and the rookie fired off a round to try to stop him before reaching the crowded roadway. As a result, Graber landed in Cedars Sinai with a bullet to the groin and Ditterand was placed on administrative leave.

Somebody leaked the gruesome details of the murder to a reporter from Entertainment All the Time! and the news went viral. The press descended like a flock of tourists at an open bar. Chat rooms everywhere buzzed with conjecture and vitriol regarding Amanda Milton's grisly murder and what it meant for the future of television and reality shows. Twits tweeted, bloggers blogged and several news outlets ran in-depth interviews of the show's previous contestants and bachelors.

The senator called in Jack Shank for spin control and Jack Shank called Peter.

By the time Jensen walked into his office, Peter Bronkowski had polished off most of a bottle of vodka and was contemplating which method of suicide would be less painful. He'd narrowed it down to swilling a handful of Xanax or wearing a Humvee.

"I'm fucked. Fucked, fucked, fucked." Peter sat slumped in his Italian leather chair, a small Baccarat crystal lamp the only illumination in the room.

"Did they at least buy you dinner first?" Jensen folded himself into the chair opposite him.

"This is it. I'm finished. Yesterday's news. Horseshit." He looked up, tried to focus on Jensen. "What're you doing here?"

"Thought I should come by, let you know we picked up Graber, but it looks like you already know."

"No shit." He attempted to lift himself to a standing position, but fell forward into the desk. He held his hands out to steady himself, missed and staggered backward into the chair.

"He's the star. What the hell are we gonna do without the star of the fucking show? Oh, yeah." He smiled to himself. "There won' be a show after tonight." It annoyed him he couldn't stop the hysterical giggle before it disintegrated into pitiless weeping. Not in front of the cop.

"I'm sure it's not that bad—"

"The fuck do you know?" Peter lurched forward and jabbed his finger in the air, then let his arm drop to his side. "Christ, I stroked this one so hard, sucked up to all those bastards. Now everybody's pulling their ads. No way I'm gonna survive this." He leaned back in the chair and closed his eyes. "What am I gonna do with Eddie?"

"Who's Eddie?"

Peter waved the question away, shook his head. "Nobody. Forget it." He narrowed his eyes at his watch, trying to make out the numbers. "Should be getting the old pink slip any minute, now. Fuck. Me. They'll be out for blood." He glanced blearily around his office, taking in the expensive Italian furnishings and modern art, his gaze settling on the new ninety-inch, Internet-ready 3-D television. Emotion welled up inside him and he choked back a sob.

Not only had he not saved any of the money he'd made, he was up to his balls in debt—the house in Malibu, the Ferrari, the villa in Croatia, Edward's new place. And oh, God, the cocaine. The weekly payment to his dealer, El Zorro, was way past most developed countries' GDP and the thought of losing unrestricted access made him shudder. He'd have to go back to smoking crack. He started to pull out the small stash of Peruvian Bliss in his desk drawer to have a reassuring snort and remembered Jensen's presence across from him in the nick of time. He eased the drawer shut with what he thought passed for nonchalance.

"If it makes you feel any better, things can get back to normal now."

Peter let out a loud belch, tipped the bottle of vodka upside down and drained it. He set it back on the desk but misjudged the distance and watched it fall to the floor. "Doesn't." He closed his eyes and leaned his head back. The room started to spin. He pitched forward and threw up in the Murano glass wastebasket near his feet.

He wiped his mouth with the back of his hand as the office door opened. Senator Runyon, Billy, Gene Dorfenberger and several of the show's crew filed in. The air around them practically crackled from the group's excitement. Probably here to witness the execution, Peter thought.

He pasted on a smile and stuck out his hand. "Senator, good to see you-"

The senator came around to Peter's side of the desk and pulled a bottle of Dom Perignon from behind his back. Peter gazed at the champagne, confused. He looked into the senator's face, searching for clarity. A cigar the size of a porn star's money maker protruded from Runyon's fat, smiling lips. The senator must be doing Ecstasy again, Peter thought. It was the only thing that made sense.

"Looks like you're way ahead of me, Pete, my boy. Isn't it fantastic? This has never happened in the history of reality television." The senator's face possessed an ecstatic glow.

Peter felt as though he was a bit player in some sort of dream sequence in a movie and didn't know his lines. He continued to look uncomprehendingly at the senator and the rest of the crew now crowded into his office. The stench from the trash can reached his nostrils and he rolled his chair closer to the senator.

Runyon looked closely at Peter. "You haven't heard?"

Peter shook his head.

The senator glanced impatiently around the room. "Didn't someone at least text the poor schmuck?" His question was met with silence and shuffling feet.

Runyon turned back to Peter and, grinning, opened his arms wide, almost cold-cocking one of the set gophers with the champagne bottle.

"My boy, great news. We thought it couldn't get any better. The ratings are through the roof. It's unprecedented. Never before in television history has this happened."

Peter sat in stunned silence, trying to suck air back into his lungs.

Senator Runyon handed the bottle of champagne to one of the crew members and told him to open it.

Then he leaned in close to Peter and whispered, "This calls for a trip to Bountiful. My treat."

Jensen slipped out of the office before the senator cornered him. Nothing like an election year to make a politician willing to bond with law enforcement.

He walked through the front doors and headed for the parking lot. He'd learned to trust his gut through years of dealing with both the guilty and the innocent. His instincts were going into claxon horn mode this time. It didn't fit. During the second interview before the arrest went down, Graber had confessed to having consensual sex with the victim the day before and that they'd planned to leave L.A. together as soon as the show's season ended. That explained Graber's semen inside Amanda Milton and why there were no signs of forcible rape.

Graber had, in Jensen's opinion, exhibited the behavior of a man who had just heard the love of his life was murdered. He acted like he was in a daze, cooperated fully with the investigation and didn't immediately 'lawyer up,' even waived his rights. On top of that, the guy volunteered to take a polygraph test and passed it with flying colors. Putnam shrugged it off, arguing that Graber was a pathological liar with no conscience: lying didn't faze him, so wouldn't register on the test.

After the arrest, when they spoke to him before going into surgery, Putnam asked why he'd run, Graber answered, "Because I know how it looks and it looks like I killed her. I'm an ex-felon. My cum was inside her, my DNA's on the towel. The fucking press is screaming for an arrest. What were my chances of getting a fair trial—or convincing a jury I didn't do it?"

Putnam insisted Graber was merely a good actor. If he was acting, then Jensen figured he must be Academy Award material.

He drove out of the parking lot and took a left. The balmy evening air ruffled his hair, temporarily distracting him. He thought of Leine Basso and wondered if he should call her and see if she was up for dinner, get his mind off of Graber for a little while. The one good thing about the arrest was that now he could work on getting Ms. Basso into bed. The more he got to know her, the more he wanted.

He pulled out his phone, punched in her number, and got voicemail. He hung up and put the cell back in his pocket. Then he made himself go over the case one more time.

All the evidence pointed to Graber. His DNA was on the towel with the victim's blood. He had one of the victim's earrings in his possession, a perfect match with the one found on the victim's remaining ear. He could have been in the building at the time of Amanda's death—he had no alibi other than he'd been at home, asleep. He knew his way around power tools and was a gym rat. He'd worked in the food industry and wouldn't eat a chicken if it was the last piece of food on the planet, and had said as much in the interview. That fit perfectly with the rambling letter the killer wrote. Several of the contestants testified that Graber had hung out with Amanda, although none could corroborate their relationship.

Putnam floated the possibility Amanda rejected Graber and Graber killed her in a fit of anger. But why the letter? He didn't strike Jensen as the manifesto-writing type.

Jensen didn't feel it. Graber didn't have a violent record and he'd seemed genuinely devastated by her death. Yes, he had the means and the opportunity, but where was the motive? Hitting on her and getting rejected was too weak, in Jensen's opinion. If Graber was convicted, the DA would seek the death penalty. Jensen couldn't let a man die for a murder he didn't commit.

Not again.

There was also another small problem.

The lab never received the forensic evidence taken from the victim's apartment. The van was robbed while the driver was getting himself a sandwich and all evidence in the vehicle had been stolen. Jensen went back with a team to work the apartment again, but everything had been wiped clean. Why would Graber wipe down the vic's apartment after he confessed to having an intimate relationship with her? Two other detectives who watched the second interview through the one-way window at the station had sided with Putnam, indicating they thought Graber's guilt was a slam dunk.

Jensen couldn't shake the feeling they were wrong.

CHAPTER 9

"KANESHA QUIT." GENE Dorfenberger shifted in his chair. He hated bringing bad news. Peter looked up from the folder on his desk.

"What do you mean, she quit? She signed a contract."

"Yeah, I know. She says her lawyer can get her out of it because the environment is what you'd call unsafe."

"What's unsafe? We hired more security, the cops caught the guy who did Mandy. Everything's back to normal." Peter tossed the folder aside. "Don't you have a niece working here?"

Gene's expression changed from apologetic to wary. "Yeah. Why?"

"She's pretty, right?"

Gene nodded.

"Put her in as a replacement."

"Uh, I don't think she's ready for that. She's pretty young, you know?"

"What is she, eighteen? Nineteen?"

"Young, as in maturity-wise."

Peter snorted. "She's gotta grow up sometime. Might as well be now."

Gene's stomach did a somersault. Ella wasn't going to like this. She'd warned him to take care of her baby, or she'd make his life more miserable than it already was.

"Her mother—"

"Fuck her mother. She's an adult. She can decide." Peter reached for the phone and pressed the intercom. "Paula? Get me Gene Dorfenberger's niece—" he glanced at Gene.

"Brenda Rawls."

"Brenda Rawls. Have her come to my office as soon as you find her." Peter leaned back in his chair, a smile on his face. Gene could swear he enjoyed making him squirm.

Bastard.

A few minutes later, Brenda walked in. Gene couldn't help but feel pride that someone from his family could produce such a classic beauty. And, she hadn't become what most of the female contestants were: narcissistic little harpies. Gene's mood plummeted. He wondered how long it would take before that changed.

"Hi Uncle Gene, Mr. Bronkowski. You wanted to see me?"

Peter offered her the chair next to Gene.

"I did, Brenda. Gene's informed me that you might be interested in becoming a contestant on Serial Date."

Brenda's eyes widened. "Are you kidding? A contestant?" She looked at Gene for confirmation. Gene glanced at the floor, trying to avoid eye contact. She nodded her head. "Yes—of course I would. But I thought this season's lineup was already filled."

"A slot recently opened up and we need someone who's familiar with the show. There's going to be some fallout from the fans. Kaneesha was popular. Think you can handle that? They're going to compare you two, at first."

"You bet, Mr. Bronkowski. I could care less what people say. It's all just made up stuff, anyway."

Peter raised an eyebrow at Gene. "Exactly. Go and see Helena. She'll set you up with wardrobe, hair and makeup. Paula will help you with the paperwork."

Brenda bounced out of her chair and threw her arms around Gene. "Thanks, Uncle Gene." She extended her hand to Peter, who shook it. "And thank you, Mr. Bronkowski, sir. This is a fantastic opportunity." She turned and bounded out the door. "Wait until Mom hears about this!"

Gene covered his face with his hands and groaned. He pushed himself out of his chair and started for the door.

"Where are you going?" Peter asked.

"Change the locks on my apartment."

Leine fired her last round at the beer can on top of the rock, hitting it dead center. She shoved the Glock back into her shoulder holster, walked over to the cans she'd used for target practice, and threw them into a grocery bag.

The theme from *The Godfather* played inside her rental car, interrupting the desert silence. Tossing the bag into the backseat, she leaned across the console and grabbed her phone.

"Leine Basso."

"Hi."

Leine stiffened at the sound of the caller's voice. "April?"

"Yeah." Her daughter sniffled like she had a cold, or maybe allergies.

"Where are you? Are you all right?" She pulled her hair out of its ponytail holder and took out the two bobby pins she'd used to keep the rest of it back and put them in her pocket.

April sighed, her impatience magnified over the wireless connection.

"I'm fine." There was a short pause, then, "I need a place to crash for a few days."

"I'm not in Seattle."

"Yeah. Del said you got a gig in L.A. Thought you said you'd never go back."

"Things change. Look, I don't know how long I'm going to be in L.A., but..." Leine couldn't squelch the hopeful emotions that surged to the surface. Maybe April was willing to work things out, become a family again.

"It would only be for a couple days. Frank should be back by then and I can stay with him."

Leine's heart sank into her stomach. Frank. April wouldn't have even called if Frank was in town.

"Where'd he go this time?" Leine found it hard to keep the bitterness from her voice. She really meant to ask who he'd gone with, but stifled the jealousy threatening to derail even the slightest chance to see her daughter again.

"Lake Como. He took Denyse."

Denyse. That piece of work. Leine always thought of her as a sterling example of the three B's Frank had taken to dating: a blonde with big boobs that gave blowjobs— anywhere. Remember, Leine. You divorced him, not the other way around.

"So—is it okay?"

"Of course. Where are you? Do you need a ride?"

"Just an address."

Leine gave her directions to the house she was renting and told her she'd be home in a couple of hours. April repeated it back to her and ended the call.

Butterflies flitted through Leine's stomach at the thought of seeing her daughter again. Maybe this time she could make her understand why she'd done what she did.

Maybe.

CHAPTER 10

Gene Dorfenberger walked along the hallway that ran past the Serial Date studios and checked office doors, making sure everything was secured for the evening. He liked this time of day, when no one else was around. No one except for Peter, who tended to work late depending on how much blow he'd done.

Not many knew it, but Gene was a solitary man. Given the option, he'd choose playing solitaire or reading over parties and titty bars any day. Of course, being an introvert wouldn't get him anywhere in L.A., so he played along, acting like he enjoyed the crowds, the booze, the women. No one had a clue his gruff exterior housed a supremely sensitive man.

Albeit with a penchant for criminal behavior.

Gene noticed the break room door was ajar and walked over to close it. He glanced inside to make sure the lights were turned off, but hesitated when something caught his eye.

He pushed the door wide and stopped, his intake of breath cut short by the dawning realization of what he was seeing. He drew closer, convinced it was some sort of morbid practical joke set up by one of the prop guys.

Illuminated by the stark light of a vending machine, a bloody head perched on the counter next to the sink, face forward, eyes staring at nothing. Blood glazed a trail down the front of the cupboard, pooling on the floor. Next to the head lay a hand, severed at the wrist, a piece of paper pinned beneath. Gene noticed the delicate French manicured tips.

Right before he vomited into a nearby trashcan.

Peter's stomach lurched sideways, the bile rising in his throat at the sight of Stacy's head. He glanced at Gene and then stared again at the severed hand, his mouth gaping in disbelief.

"My God." He took in the scene, trying to make sense of the gory sight. Both ears were missing, giving the head a gruesome, alien-like appearance. Conflicting thoughts raced through his mind like horses barreling through the gate at the Preakness.

This can't be. Graber's locked up. Peter shook his head, bewildered. *They won't let the show continue, not after this. No fucking way.*

It has to be Edward. Gotta think. He squeezed his eyes shut. *So far, there are only three people who know-me, Gene and Eddie.*

Opening his eyes, he checked the hallway to make sure no one was lurking nearby and closed the door behind them.

"This is not good, Gene."

"I know, boss."

"We gotta make it go away, for both our sakes, not to mention all the people who depend on this show."

Gene remained silent, hands clasped in front of him. Peter stared at Stacy's gray, lifeless face as the beginnings of a plan started to formulate in his mind.

"First thing, we get rid of the...Stacy. Then we clean this room like it's never been cleaned."

Gene nodded, once.

"Any suggestions where we can take her?"

Gene cleared his throat, took a step back.

"Mojave?"

Peter nodded. "Yeah. That could work." What if someone found out? Whose car would they take? DNA testing had gotten extremely precise and he wasn't about to use any of his vehicles. Not to transport body parts. They'd have to use Gene's. And a heavy duty trash bag.

"What do you want to do about the letter?" Gene asked. The piece of paper under Stacy's hand contained a cryptic note detailing what idiots the killer thought the show's contestants were and how the murders would continue until he made his point. There was no indication of what his point might actually be.

"Burn it." Distracted, Peter's mind whirled, searching his memory for a place to dump the body parts. Then an idea popped into his head.

He knew the perfect spot.

Leine slowed her pace as she neared her house. April reclined on the front porch of the California bungalow in the old-fashioned swing Leine hadn't yet used, reading a tattered paperback. She didn't notice her at first and Leine took that moment to drink in the sight of her daughter.

She was thinner than Leine remembered and still had the persistent cowlick she'd demanded be pin curled flat every night as a child. Delicate wrists poked through the sleeves of her black lace blouse, in sharp contrast to the faded and ripped cargo pants she wore. Her rope sandals were frayed around the edges.

Conflicting emotions of happiness, fear, love and dread vied for dominance inside Leine. Seeking safety from too much raw emotion, the thought she finally gave into wondered what the hell her daughter had been thinking when she got a tattoo of a snake on her neck.

April glanced up from her book, her face open and relaxed. As soon as she saw her mother standing on the sidewalk her expression changed, as if she knew what Leine was thinking.

"Been waiting long?" Leine walked up the steps, digging in her purse for her keys.

April closed her book and stood. "Not really." She placed the novel in her worn backpack. "You said a couple of hours. I took that to mean a couple of hours."

Leine sensed the old, familiar insolence. Something Leine couldn't break down, didn't know how to, but instinctively understood it was the first obstacle that needed to be overcome before the relationship could be healed. She turned to April and gave her an awkward hug. April stiffened against the overture.

Well, hell. I tried.

Embarrassed, Leine backed away, keys in hand and unlocked the door, kicking it open for her. April walked inside and Leine paused, realizing she'd left her phone on the console of her rental.

"Be right back. Forgot something," she mumbled and walked back to her car.

She found the phone where she'd left it and shut and locked the door. Taking deep breaths, she worked to compose herself.

You had no choice, Leine. You were a single mom. How else were you going to earn a living? You did what you were good at. You can't fucking type and pole dancing was out of the question. So you farmed her out to friends, but she was always safe. She never would have known if it wasn't for Eric. If he hadn't forced your hand.

She headed back to the house, thinking about what she wanted to say to April. How she could begin the conversation. As she reached the walkway, the hairs on the back of her neck stood on end. Leine kept walking, senses alert. She turned at the top of the steps and scanned the neighborhood. The old, shaggy palm trees stood silent vigil along the boulevard, their small splotches of early evening shade peppering the sidewalk. A cat dozed on the porch across the street. A lawn mower hummed in the distance.

Tranquil.

Leine shook it off and went inside the house, sure it was simply a case of nerves strung tight from the unexpected visit.

April stood in the middle of the living room, backpack over her shoulder. Leine motioned to the hallway behind her.

"The spare room's back there. Make yourself at home."

Without a word, April disappeared down the hall to the bedroom. So many questions hung in the air between them. Did this indicate a détente? How much was April prepared to forgive in order to set things right? Leine fought the need to interrogate her, find out where she'd been, who she'd spent time with. April would close down if she did that.

Leine only had a couple days, at most, to get this right. As the fear of blowing this one chance with her daughter swelled in intensity, she busied herself cleaning the already clean counters in the kitchen.

April appeared in the doorway. "Mind if I shower?"

"Of course not, no. *Mi casa es su casa.*" The smile on Leine's face felt forced, awkward. April gave her a nod and disappeared again.

Leine opened the refrigerator door to empty shelves. Well, except for a bottle of dark beer and some really rude looking cheese.

Why didn't I pick up something on the way home?

Because you're out of practice. Hasn't been much call for a hostess lately.

The word made her cringe. A hostess is what Frank had wanted. Someone to run his little soirees and dinner parties, make sure things went according to plan. Leine had tried, she really had, but realized early on that party planning was not her forte. This became abundantly clear the evening she got drunk and told all of Frank's rich, powerful and spoiled guests to go to hell.

Her inability to approach Frank's parties like everything else she did surprised her. She'd planned all her jobs meticulously, often down to the last second, but it was difficult to put her heart into something that bored the hell out of her. She never forgave Frank for expecting her to play Barbie. And for not being who he should've been.

The shower stopped and a few minutes later Leine heard the bathroom door open.

"There's not much to eat here. Maybe we should go out?" she called, rounding the corner into the hallway.

"Sure. I'm not very hungry, though." April stood in the hall next to the bedroom wearing a towel, her hair still wet.

"Holy shit." Leine stopped short at the sight of her daughter's tattoo in all its glory. The large, colorful snake began somewhere below the top of the towel and wrapped itself around her upper arm, dipped past her elbow, then cruised along her shoulder and up her neck, its forked tongue and head ending slightly below her jawline. Leine realized her mouth was hanging open and clamped it shut.

What happened to my beautiful daughter?

April's expression grew puzzled as she searched behind her for whatever had caused Leine to react so strongly.

"What's wrong?"

"Your tattoo. It's—" Leine searched for the right word, but failed. "It's interesting," was all she could manage.

April smiled for the first time since Leine had seen her on the porch. "You like? It took a long time, but it was worth it. It starts here—" April lowered the towel so Leine could see the snake's coiled section along her lower back. "I had a guy in Amsterdam do it. He came highly recommended."

Leine hated tattoos. One of her earlier hits had been a Russian mobster who'd done prison time. The distinctive symbols etched onto his torso were the last things Leine saw before he aimed an Uzi at her and pulled the trigger. Acting from pure adrenaline, she'd made the kill but barely escaped with her life.

Then there was the Frenchman.

Leine took a deep breath and slowly let it out. *I will not criticize my daughter's tattoo. I will not criticize my daughter's tattoo. Don't do it, Leine.*

"Seriously? A huge snake? Are you insane? You're marked for life. When you're an old, saggy woman with crepe-paper skin and boobs you can wrap around your ankles that snake isn't going to seem so great then, I'll guarantee it." Leine slapped her hand over her mouth before she blurted out anything else.

The hurt in April's eyes was quickly replaced with a smoldering anger that made Leine wince from the sheer force of it.

"Go fuck yourself, Mother." She stalked into the bedroom and slammed the door closed.

Good going, Leine. Yeah, just great. Now she's never going to open up to you. Not that she would have, anyway.

She started down the hallway, intending to apologize, when the theme from *The Godfather* echoed through the house from the other room. Ignoring it, she knocked on the guest room door.

"April? I'm sorry." Leine waited a beat before continuing. "I didn't mean it. Can you please come out here so we can talk?"

Silence.

"April? Please?"

She heard movement on the other side of the door. Moments later, it inched open.

"Well?" April's voice was wary. She stood with her arms crossed, now wearing a pair of faded jeans and a gray t-shirt with a black skull imprint.

Leine paused a beat, wondering what she could say to make peace between them.

"I'm sorry I freaked about your tattoos. I have…let's just say I've got issues."

April snorted, moving past her, headed toward the kitchen.

"I'll say."

Leine bit back a retort. *She doesn't know what happened, that Eric tricked you.* She followed her daughter into the kitchen, taking deep breaths with each step.

"Where are your glasses?"

Leine pointed at a cupboard. April chose a glass and filled it with water from the tap. *I'd better keep to neutral topics for now. Ease into this.*

"When'd you get back? Did you enjoy Europe?"

"It was okay. I really liked Amsterdam. The people were cool."

"I remember." Leine hadn't been back for several years, but liked to use Amsterdam as a jumping off point for European jobs. Schiphol airport was a relaxed, friendly port of entry. The people were generally laid back and happy to see you. She also knew a good weapons supplier in the city.

April walked into the living room and gazed out the front window. Leine joined her.

"Do you regret what you did?" April asked, still looking out the window.

"All the time," she answered, her voice barely above a whisper. Leine didn't tell her about the running dreams. In them, she ran from the people she'd killed, sometimes more than one. She would wake up drenched in sweat, heart pounding, right before they closed in.

"How could you...do what you did? Didn't it affect you?"

Leine sighed. "Look, I did what I was good at. Yes, it affected me. Yes, I regret some of it. Most of the targets were low-life scum who deserved a worse death than what I gave them. With me, it was over before they knew what happened. Problem is, I can't take it back. I have to live with myself every day. With all of them."

"I was talking about Carlos." April's voice held a brittle edge that echoed against the empty walls of the living room.

"Especially Carlos."

April whirled to face Leine, her face a mask of rage.

"You killed him." Her voice broke as she clenched her fists. "He trusted you. How could you?"

Leine closed her eyes against the accusation. Yes, she killed Carlos. But she'd been tricked into it. She'd tried telling her daughter that, but after Eric's campaign of deception April wouldn't believe her. She opened her eyes, saw her daughter's anguish and knew she'd never be forgiven. April adored Carlos. She never understood how Leine could work as an assassin in the first place. She swore to April that Eric misdirected her, leading to her mistakenly kill Carlos, but her efforts were futile. Eric played April like a violin. She was twelve years old at the time and highly receptive to adult male authority. He'd convinced her Leine was lying about the incident to escape responsibility and guilt.

"It's more complicated than that, April. I-"

"Don't. Don't justify what you did. You're a monster." April threw her glass against the tiled fireplace. Leine winced as it shattered on the hearth.

"My mother is a monster." April's sobs followed her as she ran down the hallway to her room and slammed the door closed.

Numb, Leine didn't follow, didn't cry. She stood by the window, unsure what to do, unable to move. Sorrow engulfed her as memories of happier times with Carlos and April surged to the surface. On a playground with April in a swing, laughing. Carlos' dark good looks, dimples deepening as he smiled, pushing April in the swing but looking at Leine, an expression of later promise meant only for her.

The sound of the door opening surprised Leine. *Now what?*

April stomped down the hallway and brushed past Leine, headed for the front door. She had her backpack with her.

"April, please. Can't we get past this?"

April wrenched the door open and turned to glare at her mother. "Don't wait up." The words fell with finality between them.

She followed her as April strode out the door. "I'll hide a key under the flower pot-" she called, but she was talking to empty space.

Leine shook her head as she wiped away a tear. The theme from *The Godfather* once again echoed from the counter where she'd left her purse. Grateful for a diversion, Leine walked into the kitchen to answer her phone.

"Leine Basso." Her voice sounded knife-sharp.

"Sorry to interrupt. This is Detective Jensen. Do you have a minute?"

Leine cleared her throat. "Of course, detective. Has anything happened?"

"No, no. Graber's still in custody. Everything's fine, as far as I know. I was wondering-" There was a brief pause. "I realize this is out of the blue, but would you be open to having dinner with me some time?"

Relief flowed through Leine like heroin through a junkie's veins. She glanced at the empty space where April no longer stood, knowing her daughter wasn't coming back until much later, if she even came back at all.

"You know, detective, you have great timing. It happens I'm free tonight."

Leine watched through the window as Jensen pulled up to the house. April hadn't come back or called since she'd stormed out of the house. Leine left fifty dollars and directions to a local grocery store on the counter. She'd placed the spare key under the flower pot on the porch. She chided herself for leaving the house after such a fight, but couldn't bring herself to back out of the date and open herself up to worrying about her angry, accusing daughter. Funny how she'd been good at hunting down targets and executing the kill, but when it came to April, she had no idea how to repair what was broken. Compartmentalizing problems she could do and she did it now.

Face it—you're just not mother material.

Leine took another peek out the window at Detective Santiago. His smooth good looks and the fact that he knew his way around a gun gave her a little thrill she'd thought long dormant. She'd actually primped and couldn't remember the last time she wore mascara and showed off her legs in a dress. She figured getting laid would help take her mind off of April. The way Jensen looked at her the last time they'd met, she was certain dinner would be the beginning of an eventful evening.

She closed and locked the front door, leaving her problems with April inside the house, and sauntered over to the black, 1969 Camaro SS. She leaned in the window to give him a nice cleavage shot. His eyes hidden behind a pair of aviator sunglasses, she noticed an almost imperceptible dip of his head as he checked the girls out.

"Nice ride." She straightened up and walked around the front, trailing her fingers along the clean lines of the muscle car. Jensen climbed out of the driver's side and met her at the passenger door, opening it for her with a hint of a smile.

"Glad you like it."

Leine smiled back and slid into the front seat, letting her dress hike up enough to expose some serious thigh. He closed the door and she inched the material back down, but not before he let out a low whistle.

Yeah. So much better than what waited for her back in the house.

Bad mother.

Bad, bad, bad.

CHAPTER 11

THEY PULLED INTO the parking lot at *Il Buon Alimento* a few minutes before their reservation. Jensen worked it like Leine was the Queen of Sheba, opening doors, offering to let her use his jacket, aware of her every need. The maître'd showed them to a table on the patio overlooking the Pacific Ocean. For Jensen, hearing the gentle crash of the waves always took the edge off.

"This is beautiful, detective, thank you." Leine sighed as she leaned back in her chair and took in the view. The sun had begun to set, the deep orange and red hues reflecting off the water like a kaleidoscope.

Jensen detected a pensive mood. He'd have to remedy that.

"It's one of my favorite places. Glad you approve." Damn, she looked good. Real. The fading sunlight brought out a hint of red in her hair as it brushed past her shoulders, framing the classic lines and high cheekbones of her face. Santiago had gotten his fill of the tucked, plucked and Botoxed women so prevalent in Southern California. In the process, he'd learned to appreciate authenticity. Especially when it came to bodies. There was something alluring about a stock pair of breasts...

The waiter appeared with a basket of breadsticks. After checking with Leine, Jensen ordered a bottle of red wine. The waiter left and Leine reached across the table, placing her hand on his. The energy snapped between them.

"I really need to thank you, detective."

"Call me Santiago." Jensen smiled his most charming smile—the one that melted the ladies. This evening was definitely heading in the right direction.

"Your call came at a good time. My daughter's here for an unexpected visit and we're not exactly getting along at the moment." Leine released his hand and took a sip from her water.

"Oh? I'm sorry to hear that." Looked like they'd be going to his place later. Good thing he straightened up the living room. Even put new sheets on the bed. Twenty points. "So, is Dad still in the picture?"

Leine frowned and shook her head. "No. He died when she was two."

"Sorry to bring it up." Jensen shifted in his chair.

"Don't be. It was a long time ago."

Time to change the subject. "I read in your file you worked security for the State Department before becoming an insurance investigator. How was that?"

Leine shrugged. "Kind of boring, actually. I worked with lower level diplomats. Not a lot of action, but a ton of travel. And waiting around."

Jensen noticed a subtle difference in her demeanor when she spoke of her past. A studied casualness. Wariness, maybe, or closing up because experience taught her not to give anything away. He wondered what she wasn't telling him.

The waiter reappeared with the wine and two glasses. They both waited to continue the conversation until he'd left.

"How long have you been with the LAPD?" she asked, cradling her glass in both hands.

"Coming up on twenty years." He laughed and shook his head in disbelief. "I guess it's true what they say: the older you get, the faster time flies."

"What made you want to be a cop?"

"Thought it'd get me laid."

"And?"

"And what?"

"Did it get you laid?" Leine's expression remained neutral.

Nice and direct. Jensen liked that. He smiled and took a drink of his wine. "Maybe."

"The real question is, why stay?"

Jensen paused for a moment before answering. "Early in my career, I watched a guy get tapped for a murder charge and knew he wasn't guilty. I mean, he was no angel by any stretch, but he didn't kill the victim. Don't ask me how I knew. Call it a gut reaction. The job was too clean and there were other indicators it was probably a contract hit. In my estimation, this guy would never have been able to pull it off. I voiced my concerns, but it went nowhere. There was an eye witness and the jury ate it up. He got the death penalty. A few years later, evidence turned up that exonerated him. I never forgave myself for not following up on my hunches. That's when I decided to become a detective."

"Were they able to catch the real murderer?"

Jensen grabbed a breadstick from the basket on the table and tore it in half. "Nope. Never did."

"You say there were other indicators. Like what?"

"The killer left a calling card. An etching on the bullet. I've seen the same symbol used in two other instances: the murder I told you about, and two more a couple months later. Then, nothing."

Leine leaned forward in her chair. "What kind of symbol?"

Jensen's smile slipped into place. "I'm sorry, ma'am, but that information is classified." He searched her face. "You seem pretty interested in the subject."

Leine smiled. "It's a hobby. Some of the guys on security detail would shoot the shit—I picked things up. Thought it was fascinating. From what I understand, contract killers take their job very seriously. I assume most would prefer to remain anonymous. I wonder why this one left such a distinctive mark?"

"Ego stroke, probably. I keep watching for a hit like the others but up to now, nothing. Evidently the shooter's working somewhere else, or he's dead. Either is fine by me."

Leine took a sip of her wine. She seemed lost in thought and Jensen didn't interrupt. He looked behind him, searching for the waiter.

"We should probably order."

The sensation of her bare foot sliding up his shin took him by surprise. It detoured to his inner thigh, then stopped as though waiting for permission. He looked up and their eyes met. There was no mistaking her intent.

"I have a better idea."

The elevator doors to Jensen's building had barely closed when Leine felt his hands slide over her hips from behind. She flipped around to face him and pulled his head down for a deep, penetrating kiss. Not breaking the lip lock, he pushed her against the wall, leaning into her, his erection obvious. A groan escaped her lips. At this point Leine was beyond caring if they ever made it to his place. All the pent up frustration from her self-imposed celibacy welled up in one giant sweep of lust that surged through her body like lightning through a metal rod.

The elevator pinged and the doors opened. Bodies still connected, Jensen propelled her into the hallway and they staggered as one to his door. He fumbled for his keys, found them and unlocked the door, all the while nuzzling her neck and earlobes.

Ten points for multi-tasking, Leine thought. She slid her hand over his ass. Nice and firm. She couldn't wait to get him inside.

They stumbled through the door and Jensen kicked it closed, flipping the dead bolt. Leine didn't waste any time and started to unbutton his shirt with one hand, while the other tugged on his belt. He smiled and brought his hand around to her back, pulled her dress zipper down, grabbed the hem and lifted it over her head in one fluid motion.

He stepped back, letting out a low whistle.

"Damn," he said, shaking his head. "You're beautiful, Leine. Really beautiful."

Leine smiled and sent a silent thank you to Victoria's Secret and her mother's good genes. Without a word, she finished unbuttoning his shirt and unzipped his slacks, sliding them down to his ankles. He kicked off his shoes and stepped out of his pants. When she moved to kick off her heels, he put his hand out.

"Don't."

Smiling, Leine turned and walked slowly into the living room, lightly stroking each surface she passed, caressing a silk covered breast with her other hand, then letting it drop, bringing his focus to the part that needed his attention most.

Jensen growled and crossed the room in two strides. He took her in his arms, pressing the length of their bodies together. Leine pushed him onto the couch and, facing him, lowered herself onto his lap. He bent his head to kiss her breast and at the same time unhooked her bra.

Unable to wait any longer, she slipped out of the matching thong and their bodies melted together, all the hard and soft parts fitting just like they were meant to.

Holy Mother of God, why did I wait this long? was the last coherent thought in Leine's head.

CHAPTER 12

"WHAT ARE THEY doing, Peter?"

Peter's stomach twisted at the anguish in Edward's voice.

"It's for your safety, Edward," Peter answered.

The locksmith Peter hired was packing up to go, having changed all the door locks to key-only entry and exit. Secure, locking shutters now graced every first floor window. A home security expert had installed perimeter cameras the day before.

Peter couldn't take a chance on Edward killing again. He waited until he'd paid the locksmith and watched him drive off, then sat Edward on the couch in the living room.

"Look, I told you if these kinds of things started to happen again, I'd have to do something drastic. You don't want to end up in a hospital, do you? It wouldn't be like the one mom was in."

Edward looked down and shook his head. His breathing was like that of a child after a tantrum: fast and heavy, peppered with little explosions of air. Peter hated locking him in the house, but didn't know what else to do. He couldn't let Edward go to a hospital. Not now.

Peter would figure out what to do later, when he had a minute to think.

"Please, Peter?" Tears streaked Edward's face. "I promise I'll be good. I-I promise I won't leave, ever."

Peter sighed. Edward's promises were like air—plentiful and free. He couldn't put it off any longer- he had to look in the freezer. Had to get that last gruesome confirmation of his brother's continued psychosis and somehow destroy the evidence he knew was there. He got up and walked through the kitchen out to the big freezer in the garage, steeling himself for what he'd find.

He lifted the lid and glanced inside. Among frozen packages of hamburger, vanilla ice cream and lima beans, the freezer held a smattering of small plastic baggies, the contents of which were various shades of brown and black. He reached in and picked a baggie at random, this one with a small tan object, and opened it. Peter's shoulders sagged.

A frost covered, furry ear. He couldn't tell what kind of animal it was from, but did it really matter?

Edward stood at the doorway to the kitchen, attention riveted on him. Peter held the bag up for him to see.

"Where'd you get this?" He looked down at the rest. "And these?"

Edward raced over and snatched the bag from his hand.

"They're mine! They were the mean ones. You told me it was okay to punish the mean ones." He clutched the baggie with both hands.

Peter leaned over the edge of the freezer and dug through the rest of the baggies, checking the few that appeared to have dissimilar contents. All contained animal parts.

He shook his head, unable to reconcile sweet, sensitive Edward with psycho-crazy Edward. "Where'd you hide the other...parts?"

Edward stared at the freezer, then Peter. "No other parts, Peter. I promise."

He must have buried them in the back. Peter slammed the freezer door shut and swept past Edward, heading into the house to the backyard. On the way, he grabbed a shovel standing in the corner. Edward shuffled behind him, wiping at the snot running down his nose.

"Peter, don't be mad at me. I won't do it again, I promise." Edward stopped at the door. More tears bubbled over, streaking a path down his face. "Please?"

Peter ignored him and walked down the concrete steps onto the patio. Waiting for his blood pressure to return to normal, he scanned the green lawn and well-kept flower beds. Better hire a service. Don't want the neighbors wondering what happened to Edward. Besides, it would only be for a little while, until Peter could figure out what to do with his brother.

Peter walked to a suspicious looking clump of grass and attacked it with the shovel. Edward's muffled sobs didn't slow him down. He stopped when his efforts revealed nothing but dirt. Spotting a freshly turned mound of soil surrounding a new lavender plant in the flower bed he yanked out the seedling and dug beneath it, but again found nothing. He rested the shovel against his hip and wiped at the sweat forming on his forehead.

Nothing else in the yard looked disturbed. Peter headed for the garbage can alongside the detached garage, anxiety dogging his steps. He lifted the lid, breathing a sigh of relief when all he smelled and saw was normal, everyday garbage. After checking inside the garage, he walked back to where Edward was furiously replanting the lavender.

"Edward," Peter said, keeping his voice even. "You have to tell me what you did with the other…pieces. I need to know so I can take care of them."

Edward continued to firm the dirt around the plant, pretending not to hear him. He sniffled, wiping tears from his eyes with the back of his hand.

"Edward, have you ever—" Peter cleared his throat, then took a deep breath. "Have you ever eaten any of the mean ones?"

Edward snapped his head around with a look of horror. "No!"

Peter was at a loss. He would have to make an appointment with Doctor Shapiro, find out if the blackouts could be controlled with new medication. Of course, he'd need to figure out a way to make sure Edward took it. Whenever the blackness won, Edward would have no memory of anything he did. Like when Peter found him standing over their stepfather. He adamantly denied having beaten him to death, even though his blood soaked clothes and the pieces of brain and bone on the bat in his hands told a different story.

As for the letter, Peter figured Edward wouldn't remember writing the disjointed, rambling manifesto. It didn't sound like him, but Doctor Shapiro suggested his personality had splintered from some childhood trauma. Shapiro didn't know the half of it.

At a loss, Peter leaned the shovel against the fence and held out his hand. Edward looked up, a hopeful smile on his face.

"Come on, Eddie. Let's go make us a grilled cheese sandwich and watch some Stooges, okay? You've had enough excitement for one day."

Edward grinned and clapped his hands. "Yes—the Three Stooges. I like the Three Stooges."

Peter took him by the hand and they walked into the house together.

"Hey, Moe!"

CHAPTER 13

"YOU HUNGRY?"

Jensen poked his head out of the bathroom door. Leine corrected herself: Santiago. They'd just had an evening of wild, no-holds-barred sex. Calling him 'Jensen' seemed somehow too removed from what they'd done to each other.

"Not really," she replied. "Hey—what do your friends call you? Santiago is nice, but it's a mouthful."

Jensen grinned. "Putnam calls me Santa. My mother calls me Santiago Reynaldo Tomàs Jensen, but that's usually when she's mad."

"I'll stick with Santiago, or maybe Jensen. Or how about Snookie-wookie-buns? Would that work?"

He laughed as he came back in the room and crawled into bed. "Yeah, that'd go over great with the guys." His brilliant green eyes bored into hers. "As long as you call me."

She could swear her knees melted. Good thing she was lying down. Jensen bent his head and nipped at her shoulder. He slid down to nuzzle her neck, followed by a slow, leisurely lick of her right nipple. Leine felt a shiver dance down her back.

"Are you ready for the red-hot tamale grandé?" he asked between nips, his voice husky.

Leine rolled her eyes and sat up. "Look, Santa baby. It's late, and I've got to be at work in less than an hour. Not that I wouldn't love to stick around, but I need to swing by my place, see if April got back all right." She sighed. "Hopefully she's calmed down and we're on speaking terms."

Jensen lay back with a smile. "No problem. But remember what's waiting for you," he said, sliding the sheet off his impressive erection.

Leine laughed as she climbed over him and padded into the bathroom. "Believe me, it'll be tough enough to function today without having that picture in my head."

Leine kicked the door to the bungalow closed and dropped her purse on the chair by the fireplace. The key was gone from under the pot on the porch. A vase of Black-eyed Susans stood on the counter, along with a twenty-dollar bill. She walked over to the fridge and opened the door. A half-gallon of two percent milk, a block of cheddar and a head of romaine took up residence on one shelf. Several cans of Red Bull stood on another.

Leine moved down the hallway and stopped at the closed door to the guest bedroom, hesitating to knock. She didn't want to wake April if she'd gotten in late. Thinking better of it, she went to her room, picked out some clean clothes for the day and headed to the bathroom to shower.

Showered and dressed, she opened the door and stepped out into the hallway. The guest room door was open and the bed made. Not sure what mood her daughter would be in, Leine walked to the kitchen, bracing for anything. April sat at the counter, wearing the skull t-shirt and a pair of yoga pants, drinking a cup of coffee. Her backpack rested against the stool next to her.

"Want some?" April indicated the fresh brewed pot of coffee next to the stove.

"Sounds great." Leine poured herself a cup and took a sip. Pretty good. Better tasting than hers.

"Did you have fun last night?"

April's tone held no trace of anger from the day before. More like polite interest.

"Look. Obviously, we got off on the wrong foot yesterday. I can't change the past, but I'm willing to start working on the future. Can we please start fresh?"

April studied Leine for a moment, ran a hand through her hair. "Where were you last night?"

Leine's shoulders relaxed a fraction. "With a friend. Detective Jensen."

"I'm sure a date with him was a lot better than staying at home waiting for a daughter you haven't seen in over three years." Her voice echoed against the kitchen walls. "You really don't care about anything or anyone, do you? But I already knew that, didn't I?"

Leine's heart broke at the hurt in her voice. Her eyes welled. She couldn't stop the tear from trickling down her cheek. Another followed. *Oh, God, not now. Maintain, Leine.* She covered her face with her hands, unable to stop the torrent of emotion that engulfed her.

When the storm passed, Leine lifted her head and wiped the tears from her eyes. April sat frozen to the stool, evidently unsure how to handle seeing her ex-assassin mother go through an emotional breakdown.

That's what I get. No one expects me to have any feelings. How can a person who did what I did for a living be human?

Leine grabbed a kitchen towel and blew her nose, leaning against the wall for support. She took a deep breath and let it go.

"Detective Jensen called at a vulnerable moment. If we hadn't had a fight, I wouldn't have left. And, I know it's no excuse, but being back in L.A. has been stressful...so weird, the old neighborhood, the memories."

April traced invisible circles on the counter with her finger. Leine stared at the delicate silver and lapis ring she wore.

"That's why I'll be staying at Frank's."

"What? I thought he was out of town."

"He gets back today."

"You don't have to do that." Leine's stomach curled into a knot. "I said I was sorry. Give me some time. I really want to talk to you, try to figure us out." When would another chance like this come along? When she was eighty?

April straightened on her stool and shook her hair off her shoulders. Like she did when she was a little girl. "It's already done. I called him last night. His plane lands at LAX in a few hours." She lowered her gaze and started with the circles again. "So what's your new job like? Del told me you were working security for a reality show. Kind of overkill, don't you think?"

Do I detect a hint of sarcasm? To her, Leine would always be a killer. No wonder she doesn't visit. She still seethed at the thought of her old boss, Eric. He single-handedly destroyed the close relationship that had existed between her and her daughter. It didn't matter to Eric how devastating killing Carlos had been for Leine. As long as he got what he wanted.

"Yeah. Well. I'm not in the business anymore. I have to pay the bills."

"You hate television."

"Hate's a strong word."

April shrugged, took another sip of coffee.

"Look, can we talk later? I need to get down to the studio. How about we have dinner tonight? I'll come by Frank's and pick you up after work, okay?"

April stared into her coffee like a fortune teller reading tea leaves. Then she looked at Leine. Why hadn't she noticed the red-rimmed eyes? Shit. *How horrible of a mother am I to make my only daughter cry?*

"I think Frank has something planned already."

"Come on, April. You need to meet me part way." Leine's heart pounded steadily in her chest. That in itself was a wonder, since she could barely breathe.

April paused a beat, considering. Then, "If you want. Sure."

Leine noticed her mouth twitch. She decided it was a smile.

She could work with that.

CHAPTER 14

LEINE LOCKED HER purse in a desk drawer in Serial Date's administration office and was just leaving to grab a cup of coffee when Gene cornered her next to the water cooler.

"We gotta talk," he said in a low voice. Large patches of perspiration bled through the armpits of his short sleeved shirt and beads of sweat dotted his forehead. He grabbed her by the arm and led her behind a cubicle, checking to make sure no one was nearby.

"Sure, Gene. What do you need?"

"Kaneesha quit…"

"Okay? And?"

"Bronkowski gave the spot to Brenda, my niece."

The worry on his face didn't jibe with what he was telling her.

"How is that a problem? They caught the killer, Gene. Don't worry." Leine made a move to leave, but he gripped her arm.

"Stacy's missing…" The words came out in a hiss.

"There you are, Gene." Peter's voice slid between them as he walked across the room toward the cubicle. Gene backed off, plastering an artificial smile on his face.

"Yeah, boss?"

"I need you to check on Javier. He's having some kind of meltdown in the dressing room."

"On my way." Gene cast a furtive glance at Leine as he left.

Peter sighed and turned to Leine. He looked gaunt. The skin around his bloodshot eyes had a grayish cast and his lips looked like a bloodless gash across his face. Leine wondered how much cocaine the man ingested that morning.

"Actors." He scowled as he folded his arms across his chest and leaned against the end of the cubicle. "So, you've heard about what happened with Kaneesha and Stacy?"

Leine decided to play dumb. No point in getting Gene in trouble. "No. What's up?"

"Kaneesha quit. I can't really blame her. Finding Mandy was pretty devastating to the girls—I mean, contestants. Couldn't quite pull it together afterward. Anyway, Gene's niece, Brenda, stepped in. I think she'll be great. Gene's a little stressed, though. He's pretty overprotective."

"And Stacy?"

Peter shook his head. "Stacy took off with Devon. They're both gone. Found a note saying they were headed for the redwoods, gonna live in wine country." He chuckled. "It's happened before. Sometimes these gals get a taste of dangerous and just can't help themselves."

Leine remained quiet, her curiosity about what Gene tried to tell her growing.

"Thought I should let you know. Bring you up to speed, so to speak."

"Are you going to replace her?"

"Paula's looking at submissions now. Should have someone within the week. I'll keep you posted." Peter rolled his eyes as he backed away toward the door. "Never a dull moment…"

As soon as he'd gone, Leine went in search of Gene. She didn't find him in a quick sweep of the building and ended up getting sidetracked by Billy and his inane questions about her past as a bodyguard. By the time she extricated herself from the conversation, she caught a glimpse of Gene and Peter leaving out a side door.

She walked back to the office to grab some cash, intending to find something to eat in the vending machine in the break room. As she bent down to retrieve her purse from the desk drawer she overheard Peter's assistant, Paula, speaking to someone on the phone.

"I understand that, Mrs. Ross, but she's no longer employed by Serial Date." There was a pause. Then, "Officially, all I've been told is that she left. I don't know why, ma'am. I'm sorry." Another pause. "Yes, ma'am, I'll have Mr. Bronkowski call you as soon as he gets in."

Paula hung up the phone. Leine walked over to her desk.

"Stacy's mother?"

Paula nodded. She didn't look happy.

"She says Stacy didn't call them last night like she always does and she's worried. Mr. Bronkowski told me not to tell anyone about the note she and Devon left about going to northern California to live. If anyone calls looking for her I'm supposed to tell them what I told her mom. He said he'd take care of any callbacks." Paula busied herself tidying a stack of papers. "If it were my mom, she'd be here in a heartbeat, looking for me. It's not like Stacy to run off with some guy. Especially one of the bachelors."

"Why not? Devon was attractive and seemed nice enough." His alibi of having dinner with his mother had checked out, too. "And, he must have made a boatload of money being on the show."

"It's not that. When she first got hired she and I became friends, I guess because of me being active in church and all. None of the other girls go and Stacy was really lonely. She told me she decided to come on the show as a way to minister to non-believers. I told her good luck. I've been around here since the beginning and I haven't figured out a way to make a dent. Basically, I keep my head down, do my work."

Leine's urge to talk to Gene ramped up a notch. "Why do you stay? It's got to be frustrating to see everything that goes on around here."

Paula's cheeks turned a delicate shade of pink. "The money's really good, you know? I've been able to tithe a lot to my church. I figure it evens out in the end."

"I guess we all have our reasons. Stacy must have had hers."

"I suppose. It still doesn't seem like her, though." The phone buzzed and one of the lines lit up. Paula gave Leine an apologetic look before answering.

Leine grabbed her purse and headed toward the break room, more determined than ever to find Gene.

The chance didn't present itself until after five. Leine was getting ready to leave to pick up April when she saw Peter and Gene walk through the front door. Gene stopped to talk to the new security guard on duty as Peter continued toward his office. Peter had fired the guard that fell asleep the night of Mandy's murder. This one wasn't much better, in Leine's opinion.

She stepped behind a column. As soon as Peter passed by and rounded the corner, she marched up to Gene, grabbed his arm and pulled him out of earshot of the guard.

"What were you trying to tell me earlier?"

Gene shook his head. "Nothing. Don't worry about it. I had a momentary lapse." He glanced down the hallway where Peter had disappeared.

"C'mon, Gene. That's bullshit. You were upset this morning. Something about Stacy missing?"

"Nah. I was over reacting. Peter told me about the note they left. Not a big deal." Gene shifted his weight, looking toward the hallway.

"Yeah, I don't think so, Gene. I know when you're lying. You forget who you're talking to."

Gene's expression hardened. Leine knew that look. His stubbornness had kicked in. She continued, ignoring his discomfort.

"I had an odd conversation with Paula this morning about Stacy. Did you know she was using Serial Date as a kind of a missionary outreach thing for her church? You know, trying to save souls and shit like that?"

Gene blinked, but didn't look away. Good. She had his attention.

"Why would Stacy go running off with Devon? Wasn't he one of the two original suspects in Mandy's murder?"

Gene closed his eyes. When he opened them, they were filled with despair. He took her elbow, dragged her into a nearby office and shut the door.

"I don't know what to do." He leaned against the wall and covered his face with his hands. Alarmed, Leine stood next to him, her hand on his shoulder.

Gene sighed and dropped his hands to his sides.

"Last night when I was locking up, I found Stacy..." He stopped, obviously trying to collect himself before he continued. "Someone had...she was dead." Gene tried to take a deep breath but it looked like a struggle. "It's gotta be the same guy from before." He leaned over like he was in pain, his hands on his knees, his breathing rapid.

Afraid he'd hyperventilate, Leine rubbed his back, trying to calm him, stunned by the implications. *They've got the wrong guy. He's still out there. I need to tell Jensen.*

"Gene." She glanced around the room, looking for something he could breathe into to calm down. Nothing looked usable. "Gene. Listen to me." She put her hand under his chin and lifted his head so she could look him in the eye.

Focusing on Leine seemed to help quiet his breathing. He stared at her through misery-filled eyes.

"Peter knows, am I right?"

Gene nodded.

"I've got to tell Detective Jensen."

Gene shook his head. "You can't tell anyone. Do you know how many people rely on this show? They'll shut it down. Peter has it under control. He's making sure it doesn't happen again."

"Are you crazy? How can he do that? Does he know who did it?"

By the look on Gene's face, he wasn't telling her the whole story. *This was insanity.* Careful to keep her voice calm she asked, "Gene, where's Stacy now?"

"I don't know."

She could tell the stubbornness had kicked back in by the set of his shoulders and his tight-lipped reply. She could also tell he was lying. *She had to tell Jensen. It didn't matter if they shut the show down. Be the best damn thing that ever happened to this fucked up little slice-of-life. Sure, she'd be out of a job along with everyone else, but for Christ's sake, people were dying.*

"You can't tell anybody, Leine." Gene's eyes glittered in the fluorescent light. His breathing had become more measured, calm. This was a look of his she'd never seen him use before. It held a strong warning mixed with something Leine had seen many times in her life.

Malice and implied threat.

"Sure, Gene. You know me. Not a word."

His face relaxed, but not by much. He wasn't convinced. She'd have to be careful.

She looked at her watch and realized she was late. "I've got to go."

"Things can happen, Leine. Remember that."

Gene was threatening her? She almost laughed, but realized she couldn't always be on alert. He did know her. Knew her habits, knew where she was living. Didn't matter how long they'd known each other. The term "thick as thieves" was never very accurate when it came to actual thieves. She'd have to rely on her instincts to stay safe. Good thing April was staying at Frank's.

"I will."

As soon as she cleared the front doors and Gene's line of sight, she called Jensen but it went to voicemail. She left a short message asking him to call her.

Leine disconnected and walked quickly to her car. She tried April's cell on the way, but no luck there, either. Then she tried Frank's. April had given her the number before Leine left for work that morning.

"Hello?"

Frank's voice set her back on her heels. God, she hated that she still felt like this. When was she going to get over him and move on? She left him. Not the other way around.

"Hi, Frank. It's Leine."

"Oh. Hi."

There were so many things she wanted to say but realized none of them mattered right now. What mattered was April.

"Can I talk to April?"

"She's not here. I thought she was with you."

"She said she was going to your place this morning. I offered to drive her, but she said you were going to pick her up on your way back from the airport."

"I swung by, but she wasn't there. She didn't answer her phone, so I assumed you two went somewhere. Did you try calling her?"

"Of course I did. It went to voicemail immediately, like she turned it off."

Leine heard him sigh and braced herself for what she knew was coming next.

"Look, she told me what happened. That you left to go on a date, didn't even try to spend time with her."

"That's not true—"

"You need to realize—"

Leine bristled at the condescension in his voice.

"You're never gonna have that fairy-tale, mother-daughter relationship you always talked about. It's not possible. Not if you're in the equation. You're incapable of loving anyone. Figure it out."

Leine felt herself grow cold. Icy.

"I loved you, Frank. I just didn't love your life. If you would have put one ounce into our marriage that you put into your businesses and not been a lying son-of-a-bitch, we would've lasted."

"I never lied to you, Leine. You assumed. Different animal." Another sigh. "Whatever. It's over. Life goes on. We need to find April, not argue."

He was right. "I'll run by my house, check to see if she's still there and call you back."

Twenty minutes later, she pulled in front of her house and parked. The dark windows didn't inspire confidence. She got out, locked the car and walked up the sidewalk. The hair on her scalp prickled, reminding her of the feeling she'd had the day before, as though someone were watching her. She kept walking until she reached the front door, sliding her hand inside her purse, reassured by the semi-automatic. Inserting her key, she went inside, ignoring the impulse to turn. She closed and locked the door behind her, drawing her weapon.

"Anybody home? April?" Her anxiety rising, she waited a beat, then walked through the house, looking for a note, her backpack, anything that might suggest where April may have gone.

There was nothing.

Her cell phone went off as she came out of the guest bedroom. She sprinted to her purse and glanced at the caller ID before she answered. Private Caller. When April called the last time, the display was the same. Relieved, she answered.

"April?"

"'I've got pieces of April...'" The melody was off-key but unmistakable.

And it wasn't April singing.

Leine's heart skipped a beat, then resumed. The man's voice was unfamiliar with a slight accent she couldn't place.

"Who is this?"

The voice chuckled. "Demanding, aren't you? How about saying hello first?"

"Who the hell is this?" Leine's hands started to sweat. Fear gripped her heart and spread to her stomach.

"That's not important. What's important is I've got your daughter."

CHAPTER 15

L EINE RECOILED at the sound of the caller's voice.
"Where's April?" *How did he know my number?*
"Now, now. Calm down." The caller paused
before continuing. "Being upset is no way to begin what
could be the start of a beautiful relationship. Besides, you
don't strike me as someone who is easily surprised. From
what your daughter tells me, you have nerves of steel,
right?"

"What do you mean? You don't have my daughter."

"Well, then I must have another April. My mistake.
Shall I describe her to you? That way we can be
absolutely certain who I've got. If she's not your daughter,
I'll hang up and our budding relationship will end. Is that
all right with you?"

The caller's breathing changed, sounding more labored
and the background noises became muffled. *He can't have
April. She took a detour on her way over to Frank's. She's
probably there now.*

The next sounds were footsteps followed by a door
opening and closing, the jingle of keys. Then silence.

"Here she is…"

Leine exhaled, unaware she'd been holding her breath.

"Let's see, I'd say she's about five-seven, dark hair-cute little cowlick, by the way – and quite the tattoo of a snake winding its way up her body, all the way to her neck. Sound familiar?"

Leine's knees buckled. She caught the arm of the chair and lowered herself into it.

April.

"Now that we've established I actually have your daughter, I'd like to get down to business." More footsteps, then a door closing.

Leine sat straight in the chair, every nerve alive. Years of training flooded back, sharpening her senses. The bastard has my daughter, she thought.

He has no idea who he's dealing with.

"What kind of business?" *Keep him talking, Leine. Find out everything you can.*

"I'm sure you're aware of my first culling?"

"Culling? What are you talking about?"

"My culling of the herd. Amanda?" He said her name impatiently, as though speaking to a five year-old.

Jesus. I'm talking to the guy who killed Amanda? Leine's heart thudded in her chest and her palms began to sweat. The dryness in her mouth made it hard to swallow. Leine used a breathing technique she'd learned in India to calm herself. She'd be no good to April if she panicked.

"And Stacy?"

"Ah. You know about Stacy. I assume there hasn't been any coverage in the press because whoever found her doesn't want the publicity, right? I mean, they caught the killer who did Amanda. L.A. is safe once again. Who told you? That moron, Dorfenberger?"

He's familiar with people who work on the show, not just the contestants.

"Why would you feel the need to 'cull the herd'?"

"Would you like the definition from the dictionary? 'Cull: to remove an animal, especially a sick or weak one, from a herd or flock'. The actors currently employed on the show are dreadful and spineless and can't or won't stand up to the horrendous script." He sighed. "It's time someone showed those idiot writers how a real killer would act."

"Why take April? She's not part of the show." She needed to keep him talking but didn't want to give him any more information than was necessary.

"Because she was available. And because you're her mother. You fascinate me, Madeleine. We're two of a kind, you know."

Leine's attention riveted on the caller's voice. *He knows my full name.*

"Why do you say that?" Her voice exited her like the crack of a whip. *Tone it down, Leine. Don't let him get to you.*

The caller chuckled. "Now, now, Madeleine, don't get testy. As our relationship progresses, you'll soon see that I'm right."

"I need to speak to April, now. How do I know she's still alive?"

"You don't. Talking to your daughter has to be earned. We're still getting to know one another. Tell you what— let's set up a point system. You do what I ask and I award you points. If you don't do as I say, then you lose points. If you reach zero, I kill April."

"I don't see how that's fair. I'm already at zero."

"Patience, lovey. I'll spot you five."

"How many points until I can talk to her?"

"Hmm. Let's say twenty-five. Would you like your first assignment? It's worth five points if you complete it in a timely manner. That will put you at ten. Only fifteen to go."

"Tell you what. How about we make a trade? Me for April."

He chuckled again. "Now where's the fun in that? It's much more fun to play the game, don't you think?"

"I feel at a disadvantage. I don't know your name. What should I call you?"

There was a momentary pause at the other end. Then, "Azazel. Like the angel."

"Where the fuck are you, Santa?" Putnam waved his hand in front of Jensen's face.

Startled, Jensen's attention snapped back to his fish taco and Putnam's raunchy story of a run in he'd had with a tranny down on Santa Monica Boulevard.

"Then, if you can believe it, she put her friggin' hand on my thigh and said, 'Cops get a twenty-percent discount...'"

Jensen laughed, but his mind remained on Leine Basso. The woman had some kind of effect on him—he couldn't think about anyone or anything but her, naked in bed, naked in the shower, naked in his arms. He even caught himself fantasizing about her naked in the interrogation room. That blew his mind. Not like the place was conducive to banging, although the table looked like it could be about the right height...

He tried to concentrate on something other than Leine as he polished off the taco. Putnam cocked his head to one side.

"I haven't seen you this preoccupied since you and Gina split." Putnam tossed his empty plate in the garbage can next to them. He leaned forward, planted his elbows on the picnic table and grinned. "Get laid last night?"

"And that'd be your business because...?"

"Because you'd be a grumpy fuck if you talked to Gina recently. This time's different, like somebody got to you, good. Gotta be a broad." He lowered his voice and looked to both sides. "So, she give head?"

Jensen stood and wadded his wrapper, lobbing it into Putnam's face. "Fuck you."

He turned and strode toward the parking lot, shaking his head as Putnam burst into laughter.

"Bull's-eye." He rose from the table, wiping his eyes and followed Jensen back to their car. "You gonna tell me who? Or do I have to bug your sorry ass until you do?" He opened the passenger door but didn't get in, watching Jensen across the roof of the car.

"I'll bet I know. Is it that new chick in the Chief's office? The redhead? Man, she's hot, hot, hot."

Jensen got in and turned the key. The engine purred to life.

"Y'know, Putz, just because you're married and not getting any doesn't mean you can live vicariously through us single guys. Besides, you told me Dana only went down if you got a boner. Oh, yeah." Jensen snapped his fingers. "You haven't gotten one of those in a looong time, have you? Dude, sorry."

Putnam snorted and got in. "Yeah, I'm a deprived man. You gotta tell me about your sex life so I know shit like that still exists."

As they drove out of the lot, Jensen's cell phone buzzed, indicating a text message.

"Can you check that?" Jensen said. He slid the phone from its holder and handed it to Putnam.

"Cargill out of Hollywood Unit wants a call." Putnam checked the number and dialed.

"Putnam here. You called?" He listened for a moment. "Yeah, be there in a few minutes." He disconnected and handed the phone back. "They've got an attempted kidnap victim. Says two women grabbed her and dumped her in the trunk of their car, talking like she was gonna be some guy's dinner. The vic escaped and called us. The patrol unit put out a description of the suspects and vehicle."

"And this concerns us, how?"

"The vic's a former contestant on Serial Date. Patrol guy thought she might have some helpful info for our case."

"Worth talking to her."

"She's with their guy who does the bureau's composites. By the time we get there, he should be done with her."

CHAPTER 16

LEINE SAT ON the chair, still as stone, the phone resting in her hand. She took a deep breath and glanced around her living room. How was it that things could seem so normal when her entire world had shifted?

He's got April. I need to find her before he kills her. Leine was certain he would. She'd more than likely seen his face. Calling Jensen was out of the question. The killer had calmly told her he would skin April alive if she attempted to bring in outside help. He also warned her he knew the places she went and to whom she spoke. Leine assumed he'd either attached something to her car and was tracking her, or he'd somehow installed listening and tracking software on her phone without her knowledge. The possibility seemed remote. She was hyper-vigilant about password protection and encryption on everything she owned and rarely let her phone out of her sight. Still, it was something to keep in mind. She could easily pick up a disposable.

A more probable explanation could be he'd somehow gotten a hold of something she kept with her every day:

her purse, maybe? What else did she have with her all the time? Her watch?

Leine studied the multi-function time piece on her wrist. A gift from Carlos, the waterproof chronometer incorporated an altimeter, compass, thermometer, barometer and clinometer. She only removed it when she took a shower. *He would need to have been in my house to gain access.* The idea chilled her. She made a mental note to pick up a bug detector and do a sweep of her house and car.

He was familiar with people on the set of Serial Date other than the contestants, which meant he'd either been on set at some point, knew someone who worked there, or was a previous or current employee of the show. Leine couldn't place the voice. She detected a slight accent, but it wasn't pronounced enough to reveal its origin.

He knew her name, knew she had a daughter. But how did he know April was here? Nobody on the set was aware she had a daughter, other than Gene. Leine flashed to the day before when she felt someone watching her as she walked back to the house after retrieving her phone from her car. Today she sensed it again. She'd ignored it the first time, convinced it was stress. Leine wanted to kick herself. *When had those feelings ever been wrong?* She was out of practice. She'd never have disregarded that kind of indicator when she was active. It was one of the things that made her so effective in her job. Intuition, gut feeling, whatever it was, Leine had it in spades.

Azazel had given her until eight o'clock that evening to finish her first task, bringing her five points closer to her goal of speaking to April. The bizarre request left Leine puzzled. Why would he waste time using her as an errand girl? It made no sense.

Then again, he wasn't exactly normal. The man dismembered women and ate them.

A chill spiraled down her back as she imagined the worst case scenario involving April. Her mind slammed the door shut on the thought and she took another deep breath. Better stick to the task.

Where the hell was she going to find a high-speed blender this time of night?

Leine parked near the post office box on Main in Venice and got out of her car. She glanced at her watch. Seven fifty-six. She leaned her head back and closed her eyes, attempting to calm herself. In order to find the exact model of Blendo-matic high performance blender Azazel specified she'd called three box stores and visited one who mistakenly told her they had the model she was looking for. Finally, the clerk took pity on her and called a sister store in another location to see if they had the SZX5000. They did, and the clerk asked the other store to put it on hold for her.

"These little puppies are really popular with the juicing crowd. They've been flying off the shelves. You're lucky to find one in stock within fifty miles," the clerk said.

Anxiety ratcheted to threat level, Leine drove like a madwoman to Culver City to pick the thing up, arriving back at the specified drop site with only minutes to spare. While in the store's parking lot, she'd unfastened the bottom of the blender base and placed a tiny tracking device inside, just under the motor. Then she secured the base and placed everything back in the box.

Frank had called twice, but she hadn't bothered to answer. Undecided on what to tell him, she didn't have the time or patience to deal with his questions. Yes, he cared for April, but he wasn't her father. Leine needed complete control as to how things went down. Frank would immediately call the police and that was the last thing Leine wanted.

At precisely eight o'clock, her phone rang. Caller ID showed Private Caller.

"Hello?"

"Did you find the SZX5000?"

"Yes." Leine bit back a sarcastic comment. "How do I get it to you?" She'd fantasized about putting a bullet through him when he came to pick it up.

Azazel chuckled. "Wouldn't that be convenient? If you succeeded in killing me, how would you find your daughter? She'd die of thirst before you tracked her down, if you could even find her."

How would he know I was thinking that? Lucky guess?

"Set the package under the post office box and leave. And Madeleine?"

"What?"

"I'll know when you leave. Don't try anything stupid. It'll get your daughter killed."

Azazel ended the call. Her desire to find Jensen and explain everything hit her full force, but she shook it off. She had to play this one carefully. Calling in law enforcement too early was risky. Not when the killer was testing her, getting to know how well she complied with his 'requests'. No, first she'd lull him into a false sense of trust. Then she'd contact Jensen.

"It was your fault, you know. Shit—" Sissy swore as a can of cream of mushroom soup fell onto the sidewalk and rolled.

Gwen whirled around, an angry grimace on her face. "It wasn't even close to my fault, bitch. She escaped, plain and simple."

Sissy placed the soup back in the grocery bag and proceeded up the walkway toward the house. "Yeah, well, plain and simple ain't gonna cut it. What're we going to tell him? He's so going to be pissed."

They reached the back door and knocked. Not hearing anything, Gwen inserted a key in the lock and opened the door.

Inside, the old built-in gloss-white cupboards and newer stainless appliances gleamed, as did the tile floor. Must be cleaning day, Sissy mused. She set the groceries on the tan Formica counter and opened the refrigerator. Gwen began to put away the canned goods while Sissy replenished the veggie drawer.

"This is new, isn't it?" Gwen pointed at the shiny red blender on the counter.

"Yeah. It's the one he's been talking about for ages. Looks like he finally found one."

The two women glanced at each other, both silently wondering if they'd be the one he would ask to use it first.

Sissy opened a can of soup and poured the contents into a bowl she picked out from the cupboard, which then went into the microwave. She set it at two minutes and returned to the fridge, selecting a stalk of celery, one carrot and a clean head of iceberg lettuce.

"Wait a minute." Gwen shoved Sissy out of the way and began to slice the vegetables, putting them into another bowl. "It's my turn to take him lunch."

"I don't think so." Sissy held the chef's knife aloft, angling the blade toward the top of Gwen's head. Gwen gave her a dark look, but moved out of the way. Sissy wasn't about to let her talk to him first. Not after their latest debacle with that homeless ho from the first season.

"Good idea, switching plates on the car. Think she memorized the old ones?"

Sissy smiled to herself. Gwen was shifting tactics. She's such a suck up. Sissy didn't mind letting her have the leftovers. Not if it meant she could manipulate her into doing the jobs she didn't like.

"If she did, they'll come up with a sedan belonging to an old man who's been missing for six weeks. No way they'll be able to track it here."

"What do you think he did with him?" Gwen whispered.

Sissy shrugged. It was none of her business what he did with the 'offerings' as they called them. She was pretty sure it wasn't catch-and-release. As long as he let her stay she didn't care.

Sissy finished making the salad and removed the now-hot bowl of soup from the microwave, setting them both on a tray with spotless silverware, a single rose (thorns removed) and the current Men's Health magazine. She added a linen napkin and a bottle of pre-squeezed barley juice she'd picked up at Whole Foods before taking everything through the living room and up the stairs.

As she neared the top of the stairway her hands began to shake. The bowls on the tray rattled against each other. She stopped and took a deep breath, willing herself to be still. When she was sure her hands wouldn't betray her excitement she continued down the hall to the closed door. Transferring the tray to one hand, she rapped on the door with the other.

"Come in."

Still holding the food in one hand, Sissy turned the door handle and entered the dark room. He used the extra bedroom as an office of sorts. At least, that's what he'd told Gwen. Sissy knew it was really his trophy-slash-gaming room. Only she was allowed to go inside.

He sat at his computer console, playing a video game. The screams emanating from the screen told her it was his favorite, Sluts and Guns. One wall was covered in black and white photographs of young women, most of them no older than twenty. Their poses fascinated her— each was nude and looked as though asleep. He'd taken the photos from differing angles in order to capture every limb, every back, every buttock in minute detail. Sissy had no idea if or how each woman died although he'd told her he had no interest in them sexually. That's what Sissy and Gwen were for, he assured her.

Sissy was still trying to figure a way to take Gwen out of the picture. She had to admit, the bitch did come in handy when one of their catches got a little too rambunctious, but most of the time she was more work than she was worth. It was a tough job trying to keep her in second position. Besides, Sissy had access to a hypodermic needle filled with anesthetic to quiet the active ones.

This latest problem with the woman who'd escaped was going to take some finessing on Sissy's part. She walked over to the filing cabinet next to him and set the tray on top, waiting for his acknowledgment. He was wearing one of her favorite shirts, a dark blue button down. Her tongue darted between her lips. She could almost taste him.

"I'll eat later."

The sound of his voice reverberated through her. The tingle from the adrenaline rush of standing so close to someone who wielded such power cascaded down her body in waves. Only she and Gwen could slake his desire.

More often than not he called on Sissy. She couldn't begin to describe how much it turned her on he needed her that way.

If she'd have stopped to think about it, she'd probably have to admit the sex wasn't great. It was more the idea that was so exciting; the idea he chose her, Sissy Nelson, as his partner above all others. Gwen was an at-bat as far as she was concerned.

He hit the pause button on his console.

"You have something to tell me?"

Sissy averted her eyes, unsure how to spin it so she came out better than Gwen.

"We found the woman you told us about. The homeless one from last season?"

He remained silent, his attention on her. Sissy would've killed for this kind of focus from him and here he was, listening to her every word.

"There was a slight problem—" The words came out in a whisper. She cleared her throat.

He rose from the chair. Sissy backed up until her legs hit the filing cabinet, her palms wet. He placed his arm around her shoulder, dipping his head in order to hear her better.

"What do you mean, a slight problem?"

"I-I mean we don't have her."

"You don't? Why?" He gripped her shoulder, hurting her.

"It was Gwen's fault. It was her idea to put her in the trunk. The little bitch figured out how to trip the release."

He let go of Sissy and stepped back, his dark eyes smoldering with anger. Sissy stared at the floor, her shoulders tense, inching their way up toward her ears.

"She escaped?" His tone was measured, but Sissy recognized intensity behind the words. "Why did you feel the need to put her in the trunk? We've talked about this at length. You're not to arouse their suspicions. You can do anything else you deem necessary, but I reserve the right to witness their fear. It's my reward since I'm letting you two find them for me."

"I know, I know. I'm sorry. I have no idea what got into Gwen, but she started hinting at what was going to happen. The woman was no dummy. She figured it out and got scared. We had to restrain her, but Gwen didn't put the ties back in the car from the last time, so we stuffed her in the trunk." It was actually Sissy's responsibility to make sure the car was stocked, but he didn't have to know that.

"Did it not occur to you that there are built-in safety features in cars? Especially the trunk?" His rigid posture and clenched fists belied his soft, calm tone. Sissy wasn't sure if she should stay and take the brunt of his anger in the hopes that he'd be aroused, or if she should go downstairs and find Gwen.

She didn't have to make the choice.

"Get Gwen up here, now. There's a way for you both to make amends."

Leine stepped through the doors of the Serial Date offices, intent on finding Peter. The tracking device hadn't worked. Either Azazel figured out that the blender was wired and removed it, or the tracker was a defective piece of shit. If he knew about it, he hadn't let on.

Frustrated, she'd tried to figure out another way to track Azazel and her daughter while working but didn't see how she could. Gaining access to April's phone would be the best, but she needed to find someone with that kind of knowledge. She knew a thousand ways to kill someone and nothing about how to hack someone's phone or email. The agency used a whole contingent of hackers and communications experts. She'd never needed to learn.

She had to have time to plan. Azazel's next victim would not be her daughter, not if she could help it. She hoped her story of needing to take care of a sick relative would work and Peter would give her a couple of days off. Not that she had any illusions they'd be paid for.

Paula, the receptionist, stopped her in the hall on her way to Peter's office.

"A package came for you this morning. I left it on the desk where you usually put your purse."

"Thanks, Paula. Is Peter in his office?"

"I'm not sure. He's around, though."

Leine walked down the hall to the door with the brass name plate and knocked.

"Come in."

The door clicked and swung open, revealing Peter sitting at his desk, the lone Baccarat lamp the only source of light in an otherwise dark room. Leine walked over to one of the drape-covered windows and pulled it open, allowing bright morning sun to stream into the office.

"What the hell'd you do that for?" Peter shielded his eyes with his hand.

"How can you stand working in such a dark place? It'd drive me crazy."

"I like it dark. No distractions." He squinted at her. "To what do I owe this visit? Anything wrong?"

"No, everything's fine on set. I wanted to ask you for a couple of days leave to care for my sick aunt in San Diego. She recently had hip surgery and needs my help."

"Isn't there someone else? I can't really spare you right now."

"Why not? It's not like a murderer's hanging around, right?" Leine watched Peter closely. No reaction. "Besides, the cons and contestants appear to be settled and working well together."

"Still, I hate to not have you on set. Gene doesn't have your experience. Everyone feels better when you're around. The cons are on their best behavior when they know you're here."

"Gee, thanks for that. But wasn't Gene good enough until Mandy was murdered? He knows his way around a Taser and pepper spray. I'm only talking about a couple of days here, max. It's important, Peter."

She could tell he was trying to think of a way to refuse. In the end he must have weighed the option of losing her entirely.

"All right. But only for a couple of days. I need you back by the time we tape. As it is, you're going to miss rehearsals."

Yeah, and that would break my heart, Leine thought.

"Thanks, Peter. Will do."

She remembered the package as she was walking out the front door. Backtracking to the administration offices she spotted the small cardboard box sitting on the desk where Paula said she'd left it.

It was addressed to Madeleine Basso, Serial Date Security but there was no return address, no postage. Must have been hand delivered, Leine thought. Wariness from the old days kicked in, but she shook it off. No one from her past knew where she was, or even that she was still alive, except for Gene. Curious, she held up the box and shook it. Too light to be anything serious except maybe ricin or anthrax, and that was a stretch. She hunted through Paula's desk drawer for something sharp and grabbed a pair of green handled scissors. She sliced through the packing tape on the top of the box and pulled the flaps open.

Inside the box, nestled between several cotton balls, was a slender finger, severed at the joint, wearing a delicate silver and lapis ring.

CHAPTER 17

L
EINE FOLDED THE cardboard flaps back into place with care, surprised her hands didn't shake. She closed her eyes as rage overwhelmed her. Every nerve screamed, adding to the cacophony that coursed through her mind, rising to demand action, then collapsing in impotence and frustration.

Think, Leine. This is not April's finger. He's toying with you. Testing you. Get it to a lab. Have the box tested for fingerprints. You can think about this later, if it's a match.

But whose finger was it, if not her daughter's? Leine had to believe it wasn't April's. It was her ring, yes, but that would be easy to swap with another woman's hand.

Leine carefully slid the box into her purse and walked through the office to the hallway. She turned left and willed her legs to take her out to the parking lot and her car, glad for the psychological manifestations of shock. The numbness was the only thing that enabled her to keep moving.

As she neared the entrance, Frank exploded through the front doors, his face a dark mixture of anger and worry.

"Why the hell don't you answer your goddamned phone?"

Leine seized his arm and spun him around, shoving him through the entry to the sidewalk outside.

"Keep your voice down, Frank." Her voice held a feral warning even he couldn't ignore.

He turned to face her, arms crossed, his fury surrounding him like a force field.

"Where is she?"

"Calm down. Your anger doesn't help."

"Don't tell me to calm down, Leine. Where the fuck is April?"

Take it easy, Leine. He's scared. Like you are. "I haven't located her yet."

"Did you call the police?"

"Yes. I'm sure they'll contact you shortly to get a statement. I gave them your number. In the meantime, I'm doing whatever I can."

"Who's the detective in charge? I want to speak to him."

"And they want to speak with you. Just remember, you're not her father. They won't give you any information. You'll have to get that through me." Leine only had one chance to get him off her ass. She'd apologize for the lies later. "They've expressed an interest in where you were when she disappeared."

His eyes widened in surprise. "And you told them what?"

"I told them you would never have anything to do with this, but they need to follow up. A huge percentage of abductions involve people known to the victim. They did the same to me." Lying left a bitter taste in Leine's mouth, but she couldn't think of a better way to get Frank out of her way. She understood his need to act, to help, but couldn't risk his involvement. He'd be like a raging bull in a china shop. Finesse was not a word anyone would use to describe Frank.

"Fine. My phone's on. What do you need me to do in the meantime?"

"Do you have a recent photograph of her? Something more current than this?" Leine reached in her purse, avoiding the box and slid out her wallet. The picture she produced showed an eleven-year old April grinning with arms outstretched, about to catch a whole salmon being thrown her way at one of the fish stalls at Pike Place Market in Seattle. Carlos stood in the background, laughing. It was their last trip together.

"Yeah, I've got several she emailed while she was in Europe."

Leine's heart twisted at the thought her daughter hadn't bothered to contact her in three years, but was in direct communication with Frank. Her resolve to find April hardened. She'd set things right. She had to.

"Great. Can you make copies and start circulating them around the city? Start in my neighborhood and spread out. Homes, businesses, restaurants, gyms, whatever. The detectives will want more recent photos, too. You can email them to me." Hopefully, Frank would stay occupied for a couple of days, give her time to find April and Azazel so she could obliterate his sorry ass from the face of the earth. The sooner, the better. Leine was under no illusions when it came to how much time she had. "Can you get me a list of her friend's names? Anyone she may have mentioned?"

"She's always been pretty tight lipped about her private life. Can't blame her, though. She doesn't want anyone telling her how to live."

A glimmer of satisfaction raced through her. So she didn't trust him completely.

Frank's gaze met Leine's. "Have you thought about calling Eric?"

"The conversation is over." Leine slipped the older photograph of April back into her purse, turned and walked away, leaving Frank standing on the sidewalk.

The idea of calling Eric had occurred to her, but she'd be damned if she'd ask for help from that low-life, even though he owed her.

She reached her car and was about to get in when she spotted Paula walking toward her.

"Did you find the box?" Paula asked.

"Yes. Thanks. Who delivered it? There wasn't a return address."

"A thin woman with strawberry-blonde hair and really white skin. When I asked who she was, she didn't answer. She acted kind of weird." Paula gave Leine a shy smile. "I hope you don't mind me saying so. I mean, if she's a friend—"

"Not a problem. Doesn't sound like someone I know. I'm going to be gone for a couple of days, taking care of my aunt in San Diego. If you get any more of these kinds of deliveries, could you give me a call?"

"Sure. I hope your aunt's okay."

"She'll be fine—she needs help planning things, is all. Thanks for asking."

Leine waited until Paula had walked into the building before she stepped behind an oak tree and vomited into a rosemary bush.

Leine showed her ID to the woman sitting at the front counter at DNAsty Lab who directed her to Zephyr Cornell's office. The guitar solo from Santana's *Smooth* filled the hallway and flowed past her as she neared his open door.

He stood at his window with his back to the door, pumping and gyrating through an air guitar rendition of Carlos Santana's hit song. Zephyr had always reminded

Leine of an irrepressible mad scientist with his black, curly hair, round John Lennon specs and white lab coat.

She waited quietly in the doorway while he finished.

The song ended and he reached over to turn down the stereo, noticing Leine for the first time.

"Leine. It really is you." Arms wide open, he bounded over to where she stood and enveloped her in a deep hug. "I had my doubts. They told me you were dead."

Leine hugged him back. "They told everyone that."

"So how've you been? You look like shit."

"Thanks. I've been better. The woman at the front told me you're the majority owner now."

Zephyr grinned. "Yeah. Those early stock options came in handy." His expression grew serious as he glanced at the plastic bag in her hands. The box was at a private forensics lab she'd used in the past. "Is that what you called about?"

Leine nodded and handed it to him. He set it on his desk.

"I won't ask you what happened." The concern in his eyes was obvious. "I'm doing this for you and for Carlos. God, I miss him."

"Yeah." Leine cleared her throat and took a small step back.

Zephyr sighed and pushed a form across the desk.

"Fill this out and take it with you to the back. Have Trudi get a sample. I'll do the test myself and call you as soon as I can."

"I really appreciate this, Zephyr."

Zephyr's soft brown eyes met hers. "It's no problem, Leine. Anything I can do to help."

She gave him her new disposable phone number and then left to find Trudi. Back in her car fifteen minutes later, her other phone rang. Private caller.

"Did you get my little present?" Azazel's breathing echoed through the earpiece.

Leine covered the mouthpiece as she fought through the rage his voice elicited.

When she thought she had her emotions under control, she answered, "You're not playing by the rules."

"Oh, yes I am, Madeleine. I only said I wouldn't kill her unless you lost all your points. I haven't yet, because you haven't yet."

He paused, waiting for Leine's reply. When she didn't answer, he continued.

"She had to be punished. That little trick of yours with the blender was a good try, but really, I expected more from you."

Leine clenched her fists, digging her nails into her palms. Her vision clouded as she fought the nausea welling up within her.

"Are you still there? Don't worry, Madeleine. I don't need to kill her yet. I have a season's worth of smoothie makings stored in my freezer, and, unless the show's writers step up their game, there are plenty more where that came from. I can wait until this little charade of ours plays out."

The nausea began to recede. In its place was a sharp clarity she hadn't experienced in years.

"What do you want?" she asked.

He chuckled. "We're not so different, you and I. You've taken life, I've done the same. I've given this a lot of thought, you know. The only thing separating your true nature and mine is you repress your natural tendencies. I merely act how God created me."

Leine stopped breathing for a moment. *How does he know what I've done?* The possibility Azazel may be a remnant of her past hadn't occurred to her.

Until now.

"Your information is false. I worked security for diplomatic envoys, and not very important ones at that. I had no cause to 'take life' as you so poetically phrase it."

"Oh, but you have. I'm aware of several. You were considered one of the best. This is where we both excel. I am undoubtedly one of the premier killers in my field. Read up on the contenders—Gacy, Manson, Bundy, Miyazaki. You'll see I'm far superior to their rudimentary methods. The thinking man's killer, if you will."

"Again, what do you want?" Leine ground her teeth. *Play along. It's the only way forward.* Certain her brain would explode if she didn't disconnect soon, she worked to slow her breathing to take her mind off the reality.

"I have a special assignment for you—worth ten points if you succeed. I need you to find an object for me. A very important object. It's currently being displayed in the back office at Nadja Imports in West Hollywood."

Nadja Imports. For some reason the name rang a bell. "What kind of object?"

"A trade gun."

"Forgive my ignorance, but what kind of gun would that be, exactly?"

"It's long, about four feet. Popular with trappers in the nineteenth century."

"So it's a flintlock?"

"Yes. Wood stock, blue barrel."

"And you want me to go to this place called Nadja Imports and purchase the gun for you?"

"Not exactly. It's not for sale."

"You want me to steal it, then."

"I don't consider it stealing when it belongs to me." Azazel's voice had a hard edge.

West Hollywood was known for its large Russian community, along with a fair-sized contingent of Russian mafia. Leine had no illusions about what this request would entail. "Have you checked Ebay? Craig's List?"

"You're questioning me?" Azazel's voice rose several decibels. "Never do so again. I'm in control. Not you. Do you understand?"

Alarmed, Leine answered, "Of course. I was merely curious—thought it might make things easier." She hoped she sounded placatory. It was hard to mask her growing anger. *Calm down, Leine. Stay in control. Save it. Let it build for when you find him. String him along.*

"The gun has...sentimental value. There are specific markings on the stock. I'll know if you bought it elsewhere." His words were calm, but his voice held menace.

"How long do I have to find it?"

"Twenty-four hours. If you haven't secured it by then, you'll lose the points you've earned. You know what happens then."

The line went dead.

CHAPTER 18

JENSEN HIT SPEED dial on his cell phone. After several rings, Leine's voicemail picked up. For the third time, he left a message asking her to call him.

Why isn't she picking up? She wouldn't avoid him. Not after the night they'd had together. *Maybe she's dealing with her daughter, butthead. Leave her alone. Give her some space.*

This was an entirely new experience for Santiago Jensen, babe-magnet detective, as Putnam liked to call him. Usually it was Jensen avoiding the phone calls.

All day, he'd been unable to concentrate for any length of time before she would invade his thoughts and it was pissing him off. His problem reminded him of what the junkies always said. The dearth of the drug in their system induced a need so deep, the only thing to turn it off was more of whatever they didn't have.

He knew how they felt.

His phone hit the wall with a thud. Putnam was walking back from the john and leaned against the desk, a wide grin on his face.

"Thinkin' 'bout the broad again, eh, Jensen?" When Jensen didn't respond, Putnam crossed his arms, a frown on his face and took a good, long look at his partner.

"Something else bothering you?"

"It's nothing," Jensen replied. "Worried about the case, is all." He'd hear no end of it if he admitted his obsession to Putnam.

"Bullshit. Some homeless babe got picked up by a couple of freaks and she escaped. End of story."

"Yeah, and a contestant on the first season of Serial Date. Doesn't that mean something to you?"

Putnam waved his hand dismissively. "We already followed up on that. Besides, Graber's still locked up. So no, it doesn't mean anything to me."

Jensen stared at the phone on his desk, willing it to ring. Pathetic.

"I know you, Santa, and this ain't worry about a case we're working. Your sorry face tells me it's about a broad. And I'm thinking it's the same one who rocked your world the other night. What, she's not calling and falling?"

The look on Jensen's face must have given him away. Putnam's cackle of laughter erupted as he leaned over and slapped him on the shoulder. "Buddy, you gotta get a hold of yourself. Either that, or go out and drag her back to your man cave. You're off the clock. Why don't you just go?" Putnam walked away, laughing. "Ha. The swinging dick's in deep, now."

Putnam had a point. Jensen wasn't the type of man to wait around for a phone call. He knew where she lived.

Probably find out it's nothing, he thought. He grabbed his keys and phone off the desk and left.

No lights were visible through the windows at Leine's place and her car was nowhere to be found. Jensen shifted into neutral and idled for a moment as he watched the house, trying to decide what to do. He tried to talk himself out of staying, but it didn't work. He eased the car into first gear and turned off the engine.

Jensen wasn't about to admit to himself he wanted to see if she'd been out with another man.

He made himself comfortable and turned the radio on low. The classic rock station he always listened to was airing a Rolling Stones retrospective. He settled in to pass the time, accompanied by the familiar strains of *Gimme Shelter*.

He didn't have long to wait. Her green sedan pulled to the curb fifteen minutes later. He watched as she opened the door and climbed out, then shut and locked the car behind her. When she reached the walkway leading to the front door of the house, Jensen got out of his car and crossed the street.

"Leine."

She stopped but didn't turn.

"You need to go." Her voice rippled through the still evening air.

He covered the distance between them and placed his hand on her arm. She turned and he could see by the light of the street lamp she'd been crying. Surprised, he let go.

She turned and walked the rest of the way to her door, fumbling in her purse. Jensen followed slowly, not wanting to spook her.

"Listen, Leine. If there's something wrong, I can help. Just tell me." All of his senses were heightened, being so close to her. He could feel her body heat and smell her hair, her perfume. Something by Chanel, she'd told him the other morning.

"No. You have to leave. Don't ask me to explain." She found her key and slid it into the lock, but didn't open the door.

Jensen edged closer and placed his hand on the small of her back. She didn't move. He buried his face in her

118

hair, inhaling her scent and encircled her waist with his other hand, bringing her closer to him. The feel of her body against his left him unhinged and he bent his head to devour her neck, acting like a man who'd found water after days without. Her breath caught; she offered no resistance.

Her body began to relax into him and a soft moan escaped her. He continued to nuzzle her earlobe and neck, his heartbeat matching his excitement. All sense of time and space vanished. Nothing mattered except Leine.

Without warning she stiffened and pushed him away. Confused, he drew back.

"I can't see you anymore," she said, as she unlocked the door. Before he could protest, she slipped inside and closed it, sliding the deadbolt into place.

What the fuck? Jensen took a second to recover before knocking. He peered through the door's stained glass, her outline barely visible as she moved through the living room.

"Leine. What's wrong?" he said through the door. "Talk to me. I can help you, whatever happened. Trust me."

She paused for a moment, then disappeared from view.

Jensen stepped back, staring at the door. His inherent belief in himself and his abilities rose to the surface to smash any self-doubt the encounter may have summoned. He'd never had a woman turn him down. The only acceptable explanation was she'd gotten in deep and didn't want to involve him.

He returned to his car determined to find out what kind of trouble had found her.

Leine sank against her bedroom door, fighting the urge to go after Jensen. There was work to do and she couldn't risk involving him. She glanced at the detection equipment stored in a case on her bed, ready to go. Purchased that afternoon from an old contact downtown, the guy gave her the agency discount after she told him she was freelancing.

She'd swept her car and smart phone earlier. Both were live, along with her watch. An inexpensive Timex and second rental car soon followed.

Keeping the lights off in case Azazel installed video, Leine made a sweep of the house, noting where the signal indicated a possible plant. It didn't surprise her he'd employed both audio and video feeds. What did surprise her was the sophistication of the hardware. Most amateurs wouldn't have a clue how to position the minute cameras and microphones for optimal observation. Except for her detached, one-car garage, her entire house was one giant surveillance system.

That's how he knew about April. And about my former life. She slid the kit onto the upper shelf in her closet and parked herself on the bed to think. If she disabled the bugs, Azazel would know and Leine didn't understand him enough yet to predict his reaction. Her daughter's life was on the line. She couldn't risk it. Besides, if she played it right she might be able to work the feeds to her advantage.

She walked out to the detached garage and turned on the new tablet she'd purchased that morning. First, she memorized the directions for Nadja Imports, then went to Google Earth to map her exit strategy. Another site from her old life gave her the building's floor plan from a recent remodel permit. Then she searched "trade guns" to get a better idea of what she was looking for, and ran a quick search for news articles regarding known Russian gang activity in L.A. Several identified incidents in the area. Her experience with the tattooed Russian was going to come in handy.

Last, she typed in the word 'Azazel'. The name came back with references to the devil and the Day of Atonement. Great name choice, Leine thought. *Day of Atonement?*

Before heading back into the house, Leine stepped behind an old lawn mower and slid a keychain with one key from her pocket, unlocking the door to a small room. A single bulb illuminated several weapons stored in the small, cramped space.

Leine chose a forty-five semi-automatic with two full mags, a night vision monocle, two smaller electronic devices and a switchblade, which she strapped to her calf.

Armed with the weapons and information, Leine closed and locked the door to the room and walked back toward the house, slipping the gun and electronics under her shirt. No sense letting Azazel know where she kept the firearms.

The import store was dark except for a couple of burglary-deterrent spots in the front showroom. Leine watched the entrance for activity before she drove down a block and parked. She made her way up the alley to the back of the building, avoiding the pools of light cast by the intermittent street lamps. Dressed in black, she all but disappeared in the shadows.

A security camera stood watch above the well-lit back door. Leine scanned the surrounding area for additional security. Not seeing any, she edged closer to the building. A loading bay door stood next to a separate man door, which appeared to be made of solid metal and had an electronic keypad mounted near the handle.

She aimed one of the electronic devices she'd brought toward the camera, jamming the feed. The

camera's security light blinked twice and she closed the distance to the door. Keeping the device pointed at the video equipment with one hand, she slid the second device into a slot on the keypad with the other. Then she pulled out her phone and entered a pre-programmed sequence of numbers. Its amber light blinked once as electronic impulses scrambled the code. A pause of a few seconds was followed by a click. The red light on the keypad blinked off.

Leine retrieved the electronic lock pick and inched the door open. The immediate area was clear. She stepped into the dark interior and slid the small night vision monocle over one eye. Shipments on wood pallets covered in shrink-wrap littered the cavernous room's concrete floor. Deep shelves filled with various decorative items lined two of the walls. The flashlight's beam illuminated a hallway to her left.

She passed a pair of bathrooms and a utility closet before she found the office. The light under the door stopped her cold. As Leine took stock of the situation, a cold, hard gun barrel pressed against her temple.

CHAPTER 19

W HO ARE YOU and why shouldn't I kill you?"
Leine pegged the accent as Ukrainian. She
answered him back in his language.

"Would you have the blood of a friend on your
hands?"

The gun eased off a few inches. The man stepped
beside her and peered into her face.

"I know you?"

His breath stank of garlic and onions and bad gums.
He was blonde, medium height and had massive
shoulders with no neck. 'Roid boy, she thought. Leine
matched his stare.

"We know some of the same people." Leine searched
her memory for the news articles she'd seen earlier.
"Zaretsky was my cousin." She felt secure invoking his
name; his entire contingent had been wiped out in a
brutal takedown by a rival faction the previous May.

'Roid boy wasn't all the way convinced, but the gun
dropped an inch.

"You knew Gregor?" He turned to look down the
hallway, toward the loading bay. "How did you get in?
The door was locked. I make sure—"

As he turned back toward her, Leine wrenched the gun from his hand, twisted his arm up between his shoulder blades and shoved the barrel against his neck, under his chin. Thankfully, his over achievement in the physical arena hadn't been matched in the mental.

"We're going to go into the office, now. How many?"

When he didn't answer right away, she yanked his arm higher, pressing the gun hard enough to make him swallow. He grunted in pain.

"Two."

She shoved him the few steps to the door marked Private.

"You first," she said. "Make one move I don't like and I'll kill you."

He grabbed the handle and pushed the door open. A fair-haired man with long legs sat in a club chair on the left. Another man, more compact with a darker complexion, sat at a desk. Both were laughing at something one of them just said. They looked toward the door in unison. Leine knew the exact moment they realized their friend was a hostage; their smiles faded and they both reached for their guns.

"Do it and he's dead."

The fair-haired one glanced at the man seated behind the desk, who eased his hand off the semi-automatic lying front of him. He leaned back, a calculating look in his eyes. The fair-haired man mirrored him.

The room was a typical office; a desk flanked by two club chairs, filing cabinets along one wall, with a copier and a safe along another. On the wall to Leine's right hung a gold-leafed crèche, spanning well over three feet. Another wall showcased a painting of several wolves in a snow-laden forest, blood dripping from their mouths, staring at the viewer from a recent kill. Leine was only interested in the object displayed behind the desk; a long barreled gun, similar to the pictures she'd seen earlier.

"What can we do for you?" The dark haired man's accent was definitely Russian, probably near Moscow. He remained still, his eyes riveted on Leine and his gunman.

"Toss your weapons over here. Now."

They glanced at each other. The Russian shrugged, leaned over and slid his gun across the floor. The other man followed suit. Leine kicked them both out of the reach of the Ukrainian.

Leine nodded at the wall behind the desk. "I want the gun."

The Russian swiveled in his chair to look at the piece. When he turned back, a smile played at the edges of his mouth.

"Now why would you want an old, rusted gun when we have a warehouse filled with many more valuable things?" He shook his head in disbelief and added, "It doesn't even fire."

"Take the gun off the wall and slide it across the floor to me. If you don't, I'll use the Ukrainian as a shield and kill you both. I've done it before. It's your choice. Either I get the gun and you live, or I get the gun and you die."

The Russian watched Leine for a moment. "First, you must answer a question." He braced his elbows on the desk. "Who sent you? I don't believe it is you who wants this gun. Tell me this and the gun is yours."

"He goes by the name Azazel. That's all I know."

The guy in the club chair moved as if to rush them. Leine pivoted the Ukrainian toward him, tightening her grip on the gun.

"Don't even try, asshole."

The Russian shook his head. The long-legged man slumped back in the chair with a scowl.

125

"This Azazel is not a good man, asking you to enter a nest of scorpions for an old gun with no value. Only someone with ties to this piece of shit would ask for such a thing." He looked directly at Leine. "I think this Azazel has something to do with the previous owner, yes? Someone we knew as the Frenchman."

Leine stiffened. The Russian cocked his head to one side.

"You know of this despicable son of a goat?" He narrowed his eyes. "It was rumored he found death by a woman's hand, although there were no witnesses."

"Slide the rifle to me, now, or I kill the three of you and take it. I don't have time for your shit." Leine renewed her grip on the Ukrainian's arm and shoved the gun into his temple.

"Calm yourself. If you are the woman who did such a valuable thing, you are entitled to anything I possess." He rose from his chair, palms raised. Leine tracked him, keeping a tight grip on the Ukrainian.

He took down the trade gun and laid it across the desk.

"This calls for a drink. May I?" He reached toward a drawer, his eyebrows raised.

"Just give me the fucking gun and we're done." *Russians. Anything's an excuse to celebrate.* She was having a hard enough time corralling the thoughts racing through her brain from what he'd said. The Frenchman?

The Russian sighed. He bent over as though to pick up the gun, then reached behind him and pulled out a mini-Uzi hidden in a side pocket of his chair. A spray of bullets erupted from the barrel of the gun, covering one end of the room to the other. Leine shoved the Ukrainian into the line of fire and rolled to the side. She shot out the ceiling light, plunging the room into darkness.

She had a clean shot at the Russian through the night vision goggle but she hesitated and he dropped behind the desk. The Ukrainian lay on the floor near the door and wasn't moving. The long legged one had ducked behind his chair, but part of his body was visible. She drew the knife strapped to her calf and waited until he peered around the chair, then let it fly. There was a muffled thwack as it buried itself in his eye socket. He screamed in pain as he pitched forward and hit the floor with a thud.

Leine turned her attention back to the Russian. He poked his head up over the edge of the desk and looked toward where the other guy had fallen. Leine aimed the Ukrainian's 9mm at him and squeezed off a shot. The bullet missed, embedding itself in the wall. The Russian disappeared behind the desk.

"Take the gun. It is my gift to you," he called. His voice held a hint of bravado.

His hand appeared and groped for the flintlock. Successful, he grasped the gun and shoved it across the desk. It landed on the floor a few feet from the Ukrainian. With a watchful eye, Leine crawled across the linoleum and picked up the rifle. Without a word, she backed out of the room.

She ran through the hallway into the warehouse and walked out the door, making sure to jam the camera as she left. She didn't want her face all over the Internet for every Tom, Dick and Yakov to see. Becoming a target of the Russian underworld would not be a good life choice. She cleared the alleyway and jogged back to her car, at the same time wiping the Ukrainian's nine clean, then tossing it over the fence.

The memory of what the Russian said kept coming back to her. *How was Azazel connected to the Frenchman?*

When she reached her car, she popped the trunk and placed the rifle inside, covering it with a blanket she'd brought. He said he'd heard a woman killed him. Azazel had to be connected, somehow. But why have her get the gun, other than to keep from getting killed? And, to continue his cat-and-mouse game.

She drove past darkened alleys and storefronts, trying to work it out in her mind. By the time she'd reached the drop point, she was no closer to an answer. She pulled into a space next to her other rental.

Butch, one of the part-time interns on Serial Date leaned against the car, waiting for her. Leine handed him the keys and a hundred dollars.

"Take it straight to my place and park in front. Lock it and leave the keys under the porch, behind the steps. No joy riding, okay? I checked the mileage."

Butch smiled. "Joy riding? In a Buick? No worries, Leine."

"Pop the trunk, will you?" she asked. He got in and hit the release.

She took the wrapped gun out of the trunk and walked into the YMCA. To prove his point Butch attempted to lay rubber with the sedan. He got a chirp out of it, she'd give him that.

There weren't many people working out at that hour, which was just as well. The women's locker room was to her right. Two different sized lockers lined the walls. Leine chose the full length one with the number sixty-two on it and placed the gun inside. An open combination lock rested on the shelf, which she removed and placed on the locker after closing the door as instructed.

Leine grabbed a towel off a clothes hook and wrapped her hair, turban-style. Then she walked to the other side of the locker room and sat down to wait with her back to number sixty-two. The mirror in front of her reflected the section of the locker room behind her. She checked her watch. Butch should be well away by now.

Ten minutes later, a thin woman with translucent skin and strawberry blonde hair walked in, gave a cursory glance around the room and headed straight for the locker. Leine slipped behind an open door and pretended to change clothes.

She fit Paula's description of the woman who delivered the finger in the box.

The woman opened the locker, pulled out the gun and, with a furtive look, walked out. As soon as the woman left, Leine tossed the towel on a bench and followed her at a discreet distance.

The woman climbed into a compact red Honda and drove out of the parking lot. Leine followed a few car lengths behind.

At first she was easy to follow. Not much traffic on the side streets. Leine stayed back, changing lanes a couple of times. The Honda headed for the onramp to the Hollywood Freeway toward San Fernando Valley and hit the gas. Leine followed.

Heavy traffic dogged them both. Leine sped up and slid into place two car lengths behind her. Even if the woman suspected a tail, she wouldn't know which of the cars to watch in the confusion of headlights behind her. They drove several miles before the Honda changed lanes. Leine checked her mirrors, waiting for an opening.

None of the bastards would let her in. Finally, a break opened up and she moved right. The Honda was several cars ahead of her, one lane over. Leine tensed, ready to slide right, waiting for the car's next move.

A tandem trailer big rig rumbled next to her, temporarily obscuring her view of the Honda. Pissed,

Leine stomped on the accelerator in an attempt to get around the front of the mammoth truck, but the asshole matched her speed. Leine immediately took her foot off the gas and let the rig pass. As soon as he'd cleared her front bumper, Leine hooked into the far right lane, ignoring the chorus of honks behind her. Realization dawned on her as she searched traffic for the familiar taillights.

The red Honda had disappeared.

CHAPTER 20

ALMOST. THERE. ALMOST—ahhh."

Peter stepped away from Tina's naked backside and pulled several tissues from a box on his desk. As he cleaned himself, Tina turned around, a pout on her heavily made-up face.

"Excuse me, Wonder Boy, but you didn't get anywhere near taking care of Miss Tina." She slid backward onto the desk and spread her legs with a wicked grin, pointing at her pubis. With a sigh, Peter finished buckling his trousers, grabbed his chair and rolled it in front of her.

If she wasn't so accommodating, he'd probably opt for paying a call girl. He didn't have time for this reciprocal shit.

He took a swig of water from a glass on his desk and sat in the chair, positioning himself for maximum air flow. A few seconds into what he figured was the best tongue action this side of the Mississippi, someone knocked at the door.

"No—don't answer!" Tina whispered as she grabbed the back of his head.

Happy for a distraction, he pushed her hand away and looked up. "Who is it?" he called.

"It's Gene, boss. The senator's here to see you."

"No problem, Gene. Hold on a sec—"

Tina shoved him away and jumped off the table with a scowl, repositioning her mini skirt so it covered the essential parts. Peter hit the hidden button under the edge of his desk and the door swung open to reveal Gene and the senator. Tina picked up her purse and walked toward them, giving the senator a provocative once-over before she sashayed out the door.

"Tina," the senator said, with a nod. He smiled as he watched her leave, then turned to Peter.

"Thanks, Gene," he called over his shoulder as he shut the door in his face.

Peter leaned back in his chair, his hands behind his head. "To what do I owe the surprise visit, senator?"

Runyon chose one of the chairs across from Peter's desk and sat down, anxiety having replaced the affable senator façade.

"I'm being blackmailed."

"By whom?"

"One of your goddamned contestants, Heather."

"You're tapping Heather? Really? I'd have pegged you as more of a tit man, myself."

"This is no laughing matter, Pete. If my wife finds out, she'll destroy me." He leaned forward and said in a conspiratorial whisper, "I think she's been talking to a publisher in New York."

Peter had to stifle a laugh at the senator's expression. He pasted a look of concern on his face, trying to act sympathetic.

"What's she asking for?"

"A house on the beach in Malibu and a Mercedes SL, for starters." The senator threw his hands up. "Christ, Pete, she's not even that good in the sack. Not like

Mandy…" His voice trailed off. He looked at Peter expectantly.

Well, dick wad, if you thought twice before dipping your wick into any old pussy, you might avoid this kind of unpleasant scenario. A bad taste had formed in Peter's mouth and it wasn't from Tina.

"Can't you pay her off? Give her a chunk of change and have her sign a confidentiality agreement?"

Runyon shook his head. "Tried that. Shank suggested it. She's not budging. Says it's the car and the beach house or she goes to the press."

"Okay, say she goes to the press. So what? It's a ripple in a big pond. There's no evidence, right?"

Runyon's face told him otherwise.

"What's she got on you?"

The senator took a deep breath. "Video."

Peter nodded, fascinated by the senator's stupidity. "Yeah, that'd be tough to shoot down."

"That's not all, Pete. Not by a long shot."

"Really? What else?" Could Runyon have shared his bizarre proclivities with another person other than Peter? If true, he deserved whatever he got. Peter half-expected to see his name listed in the Darwin awards.

"She enjoyed, shall we say, unusual pastimes. I thought I'd found my sexual soul mate, I truly did." He buried his head in his hands. "I never thought she'd betray me. Not when we were so well matched."

No fucking way. Heather was not that much of a freak. Peter sighed and closed his eyes. She was one of the favorites on the show. If he got rid of her, ratings would go down, although he couldn't be sure how far. He'd be able to fire her for breach of contract, since it stated contestants were not to participate in outside romantic relationships during the show's season, but it would leave the senator vulnerable and Peter couldn't afford to do that—yet.

He could add to the offer from the senator, but it might leave them both with their dicks in the dirt, as well as open the show up for further liability.

A surprising idea occurred to Peter, but he brushed it aside.

The idea came back.

"Let me think about this, Senator. I'm sure there's something we can do. Give me a little time to work it out."

Runyon rose from his chair. "Don't take too long, Pete. She wants an answer by next week."

"No problem. Leave it to me."

Gene Dorfenberger swallowed the Xanax dry. His sister, Ella, had been pressuring him to talk Brenda out of acting on the show since it appeared she held no sway over her daughter, at least on this issue. When Gene protested, Ella demanded he do something or she threatened to beat his ass into next Tuesday.

He had no doubt she'd make good on her threat, but didn't have the heart to disappoint his niece. She'd been so radiant the first few days on set, he couldn't bring himself to give her Ella's ultimatum. Besides, Brenda was a grown woman. She needed her independence. That's what he told himself, although the real reason ran much deeper. He'd tried to assuage Ella's fears by telling her he kept an eagle eye on her, but she laughed and told him it was funny he thought of himself as a protector, after his good-for-nothing life.

Ella was essentially a good woman, but overbearing to a fault. She was certain Serial Date harbored a den of iniquity and God only knew she couldn't have her daughter participating in the Devil's work.

Gene remembered when they were kids she would paddle him hard after he did some horrible thing young boys tended to do. Their parents had only to invoke the words, "Your sister will be home soon—" and he'd stop whatever the offending action was and be as good as he could until caught the next time. Ella enjoyed her role as enforcer. More often than not Gene ended up as the bad guy.

Still do, he thought.

There was also the specter of the second dead contestant. They may have buried Stacy's body parts, but Gene was still waiting for the other leg to drop, so to speak. The killer wasn't finished and it scared the shit out of him. His unpredictability contributed the most to Gene's sleepless nights. He lived in abject fear Brenda would be next on the list. The letter he'd found under Stacy's hand disappeared with the body parts, but Gene had committed the words to heart.

Gene was musing about how he could get out from under Ella's thumb on his way to listen to a read-through of the script when Paula stopped him in the hallway.

"A package came for you this morning." She smiled. "It's like one Leine got yesterday with no return address, but a different woman delivered it to the set. I left it on your desk."

"Thanks, Paula. You say Leine got one, too?"

Paula nodded. "Yeah. She told me to call if any more came for her."

Without a word, Gene did an about-face and headed to his office.

The plain cardboard box perched on top of his desk. He took a pen from his pocket and sliced through the packing tape. Lifting the flaps he glanced inside, at first thinking someone had sent him some kind of seafood. Soon, the realization dawned on him and he stepped back, appalled.

A piece of paper had been taped to the underside of one of the flaps. Gene peeled it off, fighting a panic attack.

Gene, you moron. I know you told her. Let this be fair warning. Your niece is no longer off-limits. If I don't get what I want, she will be next.

P.S. I saved you the best part

Gene wiped the perspiration off his forehead as fear scuttled down his back. Steeling himself, he summoned the courage to glance inside the box once more, to be sure of what he'd seen.

About the size of a fist and artfully positioned on a bright green bed of bok choy with a few cherry tomatoes strewn around it, lay a glistening, red human heart.

CHAPTER 21

"WHERE THE HELL is my daughter?"

Gene's head snapped up from the L.A. Times as Ella's imposing bulk headed straight toward him. On his feet in record time he backed up, papers sliding to the floor as he knocked over several lunchroom chairs in his attempt to get out of her way.

It didn't work.

Ella hoisted her huge Coach handbag and took a fierce swing at his head. She missed, but delivered a glancing blow to his forearm.

"Christ, Ella—take it easy, will you?" Gene tried to grab hold of the lethal accessory, but only latched onto a bulky corner, slowing its upward trajectory as she launched it toward his privates.

"I will not take it easy, Gene. Brenda is coming home with me, now. I don't care if she signed a damned contract. My baby does not work for Satan. No sir!"

A sight to behold, Ella towered over him, breathing heavily with hands on hips, legs apart in a fighter's stance and a murderous look in her dark eyes. Gene backed up as far as the break room wall would let him.

"What're you talking about? It's a reality show, for chissakes. She's not doing anything wrong…"

"Oh, HELL to the no."

It was as though someone let a wild animal loose after hours of taunting. With an unearthly growl, Ella raised her bag, spun her considerable girth a half-turn on her left foot and whirled back toward Gene with the full fury of a thousand outraged mothers.

His knees buckled from the pain and he went down like a lead weight. Gene rolled onto his back and shook his head to clear his vision, eyeing her warily from the floor where he decided he'd best remain until reason had once again visited his sister.

Evidently satisfied she'd taken care of the first order of things she blocked his exit, fists curled, anger radiating off her in waves.

"Where the fuck is my daughter, Gene?"

With a heavy sigh, Gene pointed toward the door leading to the hallway.

"Out the door to the right, third hallway on your left. She's in the dressing room getting fitted for next week's show."

Ella straightened to her full five-feet-four inches, shifted her handbag to her shoulder and nodded at Gene, still on the floor.

"Thank you." Head held high, she walked out the door to the right, a tsunami of destruction behind her.

Gene picked himself up and brushed at the back of his slacks, a smile of relief forming at the corners of his mouth.

Leine sighed as she disconnected the call. It was her third attempt at trying to locate an old contact. The woman, Keira, had worked with Leine to find several targets by hacking into their phones and laptops. She'd resigned from her cover job in the communications industry a few years back and no one knew where she'd gone. Leine left instructions to call her if anyone heard from her. Knowing Eric, he'd probably kept track of her. She'd been a brilliant asset to the company. No one except Leine and a handful of other operatives knew her identity.

She was going to have to call Eric if she couldn't find her own resources, and time was running out.

There were major problems associated with contacting him. The first being he'd be able to track her if she called. He'd assume she was interested in working again and would try to persuade her to come back. Leine didn't have the time to dick around regarding her old life. She was done. End of story.

The second problem was harder to overcome than the first: she hated Eric with a soul-eating passion.

Eric betrayed her, tricked her into killing Carlos, then ensured her complicity by threatening her only daughter. Leine vowed she would never again put herself in such a vulnerable position. The residual effects of killing someone you loved reverberated beyond what most people could endure. Recovery, if a person could call it that, took years. She knew the raw emotion elicited merely by thinking of Eric and what he put her through could morph into something she might not be able, or willing, to control. This alone stopped her from dialing his number.

As she wrestled with her emotions her phone erupted in the mafia movie's theme song. She glanced at the screen: Private Caller. *Azazel.*

A glance at her watch indicated it was exactly twenty-four hours since she'd spoken with him last. She picked up the phone.

"Leine speaking."

"Hidey-ho, Madeleine, my dear. How are you, lovey?" When she didn't answer, he continued, apparently unfazed. "Good job on the gun, by the by. Did you have to kill anyone?"

His chipper voice grated on her nerves; the Happy Cannibal act was new.

"What do you want?" It was all she could do to keep her tone civil.

"Ooh, touchy. I think you're going to be very happy with the next one. It's worth twenty points."

Twenty. He's setting me up to fail. If I do, I drop to zero and he kills April. If I succeed, I'm over twenty-five and will be able to speak to her anyway, if he keeps his part of the bargain.

Big if.

"I think you'll find it's right up your alley." He paused. "Ready? I need you to kill someone."

Leine had half-expected the request, but it still felt as though someone punched her in the solar plexus. *Relax, Leine. He's testing you. Stay calm.*

"Who's the target?"

Azazel chuckled. "I knew you'd come around, Madeleine. Like I said, we're birds of a feather, you and me."

She recognized the tone. Frank used it when they first met, but lost it when they started experiencing problems. Carlos had it all the time. Azazel's voice held a caress meant only for her. A sketchy idea began to form where only anger and frustration at being played once resided.

He's lonely.

The thought was something she hadn't allowed herself to consider, but now a glimmer of sunlight broke through the clouds that previously obscured hope.

This fucked-up monster of a human being is lonely. Leine smiled to herself.

She'd found a weakness.

CHAPTER 22

THE TARGET ENDED up being at the second location Leine checked—Hollywood Boulevard. The woman's blonde hair looked as though it hadn't been washed in weeks and her mini skirt and too-small tank top left little to the imagination. Heavy makeup obscured what might have been a pretty face. Stilettos completed the outfit.

Leine gauged her to be in her early to mid-twenties. She watched as she and two other young ladies in similar attire worked the various men who cruised by in their cars and rolled down their windows.

One of her friends scored and left with a paunchy-looking middle aged guy. Maria's other friend discreetly snapped a picture of the license plate with her phone. Leine pulled alongside the two women. She needed to have a word with Maria before she succeeded in finding a client.

Her friend noticed her first and nudged Maria with her elbow. Maria turned and stared at Leine with suspicion.

Leine rolled the passenger window down.

"Can I speak with Maria for a moment?"

With a backward glance at her friend, Maria walked up to the car window. "Do I know you?"

"We have a mutual acquaintance. I need to talk with you alone. It's important." Leine smiled. "No funny business. We can stay nearby."

Maria said something to her friend who sized Leine up as she took out her phone and snapped a picture of her license plate. Maria opened the door and got into the car.

"Good idea, in case your friend there needs to describe the vehicle, right?"

Maria nodded. "Better safe than sorry." Leine drove a few blocks and pulled to the curb outside a flower shop.

Maria turned to look at Leine. "So what do you have to tell me? Or is this your way of getting a date?"

Leine shook her head. "I wish it was that easy." She reached inside her bag and produced an envelope filled with cash. She showed it to her and then returned it to her purse. Maria's gaze lingered on the envelope before she dragged her focus back to Leine.

"Now that I have your attention: You need to understand what you decide to do is going to determine whether you live or die."

Maria's expression morphed from one of surprise at the amount of money Leine showed her to one of fear and suspicion. She reached for the door handle. Her carefully manicured nails clicked against the vinyl.

"I need to go."

Leine nodded. "I know how this sounds. Hear me out, Maria. A man we both know wants you dead. I'm here to help you stay alive, but you have to listen to me."

"Really? Who? I haven't done anything to piss anyone off that much. My customers always leave satisfied." Maria lifted her chin, defiant.

Acting on a hunch, Leine answered, "You've seen his face. That's enough."

"I've seen a lot of faces. Who are you talking about?"

"I can't tell you that. I can tell you he wanted to be sure you died by fire and to somehow include a bunch of pink gerbera daisies."

Her eyes widened. She slumped against the car door and stared out the window, her face drained of color.

"Oh, man. Callie told me the dude was bad news." She shook her head and closed her eyes. "I only went with him once. He was way too creepy."

"Why fire?"

"He paid me to talk about what scared me the most. I told him I thought being burned to death would be the worst. It got him off."

"And the daisies?"

"He asked me what kind of flowers I liked. I'd just seen those big daisy things in a store window the day before, so I told him that." She stared out the window at the flower shop.

Leine's heart beat faster. "Maria, can you describe him to me, to make sure we're talking about the same guy?"

"Yeah. Tall, wiry dude. Brown hair, dark, super intense eyes. I think he said he was Cherokee. And French."

French. He's related. "Why would you know that?"

Maria shrugged. "Gotta make small talk, right?"

"Where'd you guys go? Did he take you back to his place?"

"No. I never do that. We went to a motel down the way."

Leine hid her disappointment as she reached into her purse to retrieve the envelope.

"The cash comes with one stipulation. You have to use it to leave town. I don't care how you do it, but do it. This guy isn't someone you want to mess with. You have to leave tonight. If you don't I guarantee you will be dead."

Maria stared at the money for a minute, then nodded and held out her hand.

Leine handed her the cash. "You'll need to be discreet. Make sure no one follows you. I can take you to your apartment. He doesn't know this car."

Maria didn't reply immediately. She looked out the window for a few minutes, considering, then back at Leine.

"Go up two blocks, turn right, and follow the road about a mile. My apartment building's on the left."

"There's no way he knows where you live?"

She shook her head. "I don't usually sleep there."

"Good. I'll make sure you get out of town safely. Call your friend to let her know you're okay."

After Leine helped Maria pack up her things they drove to the bus station in downtown L.A. and bought a ticket to San Francisco, where a friend of Maria's lived. Leine waited until she saw her board and the bus pull out of the station before she continued with the rest of her plan.

Santiago Jensen parked a few lanes down from Leine's rental and slipped inside the bus station. It was risky to follow them, but he kept to the perimeter and she didn't see him. He watched as she bought the hooker a ticket and put her on a bus for San Francisco, then he trailed her to Good Samaritan. He decided to stay in his car for this one. He'd spent enough time in hospitals.

Probably going to see a sick friend, he thought. That would explain some of the odd behavior, but it wasn't enough. He had no idea why she'd buy a hooker a bus ticket, but he was confident it would all come together. He just needed to be patient.

Jensen turned his radio on and waited.

The scrubs were the easy part. Leine slipped into an empty room and found several pair, neatly folded on a gurney waiting to be put away. She pulled on a set and eased the door open, checking the hallway for people. Not seeing anyone, she walked purposefully down the corridor to a door marked "Employees Only."

Her luck held. She only had to wait a couple of minutes before a man dressed in scrubs came out. She smiled and murmured some pleasantry as he held the door for her, then walked past him into a short hallway. A door stood on each side; one for men and one for women. Leine chose the door to the women's locker room and slipped inside.

Full-length lockers lined the walls with benches in the middle. Toilet stalls and sinks were in a separate room with several showers in an adjacent space. Leine scanned the lockers, but most had combination locks on them. She walked by the lounge area where a younger woman sat on a couch, reading a magazine. She didn't look up. Leine moved quickly into the shower area.

The sound of running water led her to the far stall. A towel, a pair of slacks and underwear hung from a hook next to the shower. A plastic ID card on a cord dangled from another hook nearby. Leine slipped it into her pocket and was out the door just as the water stopped.

She took the elevator to the basement and followed the floor plan from memory to the morgue. It was unmarked but easy to find, situated next to a loading dock in the back of the hospital. Leine followed the corridor past the morgue, until she came to a fire alarm, also indicated on the floor plan. She removed two foam ear plugs from her pocket and inserted them, then pulled the alarm.

She waited until the door to the morgue opened and several employees spilled into the hallway, headed toward the nearest exit. In the ensuing chaos, no one noticed as she swiped the ID card in the reader and stepped inside.

The lights blinked on and off in the efficient white room as the alarm blared. Cold stainless steel and bleach-clean linoleum greeted her as she walked quickly through the offices into the holding area. The far wall was made up completely of body drawers. She opened several, reading the information on the toe tags until she found a cadaver about the right age. After a quick hunt in the autopsy room, she spotted a stainless tray filled with the tools of the trade. She selected a gleaming stainless bone saw and returned to the open drawer.

Folding back a portion of the sheet covering the body she assessed the hand. The fingernails sported bright pink nail polish and the fingers looked similar in size and color to Maria's, with smooth knuckles like hers. Leine judged the length of the corpse to approximate her height. She had no idea how much detail Azazel remembered about the young woman, but she wasn't taking any chances.

Leine took a deep breath as she positioned the saw at the slender wrist and began to cut. Detaching the hand took more effort than Leine planned, her concentration off because of the blinking lights and incessant alarm. Glad for the sharp blade, it reminded her of cutting up a tough chicken, but with more cartilage. If she ever had to do this kind of thing again, she thought, she'd bring an electric saw.

Once she'd severed the tendons in the wrist, she pulled an opaque plastic bag from her pocket and placed the hand inside. With a quick glance at the door, she draped the cover back over the corpse and started to close the drawer but noticed something odd and stopped.

Her heart in her throat, she carefully drew back a larger section of the covering, exposing a feminine face with a five-o'clock shadow. Further down revealed an Adam's apple. Leine didn't need to look any further. Holding her breath, she checked the information on the toe tag again.

T. Layton M, 27yo.

How did she miss the 'M'? Her anxiety rising, Leine fished the severed hand from the bag and placed it next to the stump. She slid the door shut and returned to her search, refusing to think about what just happened.

Even with the ear plugs, the alarm was distracting. Leine knew she was running out of time and hurriedly scanned the names, checking only those indicating a female. The fifth drawer yielded a fairly decent specimen.

The second try at severing the hand took more effort. Leine assumed the saw blade had been dulled by the first attempt. With a silent apology to both bodies she detached the dead woman's hand at the wrist and shoved it in the bag. Then she shut the drawer, returned the saw and hurried to the door leading to the hall. No one was visible. She removed the scrubs, left them on a gurney in the hallway and slipped out a side door.

Heather Sinclair stretched out in her bikini on the chaise longue next to the pool. The contestants on Serial Date used the outdoor pool extensively, but today she had it all to herself. Everyone else was on set, prepping for next week's show. Peter had given Heather the afternoon off, since she already shot that week's promo. Besides, when Stacy took off with Devon, it allowed Heather the chance to move into the spotlight and share top billing with Tina; which meant she didn't have to work as hard to get camera time.

She took a sip of her mojito, adjusted her sunglasses and sighed contentedly. Life was good. Her career had finally taken off. A talent scout contacted her that morning, offering a sizable contract on another reality show as soon as Serial Date wrapped. Aware she could only count on a few good years in the industry before she'd be forced to accept supporting actress roles, Heather had hustled. Blackmailing the senator was icing on the cake.

She smiled to herself. Men were so easy. Especially old, vain ones. All a girl had to do was find their Achilles' heel as her mom referred to it, and the rest fell into place. Expensive gifts, cars, and a house in Malibu. What more could a girl want? She'd emailed a link of the private YouTube video of one of her wilder encounters with Runyon to her best friend, Letitia, and to her mom in Daytona Beach for safe keeping. Both women had instructions not to release the video unless Heather asked them to.

The clear blue water beckoned and Heather languidly rose from the chaise and walked to the pool's edge. Her designer sunglasses on, she climbed down the steps into the deep end.

Careful not to get her hair wet, she breast-stroked across the pool a couple of times. Hugging the side, she turned her back to the wall and closed her eyes, letting her head fall back to soak in the sun.

A strong hand clamped down on her head and shoved her under water. Thinking it might be one of the other contestants joking with her, she tried to swim out from under their grasp. The grip on her head tightened.

This is so not funny, Heather thought, her annoyance growing. *My hair will be a mess. Wait until I see who you are, bitch. Then you won't think it's so hilarious.* She clawed at the hand but realized the glove they wore lessened the impact. Her strength was no match for theirs.

Panicked, Heather doubled her efforts, but only succeeded in being thrust deeper under water. Her ferocious kicking and clawing began to lose momentum as she inhaled the first wave of chlorinated water into her lungs.

The last thing Heather saw before she lost consciousness was the gyrating, intricate shadows painted on the pool floor by the brilliant Los Angeles sun.

CHAPTER 23

PETER TURNED UP the volume on his car radio as the announcer repeated the day's big story: Heather Sinclair, a popular contestant on Serial Date, had been found early that afternoon, floating face down in the swimming pool of the house where the contestants stayed, the victim of an apparent drowning. An outpouring of emotion from fans in the form of flowers, candles and notes to the family of the deceased littered the front of the gated mansion.

Peter hadn't experienced any remorse when Gene called him confirming Heather's death, although he'd made sure to act sufficiently devastated when informed by the LAPD. The contestants aren't the only ones with acting ability, he thought.

The lack of guilt didn't worry him much. It wasn't as if he'd killed her. He'd taken care of a problem. The ease with which the suggestion presented itself should have given him pause, but it didn't. Peter refused to delve any further into his own psyche; he didn't have time. He pulled into his spot, parked his car and walked to his office, humming the last song he heard on the radio.

Tina ran up to him, tears streaming down her cheeks.

"Oh God, Peter—have you heard? It's awful."

Peter arranged his face in what he hoped assimilated shock and wrapped his arm around her. "I know. It's so tragic."

Tina sniffed and wiped her eyes. The tears cleared quickly. She's getting her money's worth from those acting lessons, Peter thought.

"Julian and I came home from Francois' Nail Shoppe and saw her in the pool, so I went out to see how she was doing. At first I thought she was joking, you know, like playing me so I'd be scared, but when she didn't move, I screamed for Julian."

Julian was the live-in security guard. Peter hired him for his preference in dating single men in the eighteen to twenty-five year range. He enjoyed taking care of the contestants and cooked for them most evenings. They loved Julian and shared their deepest secrets with him. All for the pleasure of the audience, of course.

Tina leaned against Peter, her tears starting afresh. "Sh-she knew how to swim. I talked to her this morning and now...she's gone. It's so real."

Peter let her cry a bit and then gently extricated her. Tina dabbed at her eyes with the back of her index finger, trying not to smear her mascara. She shook back her mane of shocking white hair and took a deep breath, her smile wavering just enough to give the impression she was doing her best to be brave in the face of adversity.

"With Heather and Brenda gone, that leaves only me and LaToya as the top two. I think it's obvious who the winner should be." With a shaky smile, she ran her elaborately decorated fingernail along his chin.

Peter turned his head so she wouldn't see him roll his eyes before he replied, "Now, Tina you know we have to let the audience have the ultimate say in the finale. I'm sure you'll come out on top, but we can't take away that crucial pleasure for the fans. You understand, right?"

Tina's lower lip protruded in her signature pout and she stamped her foot on the tile. Peter wondered if she was aware how much of a spoiled snot she'd become.

As soon as he'd talked Tina into going to rehearse for that week's show, he slipped into his office and locked the door. Then he took out his cell phone and called the senator's private number.

Leine made circles with her half empty margarita on the heavily scuffed bar. *What was this, her third?* She couldn't remember. In the old days she'd come to the Happy Mermaid to get a drink and not be bothered by anyone. She glanced around the dark room at the red velvet, semi-circular banquettes hosting various versions of Marilyn, Cher and Joan. A pretty good imitation of Jackie Onassis sat in a corner booth, talking to someone dressed as Marlon Brando from On the Waterfront.

It was always festive in the Happy Mermaid. Everyone here had a story that could fill a novel. Plus, you could lose yourself in the fantasy of old Hollywood; Clark Gable, Myrna Loy, Gregory Peck and Lana Turner were usually here, along with Lady Gaga and other, more contemporary American royalty.

Leine drained her drink and ordered a shot of tequila. The Mermaid's usual magic wasn't working. Tonight she couldn't run from herself. Thoughts of April and Maria and the Russians, the morgue and what she'd done wouldn't leave her alone. Usually, a few drinks would relax her enough so she could forget. No amount of tequila or well-dressed transvestites could obliterate the fact that she was no closer to finding her daughter.

Add all of that to her undeniable attraction to Detective Santiago Jensen, and she was screwed.

Come on, Leine. You used to be a fucking assassin, for chissakes. This kind of thing never got to you before. Time to buck up.

She was getting soft. First she broke down, an emotional wreck in front of her daughter. Then she fell for the one person she should never allow herself to fall for. *Really, Leine? A detective? Couldn't you have chosen someone more suitable? Say, the head of the NSA, perhaps?*

And last, she'd actually broken into the morgue of a hospital and severed two—not one, but two- hands at the wrist in order to make Azazel think she'd gone through with his twisted instructions.

What the hell had she become? She was known for her grace under pressure. When the job became dangerous and hung by a thread, that's when she'd shine.

And those deaths were warranted. She'd done a service, brutal as it may seem. They were all scumbags. Most had killed or been responsible for the deaths of many, many people, some innocent, some not.

Except for Carlos.

Leine threw back the tequila, eschewing the salt and lime wedge and ordered another, shoving deep all thoughts of Carlos. *Maybe I should call Eric. Time is running out. I just don't have it anymore.* Leine dabbed a napkin at the perspiration on her forehead. The ceiling fans weren't cutting it tonight. Someone needed to turn on the air. She peeled off the shirt she wore over her tank top and laid it on the bar all the while eyeing her phone. The demons warred within her, telling her why she shouldn't call, and why she should.

The tequila won. She punched in Eric's number from memory. The ring changed as it transferred to voicemail.

Leine almost hung up but reconsidered, the tequila easing her hate, softening her.

His smooth, confident voice advised her to leave a message.

"Eric, this is Leine. Call me." She left her number. At least it was disposable.

"You look like you could use a friend."

Startled, Leine turned toward the sultry voice.

Long, auburn hair floated past bare shoulders, artfully arranged to make the most of the cream colored, satin strapless with matching wrap. She had that whole siren thing down; with her flawless makeup and sparkling jewels, she could've stepped out of a classic movie from the forties. You'd never know she started out as a he, Leine thought.

She offered a beautifully manicured hand. "I'm Rita."

Leine shook it and replied, "Leine. Rita Hayworth?"

"The one and only." Rita smiled as she crossed her legs and ran her fingers through her hair, appraising the room. "At least tonight," she said, with a conspiratorial wink.

The bartender swept by and they both ordered refills. Rita picked a peanut from the bowl on the bar, cracked the shell and started to nibble. "I really shouldn't eat these. They're awfully fattening." She gave Leine a sideways look. "So, man-trouble?"

The bartender came back with their drinks. Leine toyed with her glass, deciding what to tell her, if anything.

"You could say that."

"Well, honey, I'm here to tell you, there's life after loss. Permanent loss. Yesterday, as a matter of fact." Rita stared into space a moment, then snapped back to the present with a smile.

"I'm sorry," Leine said. Rita nodded and wiped at a tear.

"Thanks. It's just so damn final, you know? One day they're here, the next—poof." She snapped her fingers. "No more dancing around the apartment naked, singing Green Day tunes." Another tear slid down her cheek. Leine patted her hand.

"That's quite a visual."

Rita laughed and took a tissue from her clutch, self-consciously patting beneath her eyes.

"Sorry. I'm supposed to be the one cheering you up. What's your story?"

Leine hesitated for a moment, trying to sum up her thoughts. "I thought I'd hit bottom, but I was wrong."

"And?"

Leine gazed into her glass. *Damned tequila.* She hadn't meant to say anything.

Rita considered Leine for a moment. "You don't want to talk about it." She shrugged. "No problem. Mind if I do? It always feels better talking to someone you just met. Kind of freeing."

"Talk away. Me and Jose will keep you company." Leine raised her drink in a toast and threw it back in one swallow, setting the empty glass back on the bar. Better check my sobriety level, she thought. She shifted her focus to an older gentleman in a Greek fisherman's cap sitting across from her on the other side of the four-sided bar. Even with squinting he resembled an impressionist painting. *Perfect.* She signaled the bartender.

Rita took a sip of her champagne cocktail and began to tear her napkin into tiny pieces, turning it into a pile of confetti.

"Tanya was twenty-seven years old. Her parents wouldn't let me see her before..." The tears fell freely, now. Leine peeled a napkin off a stack on the bar and handed it to her. She accepted with a shaky smile.

"I'm going to the damned funeral, I don't care what they say. They can't stop me. It's a free country." Rita blew her nose in the napkin. Once she'd composed herself, she looked at the ceiling, as though her lover floated somewhere above them. "She was going to do it, go the whole nine yards and get the operation, but it's too late now." She drained her drink and waved at the bartender.

"How'd she die?" Leine asked. Her tongue felt thick.

"Overdose. Said she wasn't using anymore, but you know junkies. They'll tell you whatever you want to hear."

Leine shook her head in sympathy. "Man, that's tough. Losing somebody is hard as hell."

"You know it, sister."

They drank in silence a while, letting the story rest. The burn phone erupted in its snappy tune from the interior of Leine's purse. She dug it out and glanced at the screen. Unknown number.

"Basso." Her tone held a hard edge.

"Well, that's a fine hello. You called me, remember?"

Eric's oily voice floated through the earpiece. Leine's fingers automatically inched toward her purse before she caught herself. She'd left her gun in the car.

"Eric." She hesitated for a couple of seconds as she tried to collect herself. With an apologetic look at Rita, she slid off her stool and walked over to the hallway next to the restrooms.

"Thanks for getting back to me so soon. I've got a problem."

"And you need my help. Ironic, isn't it?"

She ignored him and continued. "I need to track someone. I tried Keira, but she's no longer at Stearnes."

"Hmm. That is a problem. I guess I could give you her new contact information. Would that work?"

That was too easy. "What's the catch?"

"No catch, other than I'd need to put you back on the books. The information is for employees only. You know the drill."

Leine took a deep breath. "Yeah, I know the drill. It's the same drill you used on me last time. I'm not coming back. You owe me, Eric."

"Tell you what. I'll give you access to the database and you do a little job for me. We'll call you a temp."

"You don't want me back, believe me. I'm not the same person." *If I get a clear shot, asshole, I'll shoot your motherfucking head off.*

"You're much too modest. I'm certain with a little motivation you'll be in top form in no time. We need you back here, Leine. I need you."

"The number, Eric."

"Sorry. Not without a contract. You know I can't compromise support staff. What's the hurry? Tell me. Maybe we can work something out we can both live with."

Leine imagined reaching through the phone and wrapping her hands around his throat. The visual calmed her.

"You don't need to know." *Why the hell am I negotiating with him? Fuck this.*

"Carlos—you remember him, right, Eric? One of your best. Yes? Well, Carlos left some interesting information behind." His silence told her she'd gotten his attention. "Information regarding several targets that I suspect weren't recorded in the agency's books. I believe the correct term is 'rogue op'? Why yes, I think that's it." She paused. "Where did all that money go, Eric?"

"I have no idea what you're talking about. Carlos was no longer a trusted associate. I sent the best person to take him out. Didn't matter you two had a 'thing'. It was business. That's all. What he left behind sprang from his twisted, conspiracy-filled imagination."

"You tricked me into killing him—provided all the necessary information and made sure I didn't get to him before he was in full scuba gear and in the water, alone. Hell, Eric, you even told me the color of the logo on his wetsuit so I wouldn't make a mistake. I didn't find out until the next day it was him." Leine's temper flared. "You're a cold hearted bastard. I'm not sure why the hell I thought you'd help me. Tell me, if a manila folder with the name "Razorback" printed on it found its way to Henderson's desk, you wouldn't have a problem with that, would you? I mean, everything's on the up and up, right?"

"Look, I don't know what you're trying to do, but it won't work. Don't forget, I still have the details of all of your jobs. Might get a little dicey with the fibbies, don't you think? If one were to, say, give them a suspect in a couple of cold cases?" Eric sighed. "When are you going to admit it? You're one of us. It's in your damn blood. Carlos was collateral damage. He threatened to put the entire operation in danger. I couldn't have that. Too many operatives would have been compromised. You have two choices: either you come back and I give you everything you need, or you're on your own. And Leine, it's damned cold out there."

"Not as cold as it was working for you." Leine disconnected. What the hell did she expect? Eric didn't show loyalty to anyone except Eric. His inclusion of her in his little nest of vipers stung. Things were different. She was different. She walked back to the bar and slipped the phone into her purse.

"Sorry."

"That's okay. Was it your man?"

Leine almost laughed. "Not exactly. More like an old business associate."

"Oh," Rita replied. She'd ordered another round, as evidenced by the full shot and cocktail sitting on the bar. Her head in her hand, the earlier animation had evaporated. Rita Hayworth on depressants. Not a pretty sight, Leine thought.

"Where were we?" Leine tossed back the tequila and took her place on the stool. The booze must have finally found its way into her bloodstream—she had to grip the bar rail to maintain her balance. *Might want to slow down the drinking there, Leine.*

"We were talking about Tanya." Fresh tears sliced a path down Rita's face through the heavy foundation. Leine grabbed another napkin off the bar and handed it to her.

"Tell me about her. They say it helps to talk about it, right?"

"I suppose." Rita lifted her head and took a sip of her cocktail. "Wanna see her picture?"

"Sure." Leine didn't know if she'd be able to see much of anything at the moment, but she'd sure as hell give it a try.

Rita opened her clutch and pulled out her phone. "Technology amazes me. You can carry your whole life in this one little box." She waited until the screen came to life, then typed something into the phone. "I just pinged my location," she explained.

Leine leaned closer and squinted at the screen. A small flag with Rita's face displayed on a map near the Happy Mermaid's location.

"It's easier than calling. This way, people know where I am and can come and party if they want to." She tapped on the screen again and turned the phone toward Leine.

"Her Facebook page."

The name under the picture read Tanya (Ted) Layton, R.I.P.. Leine sat back, dumbfounded. The screen may have been small, but the face staring at her was unmistakable. *No. This can't be right.* She leaned forward to check the picture again.

"You don't look so good. Need a glass of water or something?" Rita waved at the bartender. Leine grabbed her arm.

"No. It's...fine. I think I need air..." Leine clutched her purse as she lurched to her feet and walked unsteadily to the door.

How's that for a freaking coincidence? she thought. A one in a million shot, that's what that was. The same feminine face that stared, unseeing, at her in the hospital morgue, the body with the first hand she'd severed, was the same face looking out at her from Facebook.

She stumbled through the door onto the sidewalk and latched onto the light pole to keep the world from spinning. Clark Gable and Cher and someone Leine couldn't place watched her as they leaned against the building, enjoying a smoke. Unable to take a deep breath she leaned forward and put her hands on her knees.

Someone stepped in close behind her. Without thinking, she pivoted, grabbed his arm and yanked, and at the same time torqued her body, dropped her shoulder and vaulted him to the ground.

He hit the pavement with a grunt. Leine's vision cleared as she resumed her original position with her hands on her knees, taking deep breaths to stop the sidewalk from shifting. She attempted to focus on the idiot who made the mistake of approaching her from behind. The man rolled onto an elbow and squinted at her in the yellow glow of the street lamp.

"Santa?"

Jensen coughed and rolled onto his side.

"Jesus, Leine. What'd you do that for?" He climbed to his feet and brushed off his jeans. Good move, he thought, grudgingly.

"Don't...ever sneak up behind me."

She'd leaned over again, with her hands on her knees, her body swaying, looking like she was about to puke.

"Don't worry. I won't make the same mistake twice." He watched her for a minute, trying to gauge his next move. "Looks like you've maybe had enough to drink. I'll drive you home."

She shook her head. "No. I'm fine." Leine tried to stand upright, but staggered back a step and placed her hand on the light pole to steady herself.

Jensen took his time moving in. With a soothing voice he said, "Listen. You're in no shape to drive. Let me at least call you a cab."

Leine squinted at him, trying to focus. "I'm good." She started for the entrance to the bar, head high, correcting just before she walked into the side of the building. It was the threshold that got her. Jensen saw it coming and grabbed her around the waist before she fell.

"Oh, shit." Leine fell into him with a watery smile and slid part way to the ground. He kept a tight hold under her arms. "You know, I think I might be drunk."

"I think you might be right. I'm taking you home. Have you eaten anything lately? He established a better grip and hoisted her up. "Anything in there you need before we go?"

Leine turned and looked toward the bar, a frown of concentration on her face. "Jus' my purse," she said.

Jensen held her bag so she could see it. "Right here."

He slipped the strap over her head, draped her arm around his shoulders and half-dragged half-carried her away from the Happy Mermaid under the curious stares of Cher and company.

CHAPTER 24

AZAZEL SHUDDERED AND slashed viciously at the cobwebs that had appeared in the stairwell since the day before. He stopped for a moment to collect himself. Where did he leave off? *Oh yes. Eleven.*

Sissy will pay for this. He resumed counting the stairs to the bottom. Not that she'd mind. The silly bitch did anything he told her to do. His specific orders had been that the stairwell was to remain spotless. The cobwebs needed to be confined to the lower level. He positioned his special respirator to make sure there was a tight seal before he unlocked the door to the basement.

Careful to quickly close and lock the door behind him so only a small amount the basement air could escape to the upper levels, he counted seventeen steps to another door with two dead bolts. He liked the way the mask made him sound like Darth Vader from Star Wars. Azazel had an inexplicable fear of breathing the hallway air in the basement. Once he entered any of the rooms, he was fine and would remove the mask. As with most things, Azazel wasn't one to examine his neuroses, preferring to accept himself the way he was.

The bluish light from a small, single pane window cast the dark space in an eerie hue. He rather liked the effect. Made it scarier for his guests. And really, wasn't it all about the experience? Azazel liked his visitors to get their money's worth.

He remembered his older brother taking him to one of those home grown haunted houses at Halloween when he was younger, and how disappointed he'd been when the bloodied zombies and Frankensteins turned out to be actors. Really? He paid good money for this? Later, after he'd come back, he always regretted not sticking around to see the expressions on the paying visitor's faces when they realized those actors weren't acting anymore.

Now that's your money's worth.

Azazel unlocked both dead bolts and slipped through the door. To his left stood a commercial grade walk-in freezer. A down jacket hung on a hook next to the door. He removed the mask, shrugged on the coat and pulled the stainless steel handle to open the door. A single bulb blinked on, illuminating the carcasses he'd hung from hooks attached to the freezer's ceiling.

As he picked up the cordless Sawzall from its place on the shelf and carved off a section of thigh from his latest acquisition, he reminisced about his father telling him how he'd never tasted anything so good as a barbequed veal, not yet sullied by pollution or age. Of course, his father had been speaking of beef, but Azazel figured it related to his favorite type of meat, as well.

He left the leg intact, planning to use the bones in soup later that week. The flavor married well with split peas and Cajun seasoning. He ripped a sheet of white butcher paper from a roll and wrapped the cut, securing it with a piece of tape, just like the butcher at home used to do. Then he set it on the bench, next to another bag near the door, reminding himself not to forget.

His father had been intrigued when he'd discovered Azazel's predilection for killing. In his line of work, a killer in the family cut down considerably on expenses. Dad put Azazel on the payroll and for the next several years he enjoyed high rank and good pay, his talents recognized and respected. He lost count of the number of occasions when his father's associates would come to him for advice.

And then, his father was murdered. The dark, sticky rage Azazel felt as a result of his death would only lessen in intensity when he killed. He'd decided that until he avenged his father, anyone was fair game. He reverted to his default hatred from when he was a kid: actors. That threw open a whole new creative narrative in the form of the basement of horrors. Actors were always looking for work.

Easy, peasy prey.

Azazel picked up the bag from the bench that didn't contain dinner, slipped the mask back over his face and stepped out of the freezer. He resumed counting steps as he walked past the metal chains attached to the bloodied wall, past the room with the gurney and autopsy tools. Unfortunately, the last actor he'd "hired" to play a patient had hung himself and Azazel hadn't replaced him yet.

So hard to find good help these days.

The next room was his favorite. The keys came out again and Azazel unlocked the door. Lesser minds could have their obviously inferior Chainsaw Massacre rip-off. Azazel preferred a more modern type of torture. Besides the medical instruments in the other room, he had acquired several implements from a home improvement store. He'd felt like the proverbial kid in a candy shop; pruning shears, log splitters, drills, routers. So many tools to choose from. His imagination ran wild as he gleefully paid for it all with his airline credit card, racking up miles in the process.

There was nothing quite like watching someone scream in pain as you snipped off their fingers with a pipe cutter. The best, the one he was saving for her, was the Maxi Grind Oscillating 8400 Multi-tool. Lighter than most rotary tools, it was sleek and elegant. He'd only used it once before when he thought he'd found his father's killer. Sadly, it had been a case of mistaken identity, but what a show!

He walked over to a large dog kennel at the far end of the room.

"How's my little bait fish today?" he crooned as he bent closer, smiling.

April's hand shot out of the small trap door at the top of the cage. Azazel ducked as the flash of metal arced across his cheek, barely missing his eye. He seized her fingers and squeezed until the rusty knife blade fell to the floor.

"Where'd you get this?" he demanded, feeling the dampness on his face where the blood oozed from a stinging cut. April remained silent, blazing hatred evident in her eyes.

He leaned over and picked up the piece of metal, thankful for his recent tetanus shot. A quick glance of her surroundings didn't tell him where she'd managed to find it. Gwen had only been feeding her smoothies, so no knife had been needed. April hugged her knees to her chest and scowled. Azazel cocked his head to one side, considering her. No, he would not let her ruin his day. Too much was going right. He took a deep breath and imagined his anger sinking down a grounding cord, deep into the earth. Like what his therapist told him to do. Right before he gutted her for breakfast.

"I see I'm going to have to watch you more closely." He stepped back to gauge the distance of the cage in relation to other pieces within the room. Nothing looked close enough for her to reach. Pocketing the weapon, he made a mental note to have Gwen double check to make sure the small door on the kennel was always secure.

"Guess who you get to talk to tonight?" When April didn't answer, he continued with a grin, "Your mother. Aren't you excited?"

April glared at him. "I couldn't care less about my mother." She practically spit the words.

"My, you are an ungrateful little girl, aren't you? Then I'm sure you'll be happy to stick around and watch when I show Mom the utmost in hospitality." He glanced toward the tool table. "The cries of pain are delish," he said, as a small shiver spiraled down his back.

In the beginning, he'd tried to frighten April, but the girl lacked fear. He wondered if it had something to do with being the daughter of a murderer. He would've liked to have gotten to know her better before he killed her, but having similar DNA as his father's executioner nipped that in the bud.

"You need to play nice, or my little plan won't happen the way I've envisioned. Do what I say and I won't make you suffer." *Much, anyway.*

"Fuck you."

Azazel shrugged and started to walk away, the bag still in his hand.

"Oh—I almost forgot." He turned back and showed it to her. "You might be interested to know, your mother and I have a lot in common. She recently proved how closely she and I are linked. Why, we're practically soul mates." He leaned closer to the cage, though not too close, and lowered his voice, "She's one of the chosen, you know. It's in the blood."

He opened the sack and showed her the severed hand. "Your mother killed. At my request." Azazel closed his eyes and inhaled deeply, enjoying the triumph. She'd been reticent, but eventually succumbed to his obvious cunning and superiority, as he knew she would.

Images of Leine flashed through his mind, interspersed with those of his mother and scenes from his childhood. His mother, singing off-tune in the bathtub. The day of her funeral, when his father gave him that look, as though he wasn't sure to believe him when he told him he didn't kill her. The time he was almost caught by a neighbor with the lifeless body of his first community theater actor—the one who called in that awful performance of Dr. Jekyll. Pictures of Leine; in her kitchen, her bathroom, standing on her porch and next to her garage.

The familiar rage began a slow boil in his stomach, clenching, curling, slicing its way up through his chest and into his head where the voices could only be silenced by taking life.

By God, he was hard.

He opened his eyes, the urge to snap April's neck overwhelming. He felt powerful, invincible. *Not yet. You need her. Remember the plan.*

Was that a flicker of fear on April's face? Sissy commented once on the intensity in his eyes whenever 'the force' surfaced. Good, he thought. She needed to be brought to heel.

CHAPTER 25

JENSEN PULLED INTO his parking spot in the garage and turned off the ignition. Leine sat with her head propped against the window, a gentle snore emanating from her open mouth. He sighed, wondering how he was going to get her up to his apartment. It was too far to carry her. He was going to have to wake her up.

She wasn't the most willing participant. He made the mistake of leaning her against the wall once they were in the elevator and she slid to the floor with a giggle. As he bent over and hauled her to her feet, he had to admit she was a charming drunk. She threw her arms around his neck and gave him a messy kiss on the cheek.

"Y'know, you're one sexy detective…" she purred. Her gaze appeared unfocused as she took a step back, concern evident on her face. Jensen prepared to move to the side in case she blew chunks. After a couple of tense moments, the spell evidently passed and her face relaxed as she leaned her head on his shoulder and sighed.

"Nice to see you, Santa." The name brought another giggle. "I've got a little present for Mr. Santa man, yes I do." She tried to wink, but it looked more like a squint. "Jus' gotta unwrap it…"

"Sounds terrific. Let's get you to bed first. We can talk about your wrapping later." The elevator doors rolled open; Jensen pivoted and draped her arm across his shoulders. They made their way down the hallway to his apartment where he braced her against the doorjamb, hanging on to keep her from ending up on the floor. She fell against him, laughing.

He hauled her inside and deposited her on the couch, then locked the door behind them. Walking back to the couch he knelt in front of her and removed her sandals. Then he slid her purse off her arm and set it aside. Her head fell back onto the upper edge of the couch and her mouth went slack.

Did I say charming? Jensen leaned forward and patted her cheek, using a bit more force when she didn't respond. She lifted her head and opened one eye, giving him a sleepy grin.

"Must've dozed off." She studied him for a moment, then looked down at his hands, resting on her thighs. "You're so warm," she pulled him up from the floor so he was sitting next to her and snuggled under his arm. Jensen unfolded the blanket he kept on the back of the couch and wrapped it around her. She sighed contentedly and burrowed deeper into his arms.

"You remind me of Carlos," she whispered.

He reached over and gently brushed aside a lock of hair that fell across her face. Her breathing became more even as she fell asleep.

"What's your story, Leine? Why can't you trust me?" *And who's Carlos?* The tenderness he felt as he held her surprised him. *Great. Just what you need, Santa.* Fall in love with someone you had sex with once and hardly know.

And someone who wasn't what she seemed.

His concern for her had only increased with his surveillance. She used a different car, leaving the other

171

one in the parking lot of Serial Date. Why would she keep two? If she was bored with one, she could switch to another at the rental agency. This suggested she was attempting to deceive and/or evade someone, but who? He assumed it wasn't him. There'd be no point. She'd already told him in no uncertain terms she couldn't see him again.

He'd followed her to the corner where she met with the hooker. They stopped at what he assumed was the hooker's apartment before heading to the bus station. As soon as the bus left, Leine drove to the hospital. She didn't stay long, maybe twenty minutes, before returning to her car carrying a plastic bag. Then she left the hospital and drove to a strip mall on Wilshire where she entered a Mails Plus store with the bag. She returned to her car empty handed.

In his mind, Jensen argued it could all be a misunderstanding. Everything except the second car. Maybe she knew the hooker and she was helping her out. And maybe she was visiting a sick friend at the hospital, although she left through a side door well after the fire alarm had been activated. Hospital staff probably asked her to evacuate. What was in the package? Maybe she was helping her friend out, mailing something for them. But why have two cars? Nothing made sense, unless she was involved in something she shouldn't be.

The theme from *The Godfather* began to play from inside Leine's purse. Without disturbing her, he removed his arm from around her shoulders and lowered her carefully so her head rested on a pillow. Then he readjusted the blanket so it covered most of her body.

He picked up her bag and carried it into his dining room, placing it on the table. He opened it and checked the phone's screen. Private caller. Jensen turned down the volume before setting it on the table.

Rifling through the purse he discovered another phone; this one a cheap disposable. His cop radar started spinning. He checked recent call activity, recording the numbers in a small notebook he carried. The smartphone was password protected, so he left it alone.

Along with the usual wallet, car keys, tube of lipstick and address book, he found a full magazine for a nine millimeter. He let that go. Not too unusual for someone with her past.

Something shiny on the bottom caught his eye. A key chain with a key. He was in the process of putting it back when he noticed the fob on the chain itself. He held it up to the light to take a closer look.

Jensen leaned back in his chair and stared at nothing, his mind racing. It wasn't possible. He checked the fob again. The Asian symbol was still there, etched onto the side of a 40-caliber, hollow-point bullet. The same one he'd seen years before, during the investigation of the three unsolved murders.

She couldn't have known. He didn't describe the design. Unless...

The full import of the find slammed into him, taking his breath away. Either she knew the killer, or...he didn't want to think about the 'or'. Two cars, an untraceable phone, some kind of relationship with a hooker, and now this: key evidence in three unsolved murder cases. *What the fuck are you doing, Santa?* She'd gotten herself involved in something which, if he wasn't careful, could complicate things. That was one hell of an understatement.

The sound of Leine shifting position on the couch broke through his thoughts. Jensen stepped into the kitchen and grabbed a plastic baggie from a drawer, into which he placed the key chain before sliding the bag into his pocket. As drunk as she was, she'd probably think she lost it that evening. He then closed the latch on the purse, walked over to the couch and set her purse next to her on the floor.

He'd have to wait until morning before she'd be in any shape to talk.

Azazel ended the call. *Where was she?* His rage simmered beneath the surface. The affront offended him deeply. *She knew I was going to call.* He checked his computer screen. The tracking device he'd attached to her car indicated she was still at the television studio.

She usually doesn't work this late. He switched screens and pulled up her phone's GPS coordinates. He hadn't felt the need to check them the last few days. Like most people in L.A., Leine drove everywhere.

There was no avatar blipping on the screen in front of him. *She must have disabled the GPS on her phone.* He slammed his hand on the desk in frustration. The software he'd installed worked with the phone's navigation application. If disabled, the program had no way to track her. The next tab showed him a list of phone numbers she'd called. The last one had been to her dry cleaners that afternoon. Normal activity. At least he could still listen in on her conversations, although he'd have to monitor her in real time.

He checked the history on his video feeds. Nothing out of the ordinary there. He verified she hadn't somehow installed her own loop to try to deceive him. Each day was different and matched the audio. He doubted she'd had time to make distinct feeds for every day he recorded her. The muscles in his neck relaxed. She didn't know about the video or audio. That much was obvious. If so, then she probably didn't suspect the bug in her phone.

The smell from the takeout made his mouth water. He slid the bag next to him and swiveled in his chair to turn on the T.V. Using the remote, he flipped through the directory to look for his saved programs. He selected the most recent Serial Date, relaxed back in his chair and pulled out the triple bacon cheeseburger and large fries. Unable to resist, he held the sandwich up to his nose and took a deep, appreciative sniff, then settled in to watch the show.

After fast-forwarding through the show's beginning blather, one of the bachelors, Javier, presented Tina with a single, long-stemmed red rose (thornless!) as he professed his undying love for her, next to an elaborately lit backyard setting. Both were dressed in over the top evening clothes: Tina in a long, sequined strapless number and Javier in an expensive tux. Azazel snorted. It always reminded him of the campy evening soap opera from the eighties, *Dynasty*, the reruns of which he watched religiously.

Tina appeared disproportionately pleased with the offering and answered him with something equally nauseating. Azazel bit down savagely on his triple-bypass burger, cursing the writers' inane dialogue.

Good God. I would never be as lame as that. A single rose? You've got to make an impression, not be a dweeb. And, this Javier person is no serial killer, obviously. She'd be a lifeless cocoon by now, if he had any balls.

Azazel polished off the French fries and the other half of the hamburger and sucked down the sixty-four ounce cola as he watched the rest of the dreary farce, growing more incensed with every minute of show time. What they needed was a consultant. Someone who understood killers and could lend some credibility to the dialogue. Like they did with lawyers on legal dramas and law enforcement on cop shows. He'd offered his services, not even mentioning compensation, but Peter Bronkowski never even acknowledged his proposal.

Now Javier and Tina were in the pool, sipping tropical drinks with little orchid blossoms. A butler appeared, carrying a tray of canapés and assorted cheeses, with a nice little cheese slicer.

There, Azazel thought. *The perfect time to slit her throat.* The floating blood would have been absolutely ethereal in the existing pool light, not to mention easy to clean. Just drain the pool. A little bleach and you're done. Azazel punched his fists on the arms of his chair and yelled at the T.V. "Cut her throat you fucking idiot—" But Javier merely sliced off a morsel of camembert and *fed it to her.*

"Gag me." Azazel made a retching sound, never taking his eyes off the screen.

Soon, he was screaming at the show, his blood pressure spiking with every word. The force began to build inside of him, making its presence known. His deep guilt over gorging on fast food didn't help matters. He couldn't stop himself from bingeing on the artery-clogging crap. It was Azazel's dirty little secret and it vexed him to no end. He took a deep breath and forced himself to turn off the T.V.

After a few moments he calmed down and could feel the force's power ebb. He swiveled back to his computer monitor and saw none of her information had changed. Madeleine's car was still at the studio and he still didn't have a signal from her phone. She'd probably gone out somewhere with her co-workers.

Perhaps she inadvertently let the battery die? He hoped not. That would mean he was wrong about her abilities. A less worthy opponent. Careless.

No, she wouldn't have allowed it. Not when he'd assured her she'd be able to talk with her daughter once he'd verified the kill. Curious.

He would have to teach her a lesson in promptness. A smile tugged at the corners of his mouth as he texted Gwen.

Chapter 26

*T*HE DARK FIGURES *reached for her, their long, sharp fingers resembling talons, closing in as she ran without destination. All around her swirling, misty shadows danced, impeding escape as though she were mired in quicksand. She glanced behind her and realized one of them had closed the distance. Her pursuer was familiar…yet she couldn't quite make out his face. Until he closed the gap another step.*

The Frenchman, with a gaping wound across his neck. Blood flowed like a river down the front of his shirt.

She opened her mouth to scream.

Leine sat up, gasping. She shivered, remembering the dream. Confused, she scanned her surroundings. The dark room was unfamiliar at first and she tensed, wondering where the hell she was. She then became aware of the dull, throbbing ache behind her eyes.

Oh, yeah. My date with José.

As the fog of a night of too much tequila began to clear, she realized she was in Jensen's apartment on his couch, though still wasn't sure how she got here.

She groaned as she pulled off the blanket and sat up. A feeling she was forgetting something important gnawed at the edge of her brain, but she gave up trying to remember when nothing came.

Bits and pieces of the night debuted in a jumbled, dissociative mess. Leine hung her head in her hands, pleading with the pain to stop. Her tongue felt like a carpet. She stood, intending to go to the kitchen for a glass of water, but instead put her hand out to steady herself as the blood rushed to her head and the floor pitched hard to the left. She leaned against the arm of the couch and sucked in a breath. After a few minutes the apartment stopped moving. She glanced toward Jensen's room but decided against waking him. He saw her drunk last night. He didn't need to see her hung over now.

She reached for the strap on her purse by the couch when she remembered what was so important.

Azazel. He was going to call her when he received the hand as confirmation. Alarm swept through her as she dug inside her purse for her phone. She entered her password and checked incoming calls. The last entry read Private Caller.

The memory of disabling the GPS on her phone while she sat at the bar drowning herself in booze floated to the surface. She started to pull up the application to turn it back on but decided to wait until she was well away from Jensen's apartment.

What if he overreacted and killed April? The dread oozed through the hammering in her head and she found it hard to breathe. *My God. What have I done?*

Think, Leine. He's trying to lure you in. His actions screamed classic cat and mouse. The only card available to him was her daughter. He wanted his revenge, of that she was sure. The only way he could manipulate her was by dangling April in front of her as a carrot. *He's not going to kill her until he has you.*

But first, she needed to get out of the apartment before Jensen woke up. She slid her shoes on and folded

179

the blanket, laying it on the couch. Then she slipped out the door and closed it gently behind her.

She caught a cab to the Happy Mermaid to pick up her car. Little by little, the night's fog cleared as she drove, and she ran through events in her mind, trying to remember as much as possible. She cringed at the memory of her call to Eric. Shit. Now he'd know she was in the area.

Not only that, but she threatened him with the information Carlos compiled before he died. Stupid, Leine. *Why don't you just paint a bulls-eye on your back?* There were several ways for Eric to find out where she lived; she'd filed a W-4 with the IRS for her job as security on Serial Date, and she'd used her married name to rent both cars. A quick rummage in her purse located the burn phone. She removed the battery, rendering it untraceable. She'd be safe in the car, for a while.

She found her smartphone next and decided to activate the GPS once she'd switched cars, hoping Azazel would assume hardware failure. She comforted herself with the knowledge that he needed April alive. For now.

The dead tranny's Facebook page popped, unbidden, into her mind, crowding out more pressing concerns. She'd felt a twinge of guilt for having made the mistake of cutting off the hand, but told herself she needed to do it to save a life. Besides, Tanya, or Ted, hadn't felt a thing.

Rita had 'pinged' her location while they were sitting at the bar, letting her friends know where she was. Could April have done something similar? Leine wasn't even sure she had a Facebook page, much less whether she was into social networking.

Leine stayed offline except for an email account with an alias. With her previous line of work, she didn't want or need an Internet presence. As a result, social networking wasn't the first avenue she thought to pursue in locating her daughter. She gripped the steering wheel. Her stomach churned with the frustration of not knowing April the way most mothers would know their daughters. She pushed the emotions aside and concentrated on this slender thread of a lead.

She pulled into the show's lot and parked next to her other car. Then she slid the tablet out of its sleeve, turned it on and surfed to the Facebook login page. There she entered April's name in the search bar. Two possibilities appeared, and April was one of them. Her page was only accessible to 'friends'. Leine racked her brain, trying to come up with the name of a friend or two of April's to search. The only person she remembered was the kid who lived next door to them when Carlos was still alive: Cory. April and he had been inseparable, playing pirates and making each other walk the plank off the diving board in the pool every chance they got.

Leine entered his name and got back several results. She scrolled down the list and checked each photograph, hoping to find someone who resembled him. Her heart beat faster when she recognized one of the pictures near the bottom of the list.

Years older, Cory still had an endearing nerdy look, all the way down to his thick black hipster glasses. Leine clicked on his picture and was taken to his page. Using an alias she set up a Facebook account and sent him a message referencing the pirate stuff and signing it 'April's mom, Leine'. Then she did a search for a phone number, but he wasn't listed.

She put the tablet aside with a sigh. There wasn't much else she could do now except drive home and wait for Azazel's call.

And hope Cory emailed her back.

Leine turned into her driveway, got out and locked the car. She walked to the front door but stopped short of inserting her key in the lock. The place felt different.

Puzzled, she searched in the dim light of early dawn for anything out of place, inching her way along the porch. Her empty flower pot hadn't moved, the cobwebs trailing off of it were still evident. Faint footprints were visible in the dust of the painted floor, but could've been hers or April's. When she reached the picture window, she glanced inside.

To the casual observer, the living room appeared normal; the couch and chairs were in their usual places, a magazine lay open on the coffee table, waiting for her return.

But there was one thing out of place: the couch cushions. Leine's habit was to face the zippers toward the back of the couch. The end of one of the zippers was visible on the center cushion.

Leine retraced her steps to the entry and carefully ran her hand along the upper section of the window. She did the same to the top and sides of the front door. Halfway up on the left-hand side of the door, she found what she was looking for.

She bent closer to get a better look. A small device, no larger than the tip of a pen, had been attached to the wood next to the door handle. A similar-sized piece was secured to the doorknob.

Leine had used the same wireless nano-trigger for a hit in Brussels several years ago. Interrupt the connection between the device and receptor by turning the handle, and kaboom. There wouldn't be enough left of her to identify.

Eric's been here.

Azazel wouldn't be able to secure that kind of technology. Leine doubted many outside of her old agency would have access to or even knowledge of its existence.

Didn't take him long to find me, she mused. *At least he didn't get the folder.*

Leine backed away from the porch and got into her car.

CHAPTER 27

PETER WAS ABOUT to step into his office when Paula called to him from the end of the hall.

"Wait up, Peter."

He stood at the door, impatience nibbling at him. He had way too much to deal with right now. Not only did he need to handle the fallout from Heather's drowning, Brenda's abrupt resignation from the show, and Tina's incessant whining, but Edward had appeared listless and depressed the last time Peter visited. Being locked inside the house all day wasn't any way to live and Peter knew it, but he hadn't yet figured out what to do with his brother. Dr. Shapiro prescribed stronger meds, but getting Edward to take them was another matter.

Paula caught up to him and handed him an envelope.

"A package came for you early this morning. I put it on your desk. The woman asked me to hand deliver the note."

"Thanks." He glanced at the envelope. "Is that all? No more emergencies, right?"

Paula shook her head. "No, no more emergencies. I wanted to get this to you before you saw the package and wondered who it was from."

"Okay then." Peter opened his office door.

"You probably want to get to work—" Paula started to say as he shut the office door in her face.

Peter dropped his briefcase on the desk, next to the box. It was large, two-feet wide by two-feet high, and had his name written across the top. Peter opened the top drawer and found a pair of scissors which he used to cut through the packing tape on the box. He lifted the top and looked inside.

His breath cut short and he set the scissors down. His knees buckled as he dropped into his chair.

Inside the box rested a large cantaloupe on a gold-rimmed china plate supported by a gold charger. An elegant set of silverware wrapped in a linen napkin and secured with a shiny gold napkin ring lay to one side. On top of the melon lay a bloody scalp of shocking white hair. Two holes had been cut from the front of the fruit, into which had been placed a pair of human eyeballs. Blood had pooled and dried at the base of the sculpture, leaving a brick-red gash across the white china's gleaming surface.

Peter stared at the bloody white hair with dread. How did Edward escape? He'd visited him the day before and checked the locks and video cameras, made sure everything was secure. Peter had the sole set of keys. The only other way out of that house was to open an upstairs window and jump two stories to the ground.

With shaking hands, Peter opened the envelope and slid the piece of parchment free. Anxiety gnawed at his stomach with every sentence.

Dear Peter,

I realize Tina's untimely demise may come as a shock to you. Please accept my condolences. Her death was imperative, as the dialogue on the series had degraded to a point at which it was painful to watch. I was so alarmed by the latest promotional video that I realized at once the need for a fresh culling. I would have chosen the writers responsible for the scripted detritus that issued forth from her mouth, but soon realized all of them are much older than I prefer. You really must allow me to consult with them. I dare say it's painfully obvious there is nothing remotely real happening on this 'reality show'.

You shouldn't have too much of a problem replacing the woman. Besides, she wasn't getting any younger and would soon be past her pull-by date.

There's no need to thank me- your ratings should skyrocket as long as you use this opportunity to relentlessly promote her death. You mustn't allow it to be in vain.

Sincerely,

A concerned citizen

P.S. I've allowed things to slide with Stacy due to my increasingly heavy schedule. Should you decide not to publicize my latest endeavor and assign credit where due, I will take matters into my own hands and continue the culling, post haste.

Peter placed the letter on the desk, his mouth suddenly dry. He wouldn't be able to cover up Tina's disappearance. She was too popular. Besides, there'd been too many deaths and disappearances connected with the show. It wouldn't be long before the cops would be back to investigate. He raked his fingers through his hair. He'd have to report this. They'd never let the show continue. Peter's heart began to palpitate in his chest and spots appeared in front of his eyes. He reached into his desk drawer and brought out a bottle of vodka, poured himself a stiff drink and tossed it back in one swallow.

The familiar burn of the alcohol calmed him. He took a deep breath and carefully closed the box. Did Edward want to be caught? Was that it? And what about the letter? He'd never heard Edward talk like that, so articulate. Dr. Shapiro said the possibility was strong that Edward may have multiple personalities. Many cases reported at least one personality presenting as far more educated than the original patient. He shuddered at the thought of the fallout Tina's murder would bring. The show was over. Peter's career was over.

His passport was up-to-date, thank God, but what about Edward? He couldn't just leave him to fend for himself. Of course, if the evidence pointed to his brother, who was he to stand in the way of his arrest? At least then he'd have a place to stay and Peter could skip town, head for his villa in Croatia. Edward would never get the death penalty. Dr. Shapiro would ensure it by testifying that he was insane. He could then live out his days in a hospital somewhere with food, warmth and companionship. Not a bad deal, Peter thought.

But shouldn't he at least try to save the show? He'd worked so hard. Everything he'd done, everything he'd sacrificed, would be worth nothing. It wasn't right that Peter had to abandon all he'd built. At least there'll be no more trips to Bountiful.

There was a knock at the door. Startled, Peter looked up.

"What is it?"

"It's Gene. I need to talk to you."

Peter sighed and pressed the release for the door. His expression grave, Gene walked in and sat at one of the chairs next to the desk.

"We got a problem. Tina's a no-show."

The laughter bubbled up through his chest and out through his lips before he could stop. Gene watched him with a puzzled expression that bordered on alarm. Tears streamed down Peter's face as each time he tried to stop laughing he'd be overcome with a fit of the giggles.

"What's so funny? Tina's missing. She never misses camera time."

The tears were real, now, but Peter wasn't about to let Gene know he was cracking up. He wiped his eyes with the back of his hand and shook it off, taking several deep breaths.

"Sorry. I don't know what came over me. Have you checked the house?" Another giggle escaped. He avoided looking at the box on the desk. He hadn't decided what to do, yet, and wasn't sure he could trust Gene to keep Tina's death quiet.

Gene nodded, eyeing the box. "Yeah, we checked the house. I asked Julian when he saw her and he said last night. Nobody's seen her since then."

"No note or anything?"

"No note. Think he got her, too?"

Gene's anxiousness annoyed Peter. Better that he didn't tell him about the scalp.

"I'm sure she's probably out somewhere. Let's wait until this afternoon, see if she surfaces before we involve the LAPD."

"Man, you gotta call the cops if she doesn't turn up. I mean, there ain't many contestants left. You know what I'm sayin'?"

"Of course I do, Gene. I'm not an imbecile." Peter stood and grabbed his briefcase. "Keep this under your hat for now." By the look on Gene's face, that was the last thing he wanted to do. "Do this one thing for me, okay? I've got someplace I need to go first. Then, I promise, if she's not back by this afternoon, I'll make the call. Deal?"

Gene mumbled, "Yeah."

Peter clapped him on the shoulder. "Thanks. I appreciate it. We'll do right by her, I promise."

Gene rose to leave, his gaze drifted once again to the box. "What's in the box?"

Peter glanced at it and shrugged. "A gift from a fan of the show."

Peter unlocked the back door leading to the kitchen, then closed it gently behind him. Careful not to make any noise, he crossed the floor, following the sound of the television to the living room.

Edward was asleep in the lounger, a glass of milk next to him on a tray table. The remote lay on the blanket in his lap. His facial expression held the trust and innocence of a toddler. Peter glanced at the pillow on the couch. Things would be so much easier if Edward wasn't around.

He took a step toward the couch, but thought better of it and continued through the living room to a small utility closet, which he opened with a key from his pocket. He hit the review button on the monitor and watched the previous day through to present time. No one came into or went out of the house. He'd scoured the grounds and the garage prior to coming inside. There was no body, no blood. He returned to the lounger and examined Edward for signs of anything that would tell him his brother had recently murdered someone.

There was nothing.

He walked over to the stairway and took two at a time to the second floor. None of the windows were broken. All were locked and secure. He went back down the stairs and sat on the edge of the couch.

What if it hadn't been Edward at all? He'd been operating on the assumption his brother committed the murders. This was the first time he'd even considered another possibility. Peter put his head in his hands. He'd made his brother a prisoner and it was distinctly possible he hadn't done anything wrong.

Except for the frozen ears. That wasn't exactly normal behavior. Peter shook his head to clear it. He'd just now considered getting rid of his own brother, permanently. What was happening to him? He squeezed his eyes shut, unable to breathe. He needed another drink.

A snuffle emanated from the lounger as Edward turned onto his side. He opened his eyes briefly and mumbled, "Hi, big brother," before drifting back to sleep.

Peter stood and walked to the front door. Unlocking it, he went out through the porch, down the steps and over to the first set of shutters, unlocked them and threw them open. He did the same with the rest of the windows, throwing each one back with more force than the last. Back inside, sunlight streamed through the windows. Edward sat up, a puzzled look on his face.

"What are you doing, Peter?" His eyes widened and he sucked in a breath. "Can I go outside now?" Smiling, he got up off the lounger and ran to the door. He looked back at Peter as if to make sure it was okay. Peter nodded his head.

"Go ahead. You've been inside long enough."

Edward laughed and bounded down the stairs, then dove head-first onto the front lawn and tried a couple of wonky somersaults. He lay on his back, his breathing heavy, and smiled up at the sky. Then he rolled onto his side and down the gently sloping hill to the driveway, giggling like a little kid.

If only he could be like this all the time, Peter thought to himself. The blackness would be back. It always came back. Especially if Peter couldn't find another job once they shut down the show. The meds were expensive. Maybe he'd talk to Dr. Shapiro, see if there was somewhere they could place Edward that wasn't too expensive or too far away.

Peter watched him for a couple of minutes more before getting in his car.

CHAPTER 28

L EINE WAS FINISHING her Spanish omelet at a nondescript diner in West Hollywood when her phone went off. She glanced at caller I.D. It was Gene.

"Hi, Gene." Wary from their last encounter, she kept her voice neutral.

"We need to talk."

"I'm in the middle of something right now. Can I call you back?" She didn't want Azazel listening in on their conversation.

"Yeah. Don't forget."

Leine finished her breakfast and paid the cashier, then went out to her car. She'd picked up another disposable phone and called him from that.

"What's so important?" she asked.

"Where are you?"

"West Hollywood."

"Meet me at the park in twenty minutes. By the slides." He disconnected the call.

Leine checked her gun to make sure it was loaded and slipped it into her waistband. *What was Gene up to now?* She shifted the car into gear and headed for the park.

She beat him there and parked in the shade near the slides. The tablet lay on the seat next to her. So far, there'd been no response from Cory. She checked her email for the tenth time.

Still nothing.

Azazel hadn't called yet. Leine grew more nervous as the hours passed with no word on April. He was letting her sweat. She had to believe he wouldn't kill her until he had Leine.

The familiar melody of her smartphone broke into her thoughts. Leine checked to see if it was Azazel. Jensen's number appeared on the screen. She ignored the call. *Maybe I'll be able to explain all this to him, someday.* She imagined the scenario, took it to its natural conclusion.

Yeah, and he'll understand why you didn't trust him enough to tell him what was going on. She doubted he'd be willing to see it from her side. Experience told her men felt betrayed when you didn't ask for their help. She figured it'd be doubly true for a cop.

She got out of the car and walked to a vacant picnic table to wait, away from the mothers watching their children play on the Jungle Jim. The kid's shrieks of happiness brought her back to better times with Carlos and April. *Stop, Leine. Don't go there. Not now.*

Ten minutes later, Gene pulled alongside her car and got out. As he walked toward her, Leine searched his face for his intent and scanned his body for obvious bulges, indicating a weapon. The bags under his eyes were pronounced. He put his hands up.

"I'm unarmed."

Still wary, Leine slid over to make room for him to sit. "Tina's missing."

"What happened?" Her stomach churned with the thought of the unanswered phone call the night before.

"She never showed up for the promo. You know Tina wouldn't miss camera time." Gene turned to look at Leine. "She's dead, isn't she? He's gonna kill all of them."

"How do you know it's the same guy? You don't know she's dead, yet." Not that she believed it, but it was always possible it could be someone else. L.A. was a big city.

"It's the same guy. Peter had a box on his desk. The writing was the same as what was on a box I got earlier. From him." His shoulders slumped. "I was just trying to protect Brenda."

Gene got one, too? What the hell was Azazel trying to do? "Brenda? I thought Ella came and got her? She'll be fine. She isn't with the show anymore."

"There's more to it than that. A lot more."

Leine stiffened. "What do you mean?"

"He contacted me. Right before I called you about the job."

"Who? The killer? You mean you knew what he was going to do?"

"No, no it wasn't like that. He called me and told me he was watching Brenda—" A sob escaped him. Gene clamped his mouth shut, obviously struggling for control. A moment later he continued, his voice shaking. "He was gonna kill her unless I found a way to get you back to L.A."

"Me? How—what are you saying? I came down here after he killed Mandy. You guys needed additional security."

"He planned all that. I was supposed to suggest hiring you to Peter. If he didn't go for it, he was going to figure out something else. Jesus, Leine, I was so afraid. He told me where I was, all the time, like he had someone tailing me. He even knew who I talked to. Repeated my conversations back to me. When he threatened Brenda, I didn't know what else to do." Tears streamed down his face and dripped off his chin onto his slacks. "I'm so sorry."

"Where is he now?" Leine grabbed onto Gene's shirt and pulled him to her so her face was less than an inch from his.

"I don't know. He only called me. I've never seen him."

"Where's your phone?"

Gene looked confused. "My phone? It's in the car, why?"

Leine glanced at his wrist. He wasn't wearing a watch. Good. "It's probably bugged."

Understanding dawned in his eyes. "Shit. So that's how he knew."

"How did he get into the studio?"

"I-I left a key."

"Did you know he was going to kill Mandy?"

Gene hesitated. "Yes. But he said he only needed one."

"You knew he was going to murder Mandy and thought he'd just stop? How fucking stupid are you?" Leine let go of his shirt in disgust. She pushed herself off the table and started to pace.

"Look, I know I screwed up, Leine, but you gotta understand—"

Leine spun on her heel, covered the distance between them in two strides and grabbed Gene by the throat. Gene made a choking sound and grabbed at her hand, but she had an iron grip on him and wouldn't let go. She looked deep in his eyes, the rage from days of frustration reaching its boiling point.

"He has my daughter." Her voice came out low and guttural.

Gene's face was turning red and his eyes had bugged out. She pushed him away.

He sucked in a breath and coughed, massaged his throat. "Jesus, Leine. I'm sorry. I-I didn't know she was in town. I thought you and April weren't getting along—"

Leine turned on him again, her fury not yet abated as she moved toward him. She reached behind her and pulled out her gun, keeping it concealed under her button down shirt, but allowing Gene to see it. He slid off the table and started to back away.

"Whoa, there, take it easy," he said, putting a hand up. "Killing me won't help anything. Maybe—maybe I can help you find her."

Leine stopped her advance, waiting for him to continue.

"I mean, he doesn't know I told you all of this, right? Maybe there's some way we can fix things—bring him out in the open."

"Okay, say we manage that. How do I find April if we kill the son of a bitch?" One shot, Leine thought, her finger itching to pull the trigger. *Just one—I know it'll make me feel better.* Sense got the better of her and she relaxed her grip on the gun.

Gene frowned. "I hadn't thought of that. There's got to be something I can do to make up for this."

"There might be, Gene."

CHAPTER 29

S HE HEARD THE keys jingling well before the dark haired woman made her appearance. April tensed as she waited for her to open the door to the dungeon. She'd made a huge miscalculation before, trying to take out the psycho and wasted the only chance she'd had. Prepared for swift punishment, she'd been surprised when Azazel hadn't retaliated for the damage she'd done to his face. Finding the rusty knife blade stuck behind the wallboard trim had been a stroke of luck. April wondered who'd left it there and if they made it out alive.

The woman entered carrying a small tray. Lunch. The torture didn't end at being kept in a large, wire kennel. April couldn't wait to escape this hell-hole if only to eat something resembling a food source. Three times a day, she was subjected to a vile smelling green smoothie with the consistency of snot. The psycho waxed poetic about his own private concoction, extolling the virtues of wheatgrass, barley and algae, with just a hint of stevia for sweetening. The only barley April wanted to taste at that moment was a cold beer. She hadn't succumbed to her friend's reverence for eating a raw food diet, preferring a nice, juicy cheeseburger on occasion, along with a side of fries. She'd taken a lot of grief for her choices and thought it ironic she was now being force-fed the shit.

The dark-haired woman brought the tray with the plastic glass full of mossy green liquid and opened the small door on the upper half of the cage. April dutifully accepted it, itching to grab the woman by the neck, if only to lift the keys for the cage from her pocket. She always stood too far away.

"He's got a surprise for you today," the woman said in a sing-song voice, and pulled out a cellophane wrapped object from her dress pocket. She unwrapped it and held the two-inch square lump of what looked like smashed brown seeds toward her.

When April hesitated, she stepped closer and said, "Go ahead and take it. They're really yummy. His special recipe."

April brought her hand up and instead of lifting the unappetizing lump from her hand, grabbed hold of the woman's wrist and, catching her off-guard, yanked her off her feet, dragging her against the cage. At the same time, April's other hand shot out and covered her mouth, cutting short her screams. The woman scratched at April's fingers, but she held on tight.

Surprised by her own strength, she tightened her grip and growled in her ear, "Give me the key to the cage, now."

The woman nodded her head and squeezed her eyes shut. The bitch tried to take a bite out of her palm, but April leaned back and bent the woman's arm at an awkward angle. She was rewarded with a soft whimper.

"If you don't do as I say, I'll break your arm."

The woman nodded, slipping her free hand into her dress pocket. Before April could react, the woman plunged a hypodermic needle into her arm and delivered the full dose. April's grip loosened as she fought the dizziness. The last thing she saw was the smile on the woman's fuzzy face before her world turned black.

Jensen was pissed. He'd driven in circles searching for Leine, ending up at a dead end after he found one of her cars in the reality show's parking lot. When he checked with the security guard at the front of the building, he was told she'd taken time off to care for her aunt. That fit with the hospital visit, except her aunt was supposed to be in San Diego.

He'd woken up early that morning and walked out to the living room to check on her when he realized she'd left. No note, just gone. He'd gone back to the bedroom and pulled the plastic bag with the keychain out of the front pocket of his jeans. He was planning to bring it to his CO to book it as evidence in the unsolved murder cases. The only problem being, he'd have to tell his lieutenant how he'd come by it. He wasn't ready to do that, yet. If he did, he'd never live it down. He could hear him now, *"You slept with a possible suspect in a cold murder case? Well, stupid, that's what you get for thinking with your little head."*

It was a given he wouldn't be able to talk to Leine, and he wanted, needed to hear her side of the story. The lieutenant would insist he not work the cold cases since he'd had a relationship with her and he'd be required to have no contact with her until they cleared her of the murders.

If they cleared her.

Jensen pushed the idea aside. There was an explanation, he was sure. His feelings for her had grown and he realized it was making him act out of character.

He'd gone over it in his mind a dozen times. The effect she had on him defied explanation. It wasn't just sex. Even with Gina, it had been more lust than love. Jesus, he thought. This is dangerous, Santa. Love can make you stupid. He'd seen it a thousand times. Men would fall like a lead balloon for some woman and give everything up to be with them. At the time, Jensen thought they were idiots. He didn't this time.

And that scared the hell out of him.

Not once in his years on the force had his ethics been in question and he was proud of that. He realized withholding evidence, even for a brief time was a career-killer. If anyone found out, he'd be thrown out of RHD, put on patrol to finish out his days on the force. If he was lucky. He'd worked damned hard to get where he was. He could hear Putnam saying, *"You're gonna throw it away for a friggin' broad? You're nuts, Santa."* Maybe he was.

He slid the bag with the keychain into the top drawer of his dresser.

He'd wait and talk to her first.

CHAPTER 30

AFTER GENE LEFT, Leine checked her email once more. This time, there was a return message from Cory. He remembered her and had been in contact with April off and on through the years. He asked where she'd been as he hadn't seen any updates from her in a few days. Leine emailed back immediately, explaining she was concerned as well as she hadn't heard from her either, and included the new disposable phone's number. Within twenty minutes, the phone rang.

"Hi, Mrs. Basso. It's Cory."

Leine's heart leapt to her throat.

"Hey Cory. Thanks for calling. I remembered April mentioning your name once or twice and took a chance you two were still in touch."

"Yeah, but I haven't heard from her in a few days. According to her status update, she made it back from Amsterdam. I thought she told me you were in Seattle?"

Leine was surprised how happy it made her that April had mentioned her.

"I was, but I'm here now. What exactly did she put in her update?"

"That she was back in L.A. and looking to hook up with old friends. I sent her a message, but haven't heard back yet." He paused for a minute and then continued. "If you don't mind my asking, aren't you and April, you know, don't you both kind of go your own ways?"

"We were working on getting to know each other better when she dropped off the radar. I became concerned when she didn't show for a dinner date we'd planned."

"Yeah, she usually does what she says."

Yet another aspect of her daughter Leine didn't know about. She filed it away.

"Have you called the cops yet?" he asked.

"No. I thought I'd try to track her down first, and if that didn't work, I'd call."

"Have you checked GlobalPaws?"

"GlobalPaws. What's that?"

"A social tracking site. A bunch of us use it. The avatars are animal tracks. It's more accurate than most of the other tracking programs on the internet. It'll ping your location within a block of where you are. Sometimes it'll even get it right on. I figured with her going to Europe and all, you'd be one of her contacts." Cory's voice trailed off.

"No, I didn't know about it. Would you check for me?" Finally, something she could work with.

"Sure, Mrs. Basso. Hold on a minute."

Leine waited, drumming her fingers on the steering wheel. Cory came back on the line a few minutes later.

"It shows her last location as Tujunga Boulevard, seventy-four hundred block. The cross street is Sherman Way."

"Does it tell you when she last updated it?"

"Thursday. Have you talked to her since then?"

"Our last conversation was on Thursday morning." Leine's pulse was rocking now. This was what she'd been searching for. "Cory, would you like to help me with something very important? It involves April."

Her smartphone rang as she was driving to meet with Cory and Gene near the block where April had pinged her last location. Please, please, please be Azazel, she thought.

Private Caller. Leine punched the button.

"You were very naughty, Madeleine."

Leine let out the breath she'd been holding. *She's still alive. She has to be. He wouldn't call me if she was dead.*

"I know. I'm sorry. Something was wrong with my phone. I didn't realize until this morning. Can I talk to her?" Leine had to bite her lip to keep from saying what she really meant, which would have gone something like, *Get her on the fucking phone, you lunatic, and let me talk to my daughter.*

A long sigh echoed from the other end.

I'm going to kill him so slowly, he'll beg me for mercy. Fair price for keeping her in agony.

"Well, yes, I guess so. You did do everything I asked. I have to tell you, though—" He paused and she heard the jingle of keys. "Your actions caused me to vent my frustrations."

Leine's breath caught in her throat. If he touched April...

"Now, now, I know what you're thinking. Did he take it out on poor, dear April? I'll tell you, I was tempted. She's quite disrespectful. But no, I did not. I am a man of my word. Maybe this time the actors will finally figure out how to comport themselves like real killers, although I'm afraid it's for naught. They appear a little slow. You'll find when you return to work there's one less problem to deal with. You might want to suggest to the female contestants to lay off the Botox, though. Nasty stuff."

"One less? What do you mean?" Gene was right. He killed Tina.

"I won't bore you with the details. You'll find out soon enough." Azazel's breathing changed, becoming deep and heavy. It reminded her of the sound Darth Vader made in the Star Wars movies.

"Are you still there?" she asked. He didn't answer, although she could hear him breathing. More keys jangled, followed by the sound of a door opening and closing.

"Here she is. In all her glory. You look tired," he said, away from the mouthpiece. "Did the little shot Gwen gave you make you sleepy?" He chuckled and spoke into the phone. "Your daughter's exhibiting some of your tendencies, Madeleine. She's quite the pistol, aren't you, April? Would you like to talk to your mother?"

"Mom? Are you there?" April's voice barely wavered, but Leine could sense her fear. She clenched her fists to keep in control as a mixture of relief and anger flooded to the surface.

She's alive. That's all the confirmation she needed. Leine felt a fresh surge of energy flow through her, giving her resolve the boost it needed.

"I'm here, baby. It's going to be okay."

"Mom, tell Brutus I'm all right."

Azazel came back on the line. "That's more than enough time to talk, you two. Madeleine, I have one more task I'd like you to perform. I realize you have others who are anxious to see you dead, but I'd like you to complete this last request for me. If you do what I ask, April will be free."

After Azazel gave her the directions of his last request and ended the call, Leine started to formulate another plan. April mentioned Brutus, which was the name of a dog that spent most of its time in the next door neighbor's basement. April would visit with him through a window the owners would leave open while they were at work, and afterwards came home crying because she thought it was cruel to leave him inside all day and wanted to bring him home with her.

Leine assumed that April was telling her the killer was keeping her in his basement. Now, all she had to do was figure out where.

It's only a matter of time, Azazel.

Gene was the last to arrive. Leine told them to meet her one block down so they wouldn't draw suspicion. Cory sat next to Leine in the front passenger seat of the second rental. Gene parked his car so he faced her.

The block of well-kept, older homes showed freshly mowed yards for the most part, with evidence of several kids in the neighborhood; bicycles, soccer balls and Big Wheels littered the sidewalks. Leine shivered at the thought of the monster most likely living next door to these innocents. This is almost over. With any luck, he'll be dead before dark.

"Cory's an old friend of April's and has information on the last place she was before she was abducted," Leine said, by way of introduction. "It's a long shot, but I'm hoping that she entered the location just before Azazel got her.

"There's at least one woman guarding her, probably two. Paula described the woman who delivered a package to you as different than the one who dropped off mine. I've identified the one who delivered my package as Sissy Nelson through fingerprints on the box. She's approximately five feet five, thin with strawberry-blonde hair and a light complexion. She drives a late model red Honda Civic. Her last known address was some place in Ohio. She's wanted for armed robbery, so she could be dangerous. The other woman's name is Gwen. I don't know anything about her." Leine glanced at Cory. "That means you only observe. You do not attempt to follow her or stop her in any way. If you see a woman with her description, call me immediately. That goes for you, too, Gene. We don't need any heroes here, okay?" They both nodded.

"Once we have a positive ID we'll verify the house and I'll contact Detective Jensen and give him the information. The man who abducted her is extremely dangerous. He's killed three women as far as we know. This is not something to try to accomplish on our own. Got it?"

"Got it," Gene answered. Cory nodded his assent. Leine continued.

"I have to leave for a while this afternoon, but I should be back before nightfall. If I'm not, here's Detective Jensen's number." Leine handed them each a business card with her number and Jensen's written on it. "Call him if you've verified the location and you can't get a hold of me. Tell him everything I've told you. The GPS on my phone is turned on and you can track me from this." She turned on the small tablet so they could both see what she was doing and clicked the link to a website where she entered a password. The screen came to life with a map of Los Angeles and a blinking avatar labeled 'Leine.'

"Rescuing April is more important than finding me. Once she's safe, come for me if you have to. Otherwise, I'll bring you two dinner." She rolled her shoulders and stretched her neck to relieve the tension. The strain she was feeling played with the relief of a possible end in sight.

Cory frowned. "What if it takes longer than overnight? I mean, we could be sitting her for days, theoretically." His face turned red. "Where do I—you know, where do I go to the bathroom?"

Gene scoffed. "Open your door and piss on the neighbor's lawn, kid. If you gotta do something more than that, hold it."

"There's a coffee shop around the corner. Let Gene know if you have to go." She rolled her eyes at Gene. "Give the kid a break, will you? He's new."

"Yeah, yeah. Whatever." Gene reached through his window and rested his hand on Leine's door. "You sure you don't want me to come with you?"

Leine shook her head. "Thanks, Gene, but I've got this one. Cory, you take this corner, Gene you cover the other end of the block. Keep in touch with each other. She could be in any of these houses."

Cory picked up the tablet and got back into his Jetta. Gene turned his car around, heading for the far end of the street. He cruised slowly, checking both sides of the block. Leine started the car and pulled out, on her way to complete her last task for Azazel.

CHAPTER 31

GENE DORFENBERGER WAS no stranger to waiting. He'd been tapped as a getaway driver more times than he could count. It was always the same. Wait, keep an eye out, wait some more. Hope you don't hear shots fired. Wait again, until the rest of the gang comes running, jump in the car and scream at you to hit the gas, then drive like hell. Not a great way to spend your time, but safer than doing the actual job.

Gene was done playing it safe.

This time, he swore to himself he'd make things up to Leine. He'd never intended for April to be involved. The only reason he'd agreed to deliver Leine to Azazel is because he figured she'd be able to take care of herself. She was smart and had the skills to take out another killer. Gene hadn't banked on April showing up.

He hadn't banked on a lot more than that. He had no idea Azazel was going to continue to kill the contestants. The call to Ella hadn't gone well. She'd cursed him for a full twenty minutes before she hung up. Didn't matter to Gene. All that mattered was she got Brenda the hell out of town. Somewhere Azazel couldn't find her.

If everything worked out the way Gene envisioned, he'd rescue April and re-earn Leine's trust. Without April, Azazel wouldn't have a bargaining chip. Leine would then be free to hunt him down without the added stress of keeping her daughter alive. He hoped she made him suffer when she did find him. Knowing her, though, it'd be quick. Gene didn't think it was so easy to change a person's working style.

Gene sighed and lit a cigarette. Maybe he'd take the money he saved from the Serial Date gig and buy a piece of land in Montana. Sure, it was cold as hell in the winter, but there wasn't much pollution to speak of and the place was so big, he could keep to himself, live out the rest of his life reading, do some writing. Hell, maybe he'd even start a little ranch. Couldn't be too hard, right?

He glanced toward the end of the block at Cory's car. He'd have to make sure the kid was elsewhere if this surveillance thing checked out. There hadn't been a lot of activity on the street: a couple of kids kicking around a soccer ball; a woman in a jogging suit taking her dog for a walk. Typical summer afternoon.

Gene leaned his head back and blew smoke rings at the windshield. There was movement out of the corner of his eye. The side door opened on a white house about a third of the way down the block and a woman with dark hair stepped out, carrying a paper grocery bag. She walked over to a garbage can and dropped it in before she turned toward the house. Gene brought his gaze back to the door and caught a glimpse of a redheaded woman. No, make that a strawberry blonde-headed woman.

Gene sat forward and grabbed for his phone. The red haired woman disappeared behind the door as the dark haired woman walked back up the steps into the house. Gene punched in Cory's number.

"You see something?" Cory asked.

"Nah, not yet. Hey, I'm getting hungry. You up for running over to that coffee shop Leine talked about and getting me a black coffee and blueberry muffin? Get something for yourself, too. I'm buying."

"You sure that's okay? I mean, I don't want to miss something."

"Yeah, it's fine. This has to be the quietest neighborhood I ever seen."

Gene waited until Cory left and then got out of the car. He shoved his Glock in his waistband, looked down both sides of the street and crossed to the opposite sidewalk. He slowed as he reached the white house, keeping an eye on the door. Stepping behind the thick trunk of a eucalyptus tree, he waited and watched the house.

After a few minutes, he checked to make sure no one was nearby and slipped between the white house and its neighbor. He crouched, slipping down the driveway toward the one-car garage in back with an eye toward the house. What he saw told him the side door led into a small entryway next to the kitchen. He continued to the garage and looked in through the small window. A red Honda Civic was parked inside.

His heart beating rapidly in his chest, he skirted the yard and sidled up against the house so he could peek in a larger window.

The window opened onto a small room with an old fashioned closet. Several boxes of gardening tools had been stacked neatly against one wall. The closet held what looked like pairs of fisherman's waders on hangers. Gene moved on to the back door. The lack of gutters and roof overhang told him the house had been built during World War Two. Its back door had been modified somewhat by one of the owners replacing the original single door with a pair of French doors. One of them stood ajar.

Gene worked his way to the side of the door, all his senses alert. He drew his gun from his waistband and double checked that he had a bullet in the chamber. Wiping perspiration from his forehead with the back of his hand, he crept inside the house.

Leine parked a block down from her house in a vacant lot, grabbed the small pack sitting on the seat next to her and cut through the alleyway to the backyard. She had to get to her weapons stash before she did what Azazel requested. Careful to remain hidden from view of the house in case Eric stationed someone there, she slipped into the garage and went to the door of the small room. Earlier, she'd searched her purse for the key to the lock, but couldn't find the keychain. She assumed it had fallen out of her purse into her other car, or might still be in the house.

She reached inside the pack and produced a burglar's pick. Making short work of the lock, she opened the door and turned on the light.

Her heart missed a beat. The shelves were clean. Eric's people found the room. All her hardware was gone, including a simple metal file she'd thrown in when she discovered it in a drawer in the kitchen.

That left her with the nine millimeter, the night vision gear and the electronic scramblers she'd used on the Russian import store. She closed the door and exited the garage, headed back to her car.

The unmistakable sound of *The Godfather's* theme song broke through the quiet of the afternoon as she approached her car. She quickly unlocked the door and grabbed her phone.

Azazel.

"Finally." He sounded upset. "Madeleine. Listen to me closely. There is a man following you. He was waiting for you at your house. He's muscular, has blonde hair and I think he may want to kill you."

The phone went dead. Leine scanned the street in both directions. She didn't see anything, but that didn't mean much. Eric's people were experts—trained to be invisible. She was surprised Azazel warned her. Didn't he want to see her dead?

But it wouldn't have been by his hand. He'd feel cheated. For once, she was glad he'd rigged cameras outside her house.

Leine reached under the seat for her gun.

CHAPTER 32

CORY PAID FOR the coffee and muffins, drove the two blocks back to the neighborhood and pulled in behind Gene's car. He didn't see anyone through the window. Probably napping, Cory thought. He got out of his car with Gene's coffee in one hand and the blueberry muffin in the other and walked to the driver's side window. Gene wasn't there.

He set the coffee and muffin on the roof of the car and looked around. There was nothing happening in the neighborhood that he could see. A bumblebee buzzed by him and Cory took a step backward.

When Gene didn't appear, Cory placed the coffee and muffin on his dash. He wondered if Gene had seen something while he was at the coffee shop and was checking it out. Just my luck, Cory thought. He thought about walking back to his car to drink his hot chocolate when he heard two pops, one after the other. Two more followed, but further apart than the last two. Cory had never heard the sound of actual gunfire and didn't realize at first what it was. When it finally dawned on him, he sprinted to his car and dove inside, dropping to the floor on the passenger side.

Shit. Cory reached for his cell phone and punched in Leine's number. The call went directly to voicemail.

"Leine. It's Cory. I'm parked behind Gene's car. I think I just heard gunshots. I-I think they came from inside one of the houses a few doors down on the opposite side of the street. Gene's not in his car. I don't know what to do. Call me as soon as you get this." Cory ended the call still clutching the phone.

Sweat trickled down the side of his face as he weighed his options. *Should I call the police?* He looked at the card with Jensen's number on it. Leine said to call him only if they'd verified the woman's location. He considered dialing 9-1-1 to report shots fired, but thought better of it. What if it was just some kids lighting off fireworks? What if having the cops come around asking questions put April in more danger? He decided to wait for the neighbors to report it.

The only experience Cory had with guns was through watching cop shows on television. He was smart enough to know the shows didn't reflect real life. The risky heroics shown every week were to grab the audience's attention, not to be viewed as a how-to manual for dangerous situations. Still, it would've been nice to know something he could do. He resolved to check into self-defense classes and maybe even try shooting at a range.

After a few minutes, when he didn't hear anything further, he risked a peek over the dash, through the windshield. No curious neighbors were outside, trying to see what happened. No sirens wailed in the distance. Maybe Cory had been mistaken. Maybe it wasn't gun shots he heard. He slid up onto his front seat to the driver's side. Hesitant at first, he started the car and was about to shift into drive to go back to his corner when a red Honda Civic backed out of a driveway onto the street about a third of the way down the block. The car headed straight toward him. Panicked, Cory couldn't decide if he should crouch down so he wouldn't be seen, or if he should try to get a good look. He decided to look. As the car passed by, Cory caught a glimpse of the driver. It wasn't a woman with strawberry blonde hair. Cory averted his gaze as the man drove by, but not before he made eye contact.

The hair on Cory's head stood on end. A chill spiraled down his back when he realized there was a splotch of what looked like blood on the man's cheek.

Leine slid her semiautomatic out from under the seat and turned a slow three-sixty, searching the places a man could hide within shooting range. Two spindly, scrub oak trees surrounded by dry grass grew to her left. Next to them stood a mound of dirt supporting a couple of busted wood pallets and an old couch with an ugly flower pattern missing its cushions. A few older homes slumped in the distance, semi-obscured in the brown smog created by the busy freeway nearby. Large power lines and poles slashed through the scene, breaking the monotony.

Of course, he might not be using a gun. It depended on who Eric decided to send after her. Could be a sniper, although if that were the case she'd be dead by now. She'd been exposed long enough for a clean shot.

She crouched behind her car, next to the back wheel well and scanned her surroundings. A shadow moved near one of the trees. Holding the gun with both hands she pivoted and aimed, waiting. A scrawny black and white cat sprang from the tall grass behind the oak, landing with deadly finality on an unsuspecting prey. The unlucky bird flapped its wings in panic several seconds, then stilled.

Leine did another sweep of the lot. Seeing nothing suspicious she relaxed her grip. She didn't see it coming. The sharp wire snaked around her throat, taking her by surprise. He must have moved while her attention was on the cat. She dropped the gun and it glanced off the roof of the car, clattering to the ground. She slid two fingers beneath the cool metal before her attacker twisted the cord tighter around her neck, attempting to crush her windpipe. Leine grappled with the chokehold, working to loosen his grip enough so she could take a breath.

Keeping one hand on the wire she let go with the other and rammed her elbow into his solar plexus. He grunted and his grip loosened, but only for a split-second—not long enough for Leine to break free. She jerked her head back and butted him in the face, then stomped on his instep. The garrote fell slack and she slipped free. Pivoting, she slammed the heel of her hand against the bridge of his nose, but he deflected the worst of it with his left hand and punched her hard in the stomach with his right. Leine doubled over in pain and tried to catch her breath when she saw the kick coming.

She dodged right and avoided a broken nose. As his foot overshot its mark, she grabbed it and used his own momentum to lift his leg and force him backward, off his feet.

He landed on his back with a thud. Leine sprinted toward the gun. It had fallen under the car, next to the back tire. Her attacker was on his feet in seconds and lunged for it at the same time. Leine lifted her knee and brought her foot down hard, delivering a sharp blow to his shin. She was rewarded by the sound of bone cracking. To his credit, the man barely grunted. Leine turned back toward the gun, but he wrapped his hand around her ankle and jerked her backwards.

Struggling to remain standing, Leine kicked at his face, but missed. She wrenched her foot free of her shoe and dove for the gun.

Even with a broken leg he was on his feet fast and reached it first. She grabbed the barrel and gave it a vicious twist. The gun came free in her hand and she wrapped her finger around the trigger.

The first shot didn't lay him out, but the second one did. Leine backed away from him as he fell to his knees, then crumpled to the ground. The distant wail of sirens galvanized her into action and she was inside her car and leaving the scene in under a minute.

The burn phone beeped, telling her she'd missed a call. She rifled through her purse and found the phone. Leine hit speed dial and listened to Cory's message. She immediately called him back.

"Where are you? Gene's still not back—" Cory described the sounds he heard, confirming for Leine the shots fired. Then he told her about the man in the red Honda.

"Listen to me, Cory. You need to stay right where you are. I'll call Detective Jensen and explain about April being abducted, that we think she's being held in the basement of the house where you saw the red car come out of. When he gets there, show him which house it is and then follow his instructions to the letter. I'll be in touch."

Leine ended the call and dialed Jensen's number.

CHAPTER 33

TWO PATROL CARS arrived at the house and parked on opposite sides of the street, several houses down from the address in question. Cory felt the muscles in his neck relax. He got out of his car and walked over to where the officers were getting ready to go in.

"I'm sure glad to see you guys." Cory was surprised his voice sounded calm.

"Which one is it?" one of the officers asked. A large man with sandy colored hair, the name on his uniform read Blankenship.

Cory pointed at the white house.

"A guy left about forty-five minutes ago in a red Honda Civic and he hasn't come back yet. It looked like there was blood on his face. I wrote down the license plate number."

"Was he alone or did he have someone in the car with him?"

"I didn't see anyone else, but I guess there could have been somebody in the trunk or on the floor of the backseat."

"Detective Jensen said you heard gunshots. Anything else we should know?"

Cory shook his head. "No. Just the four shots. I thought it was some kids shooting off fireworks, not guns. I haven't seen Gene since I got back from the coffee place. He must have gone inside. I hope he's okay."

"Who's Gene?" Blankenship stopped what he was doing and glanced at Cory.

"Gene Dorfenberger. The security guy on Serial Date," Cory answered.

Blankenship inclined his chin. "Got it. Is he armed?"

"I don't know. His car's parked in front of mine. We were watching the block, hoping to see one of the women that works for the guy. Maybe even the guy." Cory looked down the street in both directions. "Where's Detective Jensen?"

Another officer, a smaller man with dark hair, answered. "He and his partner are on their way. Takes a little longer from downtown."

Cory could see they were busy, so he walked back to his car and slid into the front seat. He checked Leine's avatar. She was somewhere in South-Central L.A. He wondered why she wasn't back yet.

The cops stood in a huddle around one of the patrol cars. Cory watched as they moved toward the house. He craned his neck to see what they were doing, but after checking the front door and apparently finding it locked, they disappeared around the side of the house, out of his view.

Leine parked a secure distance from the warehouse address Azazel had given her. It was in a shitty section of

South-Central L.A., among rows of other rundown warehouses. Razor wire topped the chain link fence surrounding the complex, and broken glass and litter filled the parking area.

She was early. He'd told her to be there at five. It was now four-thirty. An inversion layer had created a smoggy, gritty summer day, the kind Leine loathed. Her skin and hair felt as though there was a layer of grime between her and the world, her eyes burned and the air was difficult to breathe. As soon as this is over, she thought, I'm heading back to Seattle where the atmosphere doesn't resemble the inside of a tailpipe.

Her call to Jensen went well, although his voice sounded too cool, distant. She assumed he was still pissed because she left his apartment without leaving a note. If she'd been thinking straight, she would at least have written a quick thank you for the ride to his place to sleep off the evening. When she explained about April being abducted she didn't go into how long she'd been missing. She described the box she received with the finger, and Gene's delivery, and Sissy Nelson's subsequent identification. She also mentioned Peter might know more than he was letting on. Once she was certain April was safe, she'd explain everything.

When Azazel told her what his last task entailed, Leine knew as soon as they confirmed the house where April was being held it'd be all right to call Jensen, let the police do what they did best. Especially when she realized Azazel wouldn't be near the house for a few hours. What she planned carried risk, but with April secure she'd be free to act. She'd told Cory to call her when April was safe.

She got out of her car and shrugged on the small backpack lying on her passenger seat. Out of habit, she locked the doors. Wishful thinking, she thought. In this neighborhood, she'd be lucky to have any wheels left when she came back.

Leine started off at a brisk pace toward the warehouse. *Time to finish this.*

CHAPTER 34

THE SCENE THAT greeted Jensen and Putnam as they turned onto the residential street was one of multiple patrol cars and an ambulance. Several curious onlookers lined the sidewalk across from the house. A kid with hipster glasses stood near one of the patrol cars, watching everything. Must be Cory, Jensen thought. He and Putnam got out of their vehicle and split off; Jensen walked toward the kid and Putnam went over to talk to the paramedics, who had just wheeled a body out on a gurney.

"You Cory?" Jensen asked. Cory dragged his attention away from the scene.

"Yeah. Detective Jensen?"

When Jensen nodded, Cory smiled, looking relieved. His face was blanched white, quite a contrast with his black glasses.

"Am I glad to see you. Leine said she'd call you." Cory eyed the gurney with the covered body. "I hope that's not April." His Adams apple bobbed as he swallowed. He looked ready to cry. "Did you hear if they found her?"

"None of the victims match her description, so no, I don't think so. Where's Leine?" Jensen asked, changing the subject. She hadn't said anything about not being there. *Where the hell is she? It's her daughter, for chissakes.*

"She said she had something important to do first, but that she'd be here after." A worried expression crossed Cory's face. "She said if she hadn't made it back by dinner to come looking for her. She's got her GPS turned on and gave me the password so I could track it. Want me to get the computer and show you?"

"That would be helpful, yeah."

Cory walked to his car, leaned in the window and grabbed the tablet. He came back and set it on the hood of the squad car. "The link's on her desktop," he explained as he tapped the screen and brought up the program showing Leine's blinking avatar. Jensen leaned closer to get a better look.

"What the hell is she doing in that part of town?"

"She didn't say." Cory glanced back at the house. "Gene still hasn't come out. Do you think he's all right?"

"Gene?"

"The security guy on the show. We were watching the street. I went for coffee and he disappeared."

Just then, the paramedics wheeled out another gurney carrying a dark skinned male. Still alive, judging by the oxygen mask.

"That's Gene." He turned to Jensen, his eyes wide. "Can I go talk to him?"

"Not right now, Cory. Let me do the talking, okay?" Jensen walked to where the medic was getting ready to slide the gurney into the ambulance. Cory followed at a distance.

As Jensen approached, Gene turned his head, but couldn't speak through the oxygen mask. His clothes were bloody and he had bandages on both his chest and right shoulder.

Chang, one of the patrol officers, came over and stood next to Jensen, out of Cory's hearing.

"Bullet wounds in the chest and shoulder. He's lucky. He might actually make it." Chang looked back toward the house. "Luckier than the other two." His mouth pulled down at the corners. "We found some weird shit inside the house."

Jensen glanced at Cory. "Can we make sure Cory here gets down to the station to give his statement?"

Chang nodded. "Yeah. Monroe's right over there. She wasn't here for the search." He waved her over.

Jensen introduced them. "This is Officer Monroe. She'll bring you down to the station to take your statement and then you can go." He gestured toward the tablet Cory still held in his hands. "I'd like to have the computer, in case we have to track Leine."

"Yeah, sure." Cory handed the tablet to him and started to leave, but hesitated and turned back. "April's going to be okay, right?"

"We're going to do everything we can."

"Leine told me to call her when she was safe."

"No problem. I've got her number," Jensen assured him.

Worry still evident on his face, Cory nodded and followed Monroe to the patrol car.

Jensen turned back to Chang. "What'd you guys find?"

Chang shook his head. "Photographs of young adult females tacked all over the guy's bedroom wall. Blankenship swears one of them is that contestant who got killed, Amanda Milton. But that's not the weirdest thing. There were packages in the freezer with names on the labels."

"What's weird about that?"

"Names, like people's names, and words like 'thigh' and 'buttock'." Chang shuddered. "There was a huge dog kennel in the basement with evidence they were keeping someone in there. We found chains attached to a bloody wall, medical equipment, all sorts of shit."

"But no other bodies than the two women?"

"No."

The medic began to slide Gene into the ambulance.

"Thanks, Jeff," Jensen said to Chang. "I need to see if this guy has any information."

"I'll be over there if you need me." Chang headed for his squad car.

Jensen stepped closer to the gurney and tapped Gene's shoulder. Gene's eyes opened a slit, then wider. He lifted his hand toward him, but let it drop, as though the gesture was too much effort. Jensen turned to the medic.

"Can you take off his mask for a minute? I think he's trying to tell me something."

The medic gently removed the mask. Gene licked his lips and took a shallow breath.

"Gene, it's me, Detective Jensen, remember? The murder case on the show?"

Gene tried to raise his head from the pillow, but it proved to be too much and he collapsed back.

"H-he's gone...took her..." he whispered in a raspy voice. He fell silent, unable to continue.

"Take it easy, Gene. You mean the guy we're looking for?"

Gene nodded once and closed his eyes.

"Who'd he take? April? Someone else?"

When he didn't answer, Jensen tapped his leg, trying to rouse him but Gene was out cold.

The medic replaced the mask and loaded him into the ambulance. Putnam came around the back and pulled Jensen aside.

"Two dead females and the security guy. No sign of Basso's daughter. There's enough evidence in there to put the guy on death row. Where the hell would this freak go next?"

Jensen showed the tablet to Putnam.

"I think I have an idea."

CHAPTER 35

L EINE MOVED QUICKLY around the side of the warehouse, mentally checking off escape routes in case things went south. Azazel would be expecting her to try something. He'd probably be disappointed if she didn't. It was up to her to figure out what kind of surprises he had in store.

She came around to the front and moved to the main door of the warehouse where she tried the handle. It was unlocked. He's making things easy, she thought. She opened the door a few inches. The place was dark so she strapped on the night vision monocle and checked to make sure no one was around before she walked in.

The warehouse had fallen into disrepair, evidently unused for several years. The cavernous loading bay stood empty, as though waiting for a ghost shipment that would never arrive. Despite the sweltering temperature outside, inside it was cool and not unpleasant. To her left was another empty loading bay leading to a dark corridor. She proceeded deeper into the structure, following the hallway.

After a few yards, she came to another corridor that branched off to the left of the main passageway. The faint strain of a melody floated toward her from further down the main branch. She chose to follow it, intending to return and check out the other one later. The music grew louder as she walked.

He's here already.

By the time she'd gotten close enough to identify the music as a piece by Vivaldi, she noticed a glow directly in front of her. She removed the night vision monocle and placed it in her pocket, then moved along the corridor and stepped into a dimly-lit room.

Before her stood a large, four-poster bed draped in lush fabrics; deep velvet blues and purples, shining silks and damasks, with several pillows piled at the head. The lighting was something out of a period piece, moody and dramatic, similar to that given off by gas lamps. Rich rugs carpeted the floor. Smoke from an incense burner sitting on a table next to the bed wafted upward. Dozens of long-stemmed, red roses stood in elegant vases dotting the room. The word sultan came to mind.

Four professional looking dolly-mounted cameras had been placed equal distances apart around the perimeter of the room, similar to the ones used on the set of Serial Date. A boom mic had been rigged to hang a few feet above the bed. *He's created his own studio.*

Leine slid her hand over the gun hidden in her waistband and pulled it free. She'd been in some interesting places before, but knowing this was all for her made everything surreal. The epic music ebbed and flowed in graceful, tension-filled crescendos followed by hurtling collapse, lifting once again to the pinnacle of the masterpiece, relentless in its quest for release.

She remained in the shadows and continued through the ersatz boudoir, searching for the man she would kill. Her senses sharpened, she'd reverted to her default when hunting a target; aware of every nuance and sound, possessed by a single-minded intensity.

She allowed the rage she'd been suppressing to build inside her, a match for the vivid soundtrack Azazel had chosen. Clearly, as he and Eric had both stated with such certainty—she was one of them—a killer. She would no longer fight it. Once she knew April was safe and Azazel was dead, she'd return to what she did best and make no excuses for it, although not for Eric. There were many such agencies in need of her expertise. The choice required a solitary existence, but Leine had learned to live without love.

The thought saddened her, but really, how would it be any different than how she'd been living her life? She had no doubt her daughter would refuse to speak to her once this was over. Her past had almost gotten April killed. It would be better for her if Leine wasn't a part of her life, period. She'd learned to live with the unbearable pain of having killed Carlos, a man she loved. She could live with this, too. An easier choice, since it would be her decision.

She came to a thick brocade curtain hanging the length of the room, apparently used as a sort of backdrop and felt for where the fabric overlapped. She found it and parted the folds to peek through to another section of the warehouse. Fully lit, the area looked like it had once served as a break room for the warehouse workers. A sink and cupboards lined one wall, with a table and four chairs in the middle.

A laptop sat on the table, April's face visible on the screen. Some sick kind of screensaver, Leine thought grimly.

Then the screensaver coughed.

Checking to make sure she was alone, Leine crossed the room to the laptop.

"April? April, can you hear me? It's Leine." *Where the hell is she?* It couldn't be video from the basement at the house on Tujunga. She checked her watch. They should have found her by now.

April turned her head to the left, as though she heard her.

"Mommy? Where are you?"

She looked toward Leine, but Leine realized April couldn't see her, was only looking into a camera.

"Where are you, honey? Are you still in the basement?"

April shook her head. "No. I-I'm not sure. An empty room within a larger building, but I don't know where. He blindfolded me and put me in the trunk of a car. We drove for a long time." Her voice cracked. "I'm so scared, Mom."

Leine's heart thudded in her chest. Her plan had gone sideways. Jensen wouldn't find her when they searched the house. April wasn't safe. "It's going to be okay, baby. Can you describe what the room looks like? Tell me everything you see."

April's eyes widened and she strained toward the camera. "It's a trap, mom. He showed me a room that looks like a movie set and told me what he wants to do to you. You have to get out of there before—"

"That's enough, April."

Leine froze at the sound of Azazel's voice and slowly turned. She hadn't heard him walk into the room. He stood next to the cupboards, breathing heavily. Tall and slender, his dark, curly hair brushed the collar of the button down shirt he wore loose over a pair of pressed blue jeans. His eyes slanted up at the corners, giving him a slightly exotic appearance. Studied casualness, Leine thought. It would be easy for him to lure unsuspecting victims. Except that now his dark eyes glittered with anger.

"Step away from the laptop, Madeleine."

In the split-second it took for her to realize he was unarmed, all the rage that had been building against him mixed with fear for her daughter coalesced into a single instinctual response. The short expanse between them evaporated and before he had a chance to react, Leine had him flat on his back on the floor with her gun shoved into his face.

"Where is she?" she said through clenched teeth. Leine's vision grew cloudy as she struggled with the urge to bury a bullet in his brain. *Think, Leine. You don't know where he's keeping her. Get the information, first. Then kill him.* She took a deep breath and eased her finger off the trigger.

Azazel smiled, his eyes cold. "You're early."

Leine pushed the gun into his temple. The smile threw her off balance. He was too calm. She had to make him believe she was going to kill him, regardless of whether he told her where her daughter was.

She leaned down and said in a low voice, "You know what, asshole? I don't care if you tell me where she is or not, because right now I'm going to kill you and then it'll only be a matter of time before I find her."

Azazel's smile faded. "You would have done it by now," he replied and raised his hand.

As Leine went for his arm, she felt a stinging sensation in her thigh. She glanced down in time to see Azazel deliver the contents of a hypodermic needle into her leg.

CHAPTER 36

The searing pain in her foot confused her. Leine struggled against brain fog and nausea, working to make sense of what was causing her so much agony. She opened her eyes and squinted, trying to bring the scene at her feet into focus.

She could only see the top of his head as Azazel bent over her leg, working diligently. *What is he doing to my foot?* She was on the bed, her hands crossed at the wrists and bound with zip ties to the headboard above her. The laptop sat next to them on a side table. April's face filled the screen. She's still alive, she thought. A feeling of relief mingled with the growing awareness of pain. A high-pitched whine had taken the place of Azazel's classical music selection. She tried to yank her foot away, but he'd tied her legs apart and had an iron grip on her ankle.

He stopped what he was doing when she moved and glanced up. His eyes had a glassy cast to them. Blood covered his hands and face. A folded towel had been placed under her ankle, but it was soaked with her blood. In his hand he held a bloodstained rotary tool with the sanding wheel attached. A smile spread across his spattered face.

"Oh, good. You're awake. I didn't want you to miss this part." He nodded toward the camera. "I'm filming this, so don't worry. You'll be able to see the first part in High Definition."

Leine took a deep breath and closed her eyes, trying to calm her mind and at the same time transcend the pain. When she felt she had her emotions under control, she opened her eyes to stare at Azazel and said nothing.

A look of disappointment crossed his face, but it passed and he resumed his task with the tool. Leine bit her tongue to keep from screaming and tasted blood.

A moment later he stopped and selected a dry towel next to him on the bed to sop up the blood, then inspected his handiwork from all sides.

"For this occasion I thought I'd try out my new, handy-dandy power tool. You wouldn't believe what's available at your local home improvement store." He smiled. "So much to choose from."

The pain narrowed her focus the way nothing else could. Her mind became a pinpoint of awareness as she concentrated on April's face on the laptop. Everything she was experiencing, all the pain, her fear for April's life, the rage that this monster had gotten the upper hand, she directed outward. Breathing deeply, Leine shifted conscious thought until the pain became an abstract concept.

Azazel shut the sander off and set it down. He then picked up a pair of needle-nosed pliers that were lying next to his knee, which he showed to Leine.

"I've cut the first toenail to the quick. Now I'm going to remove it." He grasped the nail and gave it a vicious jerk. It tore free and Leine screamed. He held it up to look at it, then dropped it into a dish beside him.

"Just think—you have nine more. Then we move on to your fingers."

This is going to be a long fucking night, Leine thought. She shook her head to clear the pain, fighting the nausea threatening to derail her self-control.

Azazel smiled as he laid the pliers on the damask cover.

"You're going to like what's coming next." He slid off the bed and scanned the room. "Now where did I put them? Oh, yes. I remember." Azazel started across the floor but stopped and turned to look at her. "You understand why I have to do this, right?"

Leine glared at him. "No, I don't."

"Well, you need to know. Otherwise this makes no sense, I'm sure." He walked back to the bed.

"You see, Madeleine, you committed a heinous act several years ago and now it's time for payback." He wiped his face with his forearm before continuing.

"You killed my father. You may remember him. He was nicknamed 'The Frenchman' and was well known in arms circles the world over." He watched Leine for a reaction. "No? Well that just pisses me off, Madeleine." He stepped closer. Leine prepared herself for more pain, but Azazel simply stood there, his hands shaking.

"I don't know what you're talking about. I never killed your father." Confirming his assumption would ramp up the pain factor he was going to deliver by ten. Leine ignored her throbbing foot and concentrated on him.

"You can say whatever you'd like, but I know the truth." The expression on his face had changed. His eyes appeared to snap with intensity. "I'm weary of your lies. And I'm weary of you. We could have had everything,

Madeleine. Just remember, you chose this path." He turned and walked out of the room.

What did he mean, that I chose this path? Well, she reminded herself, he's bat-shit crazy. It wasn't like she'd be able to make sense out of much of anything he said.

As soon as he was gone, Leine used her arms to pull herself as close to the head of the bed as her bound ankles would allow, giving her some slack in the plastic zip ties. She still wore the bobby pins she'd put in that morning to keep her hair back. Her hands and arms had gone numb from being tied above her head and it took several tries before she was able to grasp one of them with her fingers and pull it free.

It slipped through her fingers onto the bed behind her. Frustrated, she searched and found the other one, this time taking more care so it wouldn't drop. The seconds ticked by. After what seemed like hours Leine managed to insert a prong of the bobby pin into the underside of the zip tie and slide it free. Then she folded forward and untied the ties binding her ankles to the foot of the bed.

Once free, she hugged the headboard and climbed to her feet, careful to keep the weight off her bloody toe. A knife lay on the bed next to the sander and pliers. She tossed the few pillows remaining on the bed to the floor and threw the damask cover back, revealing the top sheet. Using the knife, she cut a strip and tied it around her toe to slow the bleeding.

Out of the corner of her eye, she saw a light flash. Silently, she slipped behind the curtain by the bed to wait for Azazel.

CHAPTER 37

JENSEN AND PUTNAM pulled in half a block down from the parking lot belonging to the dilapidated warehouse. The red Honda Civic stood out against the faded concrete walls.

"That the one?" Putnam asked.

"Same plate as what the kid wrote down."

They got out as a patrol car rolled in and parked beside them. They waited for the other two officers to exit their vehicle.

"The guy we're looking for is considered armed and extremely dangerous," Jensen said. "He's already killed three women we know of, probably a hell of a lot more. We think he kidnapped this woman," he held up a photograph of April, "and is holding her here." Next, Jensen showed them a photograph of Leine. "This is her mother. We believe she came here looking for the killer. She has extensive knowledge of firearms and is probably armed." Jensen walked to the trunk and opened it. "Garcia, you come with us. Divecchio, stay here and direct the other unit to the entry and exit points."

Jensen had radioed his lieutenant on the way to advise him there was no time to wait for S.W.A.T. and that they were going in. The team's ETA was twenty minutes—too long for them to wait. April and Leine could be dead by then. Jensen and Putnam each strapped on a Kevlar vest and closed the trunk.

They tried the first door they found, but it was locked. They got lucky on the second one. Guns drawn, they quietly crept inside. The three of them stopped to listen, but heard nothing.

The side they entered originally housed the offices for that section of the building. Destroyed by relentless sun and vandalism, the interior carpeting was ripped and faded and most of the doors were busted or off their hinges. Light fixtures hung at unnatural angles and obscene graffiti covered the walls.

Jensen went in high with Putnam covering low as they moved from room to room, finding nothing but garbage left by squatters with a couple of rats rooting through it. Garcia followed at a discreet distance. The three of them continued through the building, methodically clearing the rooms, but didn't find anything noteworthy.

Further in, they came to another suite of offices, most with their doors either missing or destroyed. Larger than the others, these rooms were more than likely where the CEO and upper management would've been located.

Putnam walked over to the only office with a closed, intact door. A large, interior window extended a few feet to the left with its blinds drawn. He tried the handle, but it was locked. Jensen nodded and they each took a side. On the count of three, Jensen kicked the door open.

April screamed in surprise. She was bound to a chair in front of a video camera and microphone. Jensen crossed the room and killed the mic, then bent to untie her. Putnam radioed they'd found her.

"He's got my mother. Please, you have to find them."

"Do you know where they are?"

April shook her head, tears streaming down her face. "I think in this building. After he showed me the area where he planned to kill her, he blindfolded me and we walked here. It wasn't far. He counted the steps."

"Can you remember which direction? Did you turn left? Right?"

"Wait." April closed her eyes to think. "We walked sixty-four steps and turned right, then I think it was fifteen and we turned left. I-I can't remember how many it was to this room. Not many. I'm sorry."

"Was he working alone? Did he have more than one weapon?"

April shook her head. "As far as I know, it's just him and he only has the one gun. He had two helpers, women, but he shot them. I heard a gun go off upstairs before he came down to the basement. He killed the dark haired woman, Gwen, right in front of me. When we got here, he hid the gun in a drawer next to the bed, but he didn't think he'd have to use it."

"There's a bed?"

"Yeah. He's got this whole weird thing set up for my mom, with cameras and stuff. Like a movie set. He thinks she's his soul mate."

"But he's still going to kill her?"

Fresh tears spilled onto her cheeks as she nodded. "He says he has to because of something she did. I-I don't know what, he didn't tell me."

Garcia walked in, Divecchio behind him.

"The other unit's in place," Divecchio said.

"I checked a little further along the hall," Garcia added. "There's a couple of bathrooms a few yards down. After that, the hall leads into what I assume is the actual warehouse. It's pitch black as far as I could see."

"Got it." Jensen pulled him aside. "I need you to babysit her. The guy has her mother and we need to go in now." Garcia nodded.

"No problem. Divecchio can go with you."

Jensen relayed the directions April gave him to Putnam and Divecchio. Jensen turned to April. "Go with Officer Garcia. He'll take good care of you."

"Can't all four of you go? I'll be fine. My mother needs your help."

"Don't worry. We'll find her." With that, Jensen, Putnam and Divecchio disappeared into the dark warehouse.

Azazel walked into the room carrying a pair of pipe cutters and froze when he saw the empty bed. Leine watched him through the slit in the curtain, silently urging him to come closer. He rotated slowly in place, searching the room. Then he lifted his head and sniffed, as though trying to locate her scent in the air.

He lowered his head and stared at the curtain. He took a step toward her, but stopped. Detouring around the bed in the other direction, he opened a drawer on the far nightstand and pulled something out. She couldn't be sure, but she thought she saw the outline of a handgun.

This way, Azazel. Just a little bit closer, Leine thought as she fingered the knife. Although larger than she preferred, it would work for her purposes.

Azazel skirted the bed and advanced toward her hiding place. As he drew nearer, Leine dropped to a crouch. He came forward a few steps, stopped and sniffed again. Incense still hung in the air. He wavered for a second as though uncertain, then moved closer.

Leine snaked the knife from behind the curtain through the space between his legs and then jerked it back with a vicious twist, slicing through his hamstring. Azazel screamed as he crumpled to the floor, clutching the back of his leg. The gun clattered to the floor. Leine emerged from behind the curtain and kicked it across the room, far out of his reach. She circled around behind him and seized him by the neck in a chokehold, running the blade of the knife up the side of his face so that he could feel the cold steel against his skin.

"Tell me where she is, Azazel. Now."

Azazel's breathing came in shallow bursts as he shook his head.

"Kill me and you'll never find her."

"Kill you and the world will be a far better place. I will find her. You can bet on that." Leaning into his ear, she whispered, "I found your house and I found you." She lifted the knife to his throat. Azazel struggled, but Leine tightened her grip.

Motion to her left brought Leine's focus away from Azazel and onto the laptop screen. April's mouth moved as though she was speaking, but it wasn't directed at the camera. Why couldn't she hear anything? *Had he turned off the sound?* Azazel's head was turned away from the screen and couldn't see what was going on. April's face grew larger as she moved toward the camera and then disappeared. For a brief instant, Jensen's face appeared on screen and then he was gone.

They found her. She's safe. Relief flooded through her. *I can kill him now.* She raised the knife but hesitated. The revenge and rage were gone, leaving her drained and numb. Leine searched her feelings and found nothing but revulsion for the monster whose life she now held.

But revulsion wasn't enough to move the knife across his throat. *Why should I take his life when surviving would be far worse for him?* Did she really want to kill again? Did she want Azazel's ghost chasing her through her dreams, where she'd never be able to escape him? There'd been far too much blood shed.

She relaxed her grip on the knife, but kept Azazel in a headlock.

"April's free." The words helped make things real. Azazel stiffened in her arms, barely breathing.

"You're lying."

Keeping the knife to his throat, Leine shifted him so he could see the empty laptop screen. A guttural cry sounded from deep within him as he realized she spoke the truth. Azazel lunged forward. Leine shifted the knife a split second before the blade would have sliced through his carotid artery.

"Kill me," he demanded.

"Never," Leine whispered.

April paced the room as Garcia watched. "Ready to go?" he asked.

"I need to use the bathroom really bad."

"Oh, sure. There's one right around the corner here. It's not gonna be close to clean, though. This place is pretty messed up."

"Believe me, when you've been tied to a chair as long as I have, it doesn't matter what it looks like."

"Here, take a flashlight." Garcia handed her the one from his utility belt.

"Thanks. I'll be right back."

He showed her where it was and told her he'd be nearby if she needed him. She thanked him, walked down the hall and stopped at the door that said Women. She turned to see if Garcia was still there. His outline was barely visible from the light shining into the corridor from the office. He waved. She waved back and stepped into the bathroom.

She let a few seconds pass and turned off the flashlight. Then she cracked the door open. Garcia was still there, but she didn't think he could see her without the flashlight on. Silently, she slipped down the hallway, counting to fifteen.

Jensen, Putnam and Garcia found the break room first. Jensen walked over to the thick brocade curtain hanging from the ceiling at one end of the room while the other two did a quick search. The sweet smell of incense reminded him of college. Muted voices filtered through from the other side of the curtain. Tracking the sound, he worked his way along the fabric, looking for an opening while Putnam searched the opposite direction. Divecchio stayed back, prepared to move when needed.

Jensen discovered where the two curtains overlapped and peered through. His eyes took a few seconds to adjust to the low light level before he saw two people on the floor by a large, four-poster bed. One of them was Leine. She held a man in a chokehold, a knife to his throat.

"Drop the knife, Leine, and back away."

Leine turned her head. Relief washed through her when she recognized Jensen standing next to the curtain. She threw the knife to the other side of the bed and climbed to her feet. "I cut through his hamstring. He's not going anywhere." She raised her hands and backed away.

At that instant, a loud shot echoed through the room. Azazel jerked and slumped sideways to the floor. Leine dropped to her knees and scanned the area. *Where the hell did that come from?* Jensen and Putnam had both taken cover behind the bed, their guns drawn and pointed at the other side of the room.

"Drop it, now," Putnam yelled.

Near the video equipment, a lone figure stood next to one of the cameras, the outline of a gun visible in her hands. The gun clattered to the floor.

It was April.

CHAPTER 38

LEINE ZIPPED HER suitcase closed and brought it out to the living room. The cop who accompanied her, Officer Hayim, grabbed hold of the handle and hauled it outside to the backseat of the patrol car. The bomb squad had been there that morning and disabled the detonator attached to her door and removed the explosives so the house was safe to enter. Leine spent most of the prior afternoon deflecting questions about the source of the bomb and the work she'd done before being hired as security for Serial Date.

The show was currently in indefinite limbo, or hiatus as the network brass liked to call it, pending the outcome of the LAPD's investigation into the missing contestants. Peter Bronkowski had disappeared at approximately the same time as the news broke about the real serial killer who'd been on a contestant killing spree. LAPD issued a warrant for Peter's arrest and were working with Interpol to locate him. He'd left a note identifying Gene Dorfenberger as a person of interest in the disappearance of contestant Stacy Ross.

A Facebook page had been created dedicated to the missing women, with over two million 'Likes'. Network executives were currently trying to figure out a way to parlay the outpouring of affection from the fans of the show into advertising dollars.

Leine took one last look around the place to make sure she didn't miss anything. Putnam and a team from LAPD were currently combing the house, searching for the audio and video equipment Azazel had installed. Not being the sentimental type, Leine wasn't sorry to leave it and L.A. behind and return to her old life in Seattle. She'd miss Jensen, but he'd acted cool during the post-warehouse interview, so she didn't hold out much hope. He also was conspicuously absent from the house. He knew she was getting her stuff that afternoon. Probably avoiding her, she thought.

As she walked out the door onto the front porch, Jensen pulled up in his Camaro and parked. Leine waited until he'd gotten out before she walked down the steps to meet him.

"Hey," she said, half hoping he was there to ask her to stay in Los Angeles. Not too realistic, she chided herself.

Jensen nodded at Hayim standing on the porch, watching them. "I need to talk to her for a minute. We'll be right back." Hayim nodded and took a seat on the porch swing. Jensen turned to Leine. "Let's walk."

They walked along the sidewalk in silence for a distance before Jensen stopped and took something out of his pocket. He held it up for her to see.

Leine stared at the keychain in the plastic baggie. Then she looked at Jensen.

"I found this at my place the night I drove you home from the Happy Mermaid. It's got the same markings as the bullets from those cold cases I told you about." Jensen's gaze bored into hers. "Where'd you get this?"

Leine closed her eyes and felt the blood drain from her face. That's where the key to the room in the garage disappeared. Opening her eyes, she took a deep breath. "It's a reminder of my old life."

"So the casing's yours?"

Leine wanted to cry from the accusing look on his face.

"No. It belongs to my old boss, Eric. I kept it to remind me of what kind of life I left behind." Leine walked to the edge of a neighbor's yard and sat on the lawn, next to a eucalyptus tree. Jensen followed but remained standing.

"Years ago I worked for a covert organization, overseen by a part of the government that neither you or any senate subcommittee has ever heard of. No one has. Our mission was to remove specific threats by any means necessary. I assumed all of the targets were legitimate. They weren't. Eric ordered me to carry out an assignment under false pretenses and when I learned the truth I left." Leine gazed into the distance. "Eric wanted me back. I told him no and foolishly mentioned I had something of his that wouldn't be good for his career advancement. He sent a team to eliminate me." She nodded at the keychain in his hands. "Your shooter is my old boss."

"Why didn't you tell me? You knew I'd been trying to find the person responsible for the shootings. All you had to do was explain." Agitated, Jensen started to pace.

"It's not that easy. You won't be able to get near him. He's too protected." Leine hesitated before continuing. "There is one way to bring him down, and I know how to do it. Once he's vulnerable, you might be able to get him on the old murder charges."

Jensen stopped pacing. "I didn't book this as evidence yet because I wanted to talk to you, get your side of the story. Once it's submitted, you'll be a person of interest."

"What does that mean?"

"It means we won't be able to see each other for the duration of the investigation. It also means you'll have to stay in L.A. for the foreseeable future—until you've been cleared of the murders."

Leine let the information sink in. Stay in L.A. She wasn't sure she'd do very well with that. She didn't have many friends there. She called Frank as soon as she'd been certain April was okay and he asked her to dinner to discuss what happened. She'd declined, not looking forward to explaining herself yet again. Maybe she needed to call Frank back and accept his invitation, try a little détente.

The only other person she really knew in L.A., Gene, was going to be recuperating from his injuries in prison. When police told him they had a letter from Peter implicating him in the disappearance of Stacy Ross, he rolled over on Peter, adding he knew Peter had held back evidence in at least one of the other murders. Apparently, the questioning finally got to Gene and he confessed to giving Azazel a key to the studio, effectively proving his connection to Amanda Milton's murder.

"I've got one more question," Jensen said. "Why didn't you trust me?"

Her heart ripped in two at the naked hurt in his eyes. "I wanted to tell you. But he threatened to kill April if I did and I knew he had my house and car wired. I didn't know how far he was prepared to go." Her voice was barely audible. "I was afraid it would put you in danger, and I swore I'd never do that to someone I cared for again." Leine could feel the tears building and looked away before he saw them. "I'm so sorry."

Jensen stared into the distance. She wondered what he was thinking. After a few minutes, he turned toward her and held out his hand. She wiped her eyes before she placed her hand in his and he helped her to her feet.

Their eyes met and Leine felt a jolt of electricity between them. Putting the tree between them and the line of sight from the house, Jensen leaned over and kissed her gently on the lips. Leine returned the gesture. They broke the kiss at the same time and began to slowly walk back toward the house.

"Do you need help finding a place?" Jensen asked.

Leine smiled. "No, I think I can manage, but thank you. I should probably find a two bedroom again, in case April decides to stick around when this is all over." April was being held on murder charges, but it was likely the district attorney would allow her to plead to a lesser charge, possibly misdemeanor manslaughter because of the circumstances. The case was a loser for the D.A. A jury would most likely be sympathetic to her as the victim, and not convict.

He walked her onto the porch and nodded at Hayim. "I'm going inside, see what they've found so far. Take good care of her."

"Sure thing," Hayim replied.

Leine watched as he walked away and then turned back to Hayim, still sitting on the porch swing.

"Ready to go?" he asked.

"Almost." She picked up a large manila envelope from the little side table next to the swing addressed to Scott Henderson, Eric's boss at the agency. At the bottom she'd written, "Re: Razorback."

Leine followed him down the steps and got into the squad car.

"Can we stop by a mailbox on the way, please?"

Jensen acknowledged the forensics guy working in the kitchen and walked down the hallway to the far bedroom. No one was working that section of the house. He'd been fighting with himself since he'd thought of the idea, but the answer always came back the same.

After checking the hall one last time to make sure no one was nearby, he slipped inside the bedroom and partially closed the door. He walked to the dresser on the far side of the room under the window, and pulled the plastic baggie from his pocket. Jensen stared at the keychain, arguing with himself once more. How do you know she's telling the truth? What if she's the shooter? There was only one answer: then you're fucked, Santa. Jensen realized this one act could jeopardize everything, put everything he'd ever worked for at risk. But he couldn't help thinking this one time he was finally going to trust his gut, all evidence to the contrary.

Opening the third drawer down, Jensen wiped the keychain and the keys with a cloth from his pocket, then dropped it in the back corner and slid the drawer closed. Without hesitation, he walked out of the room and down the hall toward the kitchen.

He'd make sure they conducted a thorough search of the back bedroom.

EPILOGUE

PETER BRONKOWSKI NERVOUSLY eyed the dog making its way down the line with its handler at the US-Mexico border south of San Diego. He'd only stashed a small amount of blow in the passenger side door, thinking getting it into Mexico would be a piece of cake. It was coming back to the U.S. that was hard. But Peter wasn't planning on coming back. The airline tickets and passport on the seat next to him had a Croatian surname Peter could barely pronounce. He'd figured it would draw less attention than an American name once he boarded the plane for his villa.

He'd left money and instructions with Dr. Shapiro to take care of Edward, however he deemed appropriate, assuring him he'd email him an address where the good doctor could contact him. Peter had bought the house where Edward lived in Edward's name and he intended to list it with a California realtor as soon as he arrived in Croatia, putting the sale money into an account for Dr. Shapiro to use on his brother's behalf.

As the dog drew nearer to his car, Peter started to sweat. *How did everything go to hell so fast?* One minute, he was flying higher than he'd ever dreamed. The next, he was wanted by the cops and had to leave the country. The phony passport and tickets to Dubrovnik wiped out what little savings he had. They'd frozen the rest of his accounts. He was gonna need to start from scratch. Again.

The border patrol walked next to Peter's car and hesitated. The German shepherd pulled him to the other side of the vehicle and started to paw at the passenger side door. The officer leaned over and knocked on the passenger side window.

Peter glanced at the airline tickets on the seat next to him as the perspiration rolled down his face. It looked like he was going to have to give the senator a call.

Senator Runyon sucked in a deep breath of the sweet, fresh, unpolluted air. This is God's country, he thought to himself with satisfaction. Birds chirped happily in the trees and the farm animals contentedly munched away at the grass in the pastures. He was thinking seriously about purchasing the little piece of land next door that had recently gone up for sale.

After he won his next term, of course.

He'd taken the unanticipated detour to Bountiful once news broke with the discovery of the serial killer and dead contestants from Serial Date. Thanks to Shank's quick thinking and handiwork the cops hadn't been able to track down the earlier missing evidence from Amanda's apartment, while Heather's 'drowning' had taken care of the blackmailing little bitch. Filled with relief at having dodged yet another bullet, the senator figured he deserved the side trip.

As he made his way back to the farmhouse and his limousine, his aide, Christopher strode toward him, his face white.

Now what, the senator wondered? Christopher covered the distance between them and stopped, opening and closing his mouth like a dying fish as he searched for the right words.

"Well, speak up, Christopher. What?" Runyon growled.

"Senator, I-I don't know how to say this—"

"It's easy, Chris. Use words. It's all the rage." Irritated, Runyon brushed past him toward the car.

"There's a video of you. On YouTube. It's gone viral."

"And that's a problem?" As far as the senator was concerned, anything going 'viral' on the internet was good press and would help with his re-election.

"It's-it's of you and—and Heather and—"

Runyon felt the blood leave his face. He stopped, as still as stone.

"My God. Oh my God." He bowed his head as Christopher's words sank in. His stomach twisted into a knot and his knees liquefied. Feeling nauseous, he blindly reached out. Christopher quickly stepped forward and caught the senator before he collapsed. They staggered to the limousine as one and Christopher leaned the senator against the hood of the car. The driver got out and stood nearby, unsure what to do.

"Do you want me to call somebody?" the driver asked.

Runyon vigorously shook his head and waved the driver off. "No," he said, his voice sharp.

The senator pulled a monogrammed, starched white handkerchief from his pocket and blotted the perspiration from his forehead. His chest grew tight as blood pounded in his ears and he attempted to wipe his clammy hands on his trousers. Clearly alarmed, Christopher ran to the side of the car and grabbed a bottle of water from the limo's fridge, brought it back and offered it to the senator. Runyon pushed it away.

"Call Shank," he commanded and handed Christopher his phone. *Dear God, how do I survive this? How the hell did it get on YouTube? Heather's dead.* Runyon shivered as he imagined Heather's ghost reaching out to choke him with icy fingers from the grave.

Christopher searched his speed dial, punched in Shank's number and glanced up, waiting for it to ring. At that moment one of the farm's beloved dogs, a spunky border collie named Ralph, ran from behind a chicken coop with something large and dirty swinging from his mouth. He scampered toward the limousine, wagging his tail and overjoyed with having found something unusual with which to play catch.

Upon closer inspection, the object turned out to be a blood-encrusted human head with no ears. Runyon's heart couldn't take it. The tightness in his chest evolved to a crushing pain and the senator fell to his knees, gasping for breath. Panicked, Christopher loosened the senator's shirt collar and attempted to lay him on his side.

His eyes wide, the driver looked at Christopher, then at the senator, then back to Christopher.

"Call a fucking ambulance, now," Christopher yelled. The driver dove into the front seat of the vehicle and picked up the console phone. Ralph trotted over to Christopher and Runyon, dropped the head next to the senator and started to lick his face, all the while wagging his tail.

It would be Senator Runyon's last trip to Bountiful.

THE END

 **DV Berkom** is the award-winning author of two action-packed thriller series featuring strong female leads (**Leine Basso** and **Kate Jones**). Her love of creating resilient, kick-ass women characters stems from a lifelong addiction to reading spy novels, mysteries, and thrillers, and longing to find the female equivalent within those pages.

Raised in the Midwest, she earned a BA in political science from the University of Minnesota and promptly moved to Mexico to live on a sailboat. Several years and a multitude of adventures later, she wrote her first novel and was hooked. *Bad Spirits,* the first Kate Jones thriller, was published as an online serial in 2010 and was immediately popular with eBook fans. *Dead of Winter, Death Rites*, and *Touring for Death* soon followed before she began the far grittier Leine Basso series in 2012 with *Serial Date*.

D.V. currently lives in the Pacific Northwest with the love of her life, Mark, a chef-turned-contractor, and several imaginary characters who like to tell her what to do. Her most recent books include *A Killing Truth, Cargo, The Body Market, A One Way Ticket to Dead,* and *Yucatán Dead.*

More by DV Berkom:

The Leine Basso Thriller Series:
Bad Traffick
The Body Market
Cargo
A Killing Truth
The Kate Jones Thriller Series:
Bad Spirits
Dead of Winter
Death Rites
Touring for Death
Cruising for Death
Yucatàn Dead
A One Way Ticket to Dead

If you would like to learn more about Leine Basso or my other thriller series featuring Kate Jones, see the links below:

Facebook: www.facebook.com/DvBerkomAuthor
Twitter: @dvberkom
Website: www.dvberkom.com
Blog: www.dvberkom.wordpress.com
Pinterest: http://pinterest.com/dvberkom/
Google+: http://bit.ly/googldvb

***Sign up for my free readers' list to be the first to find out about new releases and exclusive, subscriber-only special offers: **http://bit.ly/dvbNews** (Your email address will never be sold and you can unsubscribe at any time.)

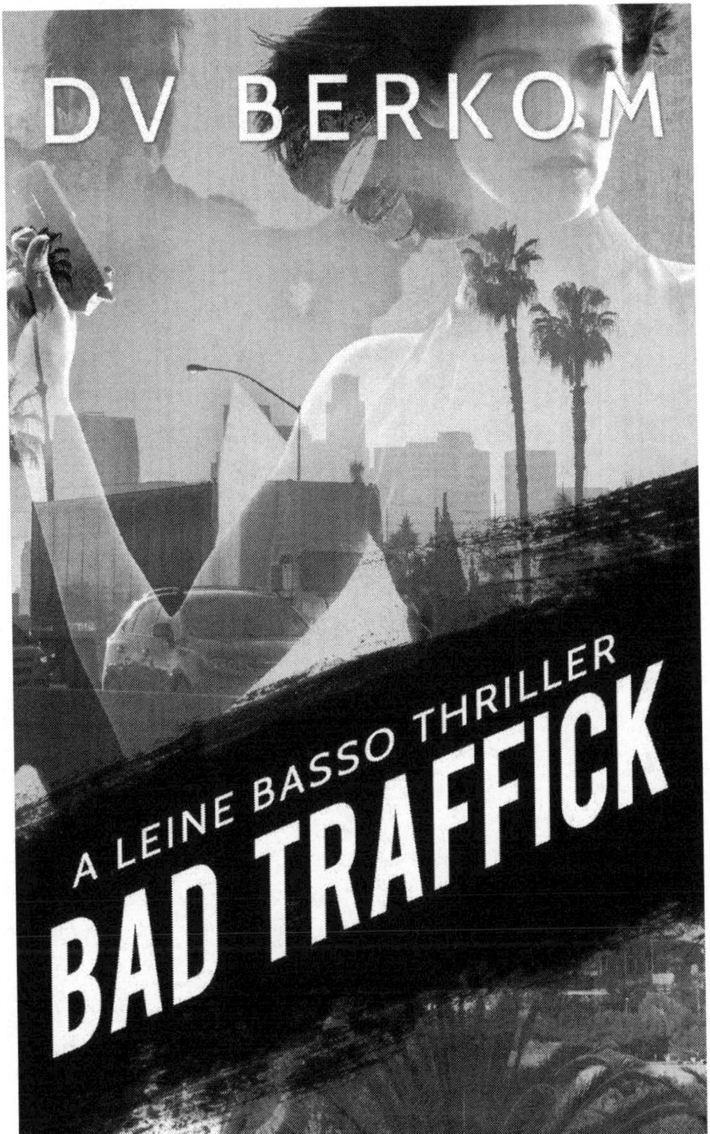
DV BERKOM
A LEINE BASSO THRILLER
BAD TRAFFICK

CHAPTER 1

A GLASS OF Macallan single malt rested on the gold inlay table beside the gentleman in the impeccable Armani suit, as he watched the images flash by on the white screen. Two other men, shrouded in darkness and each anonymous to the other, were also taking part in the video conference from different areas of the world, watching the same images. Several times one or the other would raise his hand, platinum or gold watch flashing in the darkened rooms, signaling for the Seller to pause the presentation so they could look more closely at the photographs.

The Seller was visibly sweating in the air conditioned comfort of the massive hotel suite. If he didn't make the sale this time, these clients would look elsewhere for their pleasures. His reputation as the go-to guy in the business was balancing on a knife's edge. Ever since the fiasco with the televangelist two months prior, he'd kept a sharp eye on the fiscal side of things.

One of the executives was fidgeting, apparently bored, and the Seller's anxiety level skyrocketed. He didn't have to find a mirror to know his appearance was giving his discomfort away. He could feel the cold sweat flowing down his back and armpits, running between his buttocks. *What the hell do these guys want? Am I losing my touch?* Usually it wasn't this hard to match the client to the product.

The Seller was down to his last two photographs when all three men simultaneously motioned for him to stop. The client in Saudi Arabia rose from his chair and walked to the screen, gazing at the delicate visage.

The Seller's shoulders relaxed. He shouldn't have been worried, should've known the eyes would close the deal: jade green flecked with gold surrounding deep black pupils. Everyone who saw her stopped in their tracks. She'd reminded the Seller of a famous photo he'd seen years before in an issue of National Geographic. She wore the same enigmatic expression. The silence of the buyers signaled it was time for the hard sell.

"Gentleman. I see you have exquisite taste. Mara is newly acquired and in pristine condition. I guarantee she will delight you with her generous charms. As I'm sure you'll agree, she has no equal. I always save the best for last. Mustn't trot out the most sublime too quickly, eh?"

There were murmurs of agreement between the men. The Seller's anxiety morphed to excitement as he prepared to set the hook. *My God, look at them. They're practically salivating.* A bidding war would be a welcome relief.

The client in the room waved him to his side. His unusual gold pinkie ring flashed, catching the Seller's eye. He'd seen the symbol before, but was unaware of its significance.

"Her age?" he asked.

The Seller turned and glanced at the picture of the girl. Her expression still held a trace of innocence, although churning through the American foster care system for two years had taken its toll. The photographer captured the picture before the girl had realized she wasn't going home.

"Twelve years, sir."

"Pure?"

"Most assuredly."

The man nodded his approval. He glanced back at the screen and steepled his fingers, bringing them to his lips to mask his words.

"Make sure she's mine," he whispered.

The quiet statement held the promise of a lucrative payday tinged with strong warning. The Seller's mouth ran dry. He nodded as he straightened and walked to the front of the room. The cameraman panned with him, framing his head and shoulders with the young girl's photograph in the background. The other two clients would see only the Seller with her face behind him on screen. He took a sip of water from a glass nearby and cleared his throat.

"Shall we start the bidding at fifty-thousand?"

CHAPTER 2

LEINE BASSO CHECKED her watch one more time. *How long can a lunch take?* She'd followed him to the diner and took up position on the other side of the street, out of sight behind a minivan.

Waiting had never been her strong suit. When she was in the business working for Eric, she'd learned to pass the time until the target appeared by memorizing every detail in her immediate vicinity. In fact, many times she'd arrive days early in order to scope out the activity of the area where the hit would take place. Bus schedules, vendor movement, deliveries, residents walking their pets. Nothing escaped her notice. Her attention to every facet of the job turned out to be one of the reasons she was still alive.

But, she was no longer in the business and now her impatience was getting the better of her. Catching a glimpse of him, even if for a moment, would suffice.

What if he sees you?

She shrugged off the thought and shifted from one foot to the other. The day was warm, with one of those deceptively clear skies so prized in Los Angeles. If she didn't know better, she'd think the air was safe to breathe.

She hated to admit it, but she was getting used to being in L.A. again. Breathtaking pollution aside, the city had a draw she'd always found hard to resist. The resident's frenetic, hive-like activity masked by a laid-back façade, and how everyone who stayed there, rich or poor, had the attitude they were living the dream. Deceptive.

Like her life.

The door to the diner swung open and a young couple stepped onto the sidewalk. Leine checked at her momentary disappointment and took a deep breath. *Give it a rest, Leine. He'll come out eventually.*

Minutes ticked by before the door opened again. Don Putnam emerged onto the sunlit sidewalk and slid on a pair of sunglasses. Santiago Jensen followed seconds later, jacket slung over his arm, dark hair tousled as if he'd only just rolled out of bed.

Leine's heart rate kicked up a notch as she watched him cross the sidewalk and open the door to the light-colored sedan. The force of her emotions rocked her, unbalancing her normal equilibrium. She prided herself on iron-fisted control, but when it came to Santiago Jensen the ability to think rationally deserted her without a backward glance. Viewing it as her body's ultimate betrayal, she knew enough to keep her distance. She'd be damned if she was going to add to the current problems in her life.

Or his.

Like an addict trying to kick a habit, she allowed herself the occasional glimpse. Not too close, she reminded herself. She didn't want him to know she was there. She'd done all she could to move the case against her old boss along. Once the murders were solved and Eric was behind bars, the two of them would be free to see where this attraction might take them. Until then, she had to keep her distance or Jensen could lose his detective's rank, or worse, his job.

Jensen tossed his jacket in the backseat and started to get in the car. At the last minute, he hesitated. Leine watched as his head snapped up. He straightened his shoulders and slowly pivoted, scanning the block. Leine moved to the shadows as he turned toward her, but was a second too late. His eyes locked on hers.

Leine's heart thudded in her chest. She clenched her fists, nails digging into flesh, fighting the urge to go to him. He remained motionless, his expression like a magnet. They watched each other, neither breaking eye contact. Leine sensed the electricity between them, could almost hear it snap.

The draw between them was like nothing she'd experienced with Carlos, or any other man, for that matter. She knew it was an addiction, and she was at a loss as to how to proceed. The harder she tried to forget, the more the feelings came back with an intensity she could barely fight. She woke up often having dreamt of him.

She needed to bide her time, wait until they could be together. She had to break contact or she might act on impulse and compromise the case. She wouldn't rest until Eric was behind bars. The death penalty would be too good for him.

In the end, she didn't have to do anything. Putnam reached across the seat and honked the horn to get Jensen's attention. The spell disintegrated. Jensen turned to say something to Putnam.

Leine disappeared before he turned back

Santiago Jensen sat at his desk in the Robbery Homicide Division offices in downtown Los Angeles and stared at his phone, fighting the urge to call Leine Basso. Catching sight of her outside the diner brought it all back—he wanted to see her, touch her skin, smell her. He *craved* her. All the late nights working cases only kept his mind off her so long.

"Hey, Santa. Know a good security guy who can keep a secret? I got a film star needs protecting."

Startled, Jensen looked up as Walter Helmsley leaned against his desk. Helmsley was in his mid-thirties, had a pallid complexion for a resident of southern California, and was on his way to capturing the geek award for most movies watched by a human being. His mind was a never-ending database of film trivia. If you had a question about some obscure movie from the seventies then Walter was your guy.

"What about Ben?" Jensen asked. An ex-security specialist who'd worked the Iraq war, Ben was usually available for short-term security jobs and everybody in the division knew and trusted him. With budgets stretched thin and personnel even more so, outsourcing security detail was the norm.

"He's tied up for the next couple of weeks on some rapper's detail," Walter said. "You know Ben. Likes the gangstas and their ladies."

Before Jensen could stop himself he said, "Yeah. I know somebody. She's got plenty of experience and I think she's between jobs at the moment." He had no idea if Leine would accept working a security gig, but it would give him a chance to contact her.

"She'll like this one. It's for Miles Fournier."

Jensen frowned. "Fournier. Where have I heard that name before?"

Walter snorted. "He's only the biggest thing since Johnny Depp played an effeminate guy-liner wearing pirate." He shook his head. "Where have you been? Ever heard of Jake Dread, Intergalactic Spy? Every female I know wants to meet him, and for mostly carnal reasons. He draws a crowd that's half giggling pre-teen girls, half sex-deprived mommies."

Oh. Instantly regretting opening his mouth and suggesting Leine for the job, he realized he couldn't take it back just because he might be worried about her sleeping with some movie star. Besides, weren't most of them gay? Leine wouldn't fall for some famous pretty boy.

Would she?

"I'll give her a call. What are the particulars?" Jensen asked.

"Three guys rushed him and his friends in the lobby of the Palms."

"Not paparazzi?"

Walter shook his head. "No cameras, and the friends claim they wore guns under their jackets. Some little girl got caught in the middle when she recognized Miles and ran into the mix. His friend delivered a roundhouse kick to the face of one of the attackers. Evidently, the suspects hadn't bet on anyone with Fournier fighting back, and they scattered."

"What happened to the girl?"

"Disappeared. Probably scared."

"So Fournier came to you for security recommendations?"

"The dude's spooked. Figures someone's out to kidnap him. Doesn't trust outside security companies, for some reason. He'll only accept a referral from LAPD. He wants one main person twenty-four seven that he can rely on, get to know. I suggested he have someone review security around his home, maybe hire a couple of private security guards to patrol the place. He said he'd think about it. Wants our referral to do the security assessment."

"I'll see if she's interested."

END EXCERPT

60794549R00164

Made in the USA
Charleston, SC
08 September 2016